The Wolf of Hades

To my wife Sue,
Researcher, critic, editor
And best friend

Thanks to Ken Hankinson for guidance about the rock climbing scenes. Any blunders are due to my misunderstanding of his advice or my striving for dramatic effect.

The Wolf of Hades

Michael Hillier

ROBERT HALE · LONDON

© Michael Hillier 2010
First published in Great Britain 2010

ISBN 978-0-7090-9085-4

Robert Hale Limited
Clerkenwell House
Clerkenwell Green
London EC1R 0HT

www.halebooks.com

2 4 6 8 10 9 7 5 3 1

Typeset in 10/13½pt Palatino
by Derek Doyle & Associates, Shaw Heath
Printed in Great Britain by the MPG Books Group, Bodmin and King's Lynn

- 1 -

The taxi pulled into the kerbside and stopped with a squeal of brakes. The thud of the diesel engine subsided into an untidy rattle as it idled. The driver glanced in his mirror at the young fellow who'd been easing his hand up the pretty girl's thigh for the last five minutes.

'Jermyn Street,' he announced in a loud, cheerful voice.

With great reluctance Ben Cartwright tore his eyes from their close study of Mollie's features and made to open the door. She straightened her dress as he paid off the driver with an extravagant tip. Ben was contemplating a successful conclusion to the evening.

He helped Mollie from the back seat and shut the door behind her. Then he shepherded her to the side entrance from which the stairs led directly to his second floor flat. Behind them there was a renewed clatter of the engine as the taxi pulled away from the kerb and prowled off noisily into the night. Mollie stood beside him and shivered in her thin cotton dress with the stole pulled tight around the shoulders while Ben hunted for his key and opened the door.

'We'll put the fire on when we get into the sitting room. That'll soon warm you up,' he assured her.

Her smile was appealing. He let his hand slide up her back under the stole as he ushered her into the small hallway and pushed the door shut with his foot. At the bottom stair he stopped her and kissed the nape of her neck just where the hair began. He massaged the little knobs at the top of her spine and she shivered and snuggled deliciously up to him. He started to slide down the zip on her dress.

This was the first time, after several weeks of assiduous effort, that Ben had been able to persuade her to come back to his flat for a nightcap. Mollie was no easy catch and he didn't want to spoil it now.

This evening had been perfect, without the usual crowd of friends to provide Mollie with her escape. He had caught her mood early on and had spared no expense in his choice of food and wine. They had sat side by side in a private alcove while they ate and the conversation had been romantic and personal. Then they had smooched for an hour on the crowded little dance floor, gazing into each other's eyes or murmuring intimate endearments. When he had suggested they should go back to his place there had been no sign of hesitation in her acceptance.

His flat was above the wine-importing business in which he and Toni Cimbrone were partners. The shop had been leased by his family for generations. In the past it had been an old-fashioned and slightly faded enterprise. But, after Toni had bought a half-share in the business, the place had been extensively modernized. They had installed the latest sales and display equipment. There were deep pile carpets and comfortable armchairs in the special sampling area. They sold their wines by the case, a lot of it to the hotel and restaurant trade. Ben was proud of the atmosphere of sophistication and success.

The business occupied a good position. During the day the surrounding district was busy and affluent. They were in the heart of the most expensive area of the West End. But few people actually lived in the street and it became quiet after six o'clock. Ben liked it that way. There were no prying eyes or complaining neighbours.

As they started up the stairs he let his hand slide down to rest on Mollie's right buttock and he could feel the line of her briefs below the soft fabric of her dress. She half turned towards him. Her lips were slightly apart and her eyes seemed darker than he recalled them being before. Ben felt a churning in his stomach as he thought of the night ahead.

The next second there was a crash from the shop and the alarm bell started to ring.

After the briefest pause Ben rushed towards the link door to the shop. It was locked of course. Desperately he plunged into his pocket for the keys. He fumbled with the handle in his rush to open it, managing to insert the key at the third attempt. He swung the door open wide. Then he stopped in the pitch darkness and felt along the wall for the switch.

A second later the light flashed on and he paused, blinking in its brightness as he looked around. He immediately saw one of the upright display stands had been knocked over and its contents (mainly special offer bottles of wine) were rolling across the carpet. But at first sight there seemed to be nothing else out of place. Everything appeared to be as he had left it when he closed the shop at six o'clock. This time there was none of the destruction that had been caused when some youngsters broke in one weekend when he was away. On that occasion there had been filth and excrement everywhere when he returned – nearly £5,000 worth of drunken, wanton damage. Perhaps this time he had disturbed the thieves before they could do any real harm.

Responding to the strident clangour of the alarm bell, he made for the front door. It was ajar. In a few strides he had pulled it open and was out on the street. There was no one in sight, but he fancied he could hear the clatter of fleeing feet in the distance. He hesitated, trying to decide whether he should chase after them in an attempt to get a sight of the robbers or immediately phone the police.

Just then Mollie screamed. It was a sound that made the hairs tingle on his scalp. What on earth had happened to her?

Ben spun round and dashed back into the shop. He saw her immediately. She was standing by the door leading into the rear office. Her back was towards him and she seemed half doubled up and clutching at the door jamb. She was making a soft little sound, something between a groan and a whimper, as if she had been violently struck in the stomach.

He rushed to her side, not knowing whether she had been attacked or suddenly taken ill. Then he saw the cause of her distress. Lying on its side in the middle of the office was the body of a man.

All that Ben could see from the door was his back. He had dark hair and was wearing a dirty white shirt and light-coloured trousers. His hands were secured behind his back with electrical wire and his bare feet were tied together in the same way. Ben could see where the wire had bitten deeply into the puffy, bruised flesh. There was a great dark patch below the top half of the body which was slowly spreading out over the expensive Turkish carpet. And the collar of the man's shirt was turning crimson.

Ben felt himself propelled to the man's side. As he got near he could see the start of a wound at the throat. With a horrible fascination he reached out to touch the man's shoulder. His heart leapt into his mouth as the body toppled on to its back. The head lolled at a strange unnatural angle where it had been half severed from the neck. Despite the fact that he was looking at the face of a man in the last grimace of death, there was no mistaking who it was. He was touching the still-warm body of his business partner. This was the end of life for Toni, his close friend for the last six years and the man whose life he had saved in the Italian mountains less than two years ago.

Oh, my God, thought Ben suddenly, I think I'm going to be sick.

'He didn't know why, but he felt he had to return Toni's body to the position it had been in when he first saw it. Grabbing the shoulder, he started to lift it, then pushed at the body until it flopped over loosely like a gigantic rag doll. After that he had to pause for a minute – concentrating hard on a bit of the carpet, staring at the pattern and seeing the detail of the pile – while he waited for the nausea to pass.

It was then that he noticed something out of the corner of his eye. It was a small, square object which might have fallen from Toni's hand. He reached over and picked it up. It looked like a kind of enamelled badge, small and metallic and surprisingly heavy. He had never seen anything quite like it before. Why should Toni have been holding something like that?

However it wasn't important now. He had to do something to help Mollie. The worst of the shock had passed. He got shakily to his feet, keeping his eyes averted from the body. Then he had to pause again because the world seemed to be swaying about him. His head felt as though he'd just walked into the fresh air after a drinking orgy.

To try to order his mind, Ben looked around him. The office was a complete shambles. Every filing cabinet had been pulled open and papers were strewn over the floor. Drawers had been opened on to desktops and the contents scattered about. The stationery cupboard had been opened. Notepaper and envelopes had been hurled across the room. Even the secretary's office beyond the glass screen had been ransacked. Noticeboards and calendars had been pulled off the walls. Chairs and a small table had been upturned. Obviously someone had been searching the place thoroughly.

His head began to clear and he dragged his gaze away from the scene of devastation. He turned his attention to Mollie who still looked as though she had been paralysed by the shock. She just stood by the door, quivering, without appearing to look at anything. With an effort

Ben shook off his own revulsion and turned his attention to her.

She didn't react in any way when he took her in his arms. She didn't even seem to see him there. He slid the zip of her dress up again and pulled the stole over her shoulders. He removed her hands from the door jamb as gently as possible and shepherded her back into the shop to the clients' sampling area where she allowed herself to be lowered on to a sofa. She was still mute, seemingly deep in shock. He leaned over her, wondering what he should do to help her.

What he most wanted to do was to wash his hands – the hands which had touched Toni's dead body. But he couldn't leave Mollie on her own while he went to the bathroom. And he couldn't very well take her up to his flat now.

Of course! He suddenly realized that he had to ring the police. They would want to know why that hadn't been the very first thing which had entered his mind. No doubt they would be annoyed about him touching the body. He wished he hadn't done it, but it was too late to change that now. What should he say to them?

'Just stay there a moment, Mollie. I must ring the police.'

She nodded but still didn't look at him.

He went to the extension phone on the side table. It took him less than thirty seconds to make the call. The woman at the police control centre told him to wait and not to touch anything. They would be there in less than five minutes.

Now he could sit beside Mollie, put his arms round her and start to murmur little messages into her ear. She seemed to be helped by that. After a few minutes the tears began to flow. She made no noise. There were no sobs or sniffs. It was as though a tap had been turned on and the tears and the tension poured out of her. She gradually relaxed. Her shoulders slumped and she trembled against him.

'Don't worry, darling. The police will be here in a few minutes.'

His murmured encouragements resulted in a rather watery smile. He put his arm round her again and she snuggled up to him. Ben reflected that this was just what he had hoped she would be doing by now – but in rather different circumstances.

He pulled out his handkerchief and gave it to her to mop up her tears. As he did so, the little metal object which he had found beside Toni's body fell with a thump on to the floor. He picked it up and examined it more closely. It was a small piece of metal about an inch square, and heavier than its thickness would suggest. There were some irregular scratches on the reverse, rather like rough Roman numerals. They were indecipherable to Ben.

The face was very smooth. He turned it over and studied the small picture which was enamelled on the metal. It was an image of grotesque design but exquisite execution. Around the edge was a dark green border. In the centre was a black dog with red eyes. The artist had rendered the animal in the tiniest detail, so that even the individual hairs could be picked out. it was standing with its head lowered and with blood dripping from its savage white fangs. A short chain held it by a studded collar as it sought to escape – as though to pursue some unfortunate victim. Its long-clawed paws were tearing furiously at the non-existent ground. Its face bore an expression of almost demonic hatred. It was truly a beast to terrify the most stout-hearted.

What on earth was it doing in Toni's possession? he wondered.

Then he heard the sound of an approaching police siren and the thoughts were driven from his mind as he slipped the object back into his pocket.

Within seconds the car had pulled up outside the shop. A burly constable entered wearing a waterproof jacket and carrying his mobile.

'Is there an emergency, sir?'

Ben just pointed to the back of the shop. The constable walked to the door of the office and Ben watched him recoil at the sight which met his eyes. The next minute the man was on the radio to the station.

- 2 -

Detective Inspector Paisley sat down opposite Ben in the clients' sampling area and pulled the low table towards him. He placed his interview file neatly to his left, took out the first sheet of statement paper and set it in front of him. From his inside pocket he took two cheap ballpoint pens, one of which he placed at the head of the sheet of paper. With some deliberation he removed the cap from the other and placed that alongside.

He nodded at Ben. 'I prefer to take the statements myself, face to face. That way I get a full picture.'

Ben sat mute and watched as the inspector laboriously filled out the details at the top of the form, using his second pen when necessary as a ruler to underline the headings.

He glanced at his watch. It was already half past midnight. Time was dragging. To start with he had been relegated to the role of tea-maker for the large number of people who'd turned up – patrolmen, detectives, a doctor, scenes-of-crime officers, a photographer, a specialist security man to check the locks and alarm systems, a policewoman to offer help to Mollie – it seemed to go on for ever. The inspector painstakingly tried to extract a logical statement from Mollie while Ben had been told to wait at the other side of the shop. A police car had taken her home nearly an hour ago.

Then Ben had been required to help in a minute search of the shop and offices to see what had been removed and whether anything had been left behind by the intruders. That had uncovered nothing of significance. Then he was allowed to tidy up the remains of the upturned display unit in the shop. Now at last it was his turn to be questioned.

From the office there came a soft mumble which was the pathologist

11

describing his preliminary investigation of the body in intimate detail to a recording machine, watched by a horrified young detective. The combined effects of shock and fatigue seemed to make the sound rise and fall irregularly in his ears.

'Now, Mr Cartwright. . . .'

With an effort Ben concentrated on Paisley's face.

'. . . I'm sorry to have kept you waiting, but I do like to have written statements from any other witnesses before I interview the primary witness. It saves me from having to keep returning to you to ask further questions if new points are raised. Do you understand?'

Ben nodded a little nervously. He noticed the inspector still had a faint Scottish burr to his accent.

'Now, I understand that you have known the deceased for over six years. Can you explain how you met?'

Ben tried to order his thoughts. 'I believe it was at a wine fair in Paris.'

Paisley waited a few seconds but the young man didn't add anything further. 'Any special significance in Paris?'

'Well, it's the biggest centre of wine-trading in the world.' The words started to tumble out of him. 'France is the biggest wine producer, even now. It's the place to go if you want to buy or sell wine wholesale. I had only recently taken over my father's business – this business. My father had died the previous year. It was the first time I'd been to anything like that'

'And your partner?'

'Pardon?'

'What was the reason for the deceased being at the Paris wine fair?'

'Oh, Toni is a member of the Cimbrone family.' He felt an absurd desire to giggle as he spelled out the name for Paisley. 'They have been wine producers for generations in southern Italy. They had a stand at Paris to promote their wines.' He shrugged. 'Well, somehow we got talking.'

He remembered that he had made the common mistake of thinking Italian wines were solely for the cheap, poor quality end of the market It had taken Toni a long time and several subsequent visits to Ben's shop to convince him that there was also a range of quality Italian wines which was more reasonably priced than the French but equally as good.

The inspector stopped writing and looked up at him. 'And this led to your setting up a business partnership?'

'In the end – yes. But not for nearly two years.'

'How did that come about?'

Ben thought for a minute. 'A few weeks after our first meeting he called in to see me. I agreed to try some of his wines on a sale or return basis. A lot of my customers are discerning wine drinkers who like to try something different for a change. They, like me, were pleasantly surprised and gradually the wines began to take off. So Toni started to call on me every three months or so to extend the range. We soon discovered that people were asking for his latest selections. We decided that there was a real gap in the market and in due course we formed a joint company to exploit it.'

The inspector wrinkled his nose. 'And your business relations have been – er – harmonious?'

'Yes, it has been a great success.'

'However, I understand that you were under the impression that Mr – er – Cimbrone' – he didn't quite manage to get hold of the name – 'had returned to Italy.'

'Well, yes. I haven't seen him for more than three weeks. His father died suddenly at the end of last month. He went home for the funeral and expected to be away for several weeks. In any case he spends quite a lot of his time in Italy at this season of the year. He is the buying half of the company.'

'And you heard nothing from him since he left?'

Ben shook his head. 'I didn't expect to. There was no real need for contact unless something unusual came up. We both deal with our own sides of the business. I had his mobile number. If I couldn't get hold of him that way, I could contact him through his family if necessary.'

'So you're not absolutely sure that he ever left this country?'

Ben tried to drag his disorganized thoughts into line. 'I suppose not,' he said slowly. 'But I think I would have heard from his family if he hadn't arrived.' He ran his fingers through his hair. 'I'll have to ring them first thing in the morning to ask when he left them. God knows how I'll break this to them.'

'And there was no indication that he intended to return to this country during the last few days?'

'No. I was absolutely shattered when I found him lying on the floor.'

The inspector raised his eyebrows. 'Do you mean you expected the victim to be someone else?'

'No!' Was the man trying to catch him out? 'No, of course not. I didn't expect anything like – well, like that. I thought at first that the alarm was just another break-in by young hooligans. We had one last year while I was away. At first I was surprised that there was no mess in the shop.'

Paisley nodded and opened his mouth, but Ben hurried on.

'I've suddenly thought of something. After our last trouble we installed a new alarm system with infra-red sensors. But it was the old one on the front door which went off.' He snapped his fingers. 'Why didn't I think of that before? I'm sure I switched on both alarms before I locked up this evening.'

'Who has the keys?'

'Only Toni and I – and the alarm company, of course. So they – the killers – must have used his keys. I've still got mine.' He dug in his pocket and held them out for inspection.

'That's very interesting. Can you show me the control panel?'

Ben took him to the cupboard in the secretary's office, being careful to keep his eyes averted from the gruesome scene on his own office floor. Sure enough, there was a key in the panel and the system was turned off.

'Don't touch anything,' said the inspector unnecessarily. 'Let's see your key.'

Ben passed it to Paisley. 'The one in the panel must be Toni's. The alarm company advised that we shouldn't keep any spares.'

'We'll check it for prints. This is the installer's name on the box?'

He nodded. That seemed obvious to him.

'OK. Let's carry on, shall we?' The inspector started to lead him back to the report table.

'A moment of your time please, Inspector Paisley,' said the pathologist, as they were about to go.

Ben went back on his own and sat down while the two men talked quietly out of his hearing. He put his head in his hands. He couldn't understand it. He had been so sure that Toni was 1,500 miles away in southern Italy. Why had he come back without warning? From the mess in the office it looked as though his murderers had been looking for something there. But Ben had no idea what it might have been.

He had never had any reason to suspect that Toni might be keeping any secrets from him about the business – or about his private life, for that matter. Toni wasn't that kind of person. Ben had also received no intimation that his partner might have enemies who would wish to murder him. Thinking about it, he had to admit that he knew relatively little about Toni's family and his other connections in Italy. Ben had met members of the Cimbrone family in a formal kind of way on two or three other occasions. His mind wandered back to vague memories of sunny days at the villa in Posillipo. Then there had been that holiday a couple of years ago which had ended in the tragic death of Toni's brother-in-law, Carlo. He hadn't visited Italy since.

The inspector broke into his day-dreams. 'Mr Kirkpatrick – he's the pathologist – tells me, from the temperature of the body and the state of coagulation of the blood, that your friend has been dead for less than three hours. That means, on the evidence of Miss Parkinson, that you cannot possibly be a suspect. It's fortunate that the young lady came home with you.'

There was a twitch at the corner of Paisley's mouth. It was only then that it dawned on Ben that he might have been a suspect. He suddenly felt the need to take a long, deep breath.

'He also says that the young man looks malnourished and that his body has had a considerable beating. Several of his fingers have been broken – probably deliberately – and some of his ribs may have been fractured by heavy kicks. I'm afraid it looks as though your friend was tortured before he was killed. That might mean that his murderers wanted Mr Cimbrone to tell them something, or to give them something which they thought was very important Do you have any idea what that might have been?'

Ben shook his head. For the first time the full meaning of Toni's death got through to him. There was something very nasty behind all this. He felt the floor sway beneath his feet. If he hadn't already been sitting down he would have felt the need to find a chair.

The inspector was watching him closely. 'You say that the father of Mr Cimbrone had recently died. Do you know the cause of *his* death?'

The harshness of his voice jerked Ben into alertness again. 'The cause? Er – well, I believe it was a heart attack or something like that. I know the old boy had been ill for some time. Toni had mentioned being worried about him.'

'Mr Cartwright,' Paisley spoke slowly and clearly, 'can you think of anything in your business here which the murderers might have wanted to obtain?'

'No, I can't. I've been wondering about that myself. We never keep large amounts of money here overnight. I don't know of anything valuable. Obviously, there's the drink on the shelves, but that's not enough to commit murder for.'

'It wasn't a simple theft which went wrong,' agreed the inspector. 'They weren't worried about leaving fingerprints. We've found them all over the place. They seem to have been looking for information. They've been through all your papers thoroughly.'

Ben pondered. 'I don't know what sort of information they would have been looking for. We only have the normal business paperwork – nothing of special significance. We import wines of course, as you know, but I can't see why that should be significant, unless there's some sort of hidden code on the manifests.'

The inspector asked no further questions for several minutes as he brought his notes up to date. Ben was left to ponder the mystery of why someone had wanted to torture and murder his partner – a man whom he'd always regarded as a friendly, easy-going individual.

Paisley raised his head again. 'This company of yours, Mr Cartwright – who are the principals?'

'Pardon?'

'The owners?'

'Well, Toni and I are – or were. That is – we had ninety-eight per cent of the shares split equally between us.'

'Who has the other two per cent?'

'They're held in a trust fund administered by our solicitor – James Meredith. The intention, when we set up the business, was to give somebody else a casting vote if we disagreed over anything important. In fact it has never arisen.'

'And what will happen to Mr Cimbrone's shares now?'

'I don't know. I suppose they'll go to his next of kin. That will probably be his mother. Perhaps I might be able to buy them – although I don't think I'd be able to afford it. The shares are now worth quite a lot on paper because of the success of the company. In any case, Toni's family has a big interest in our activities. They supply a lot of the wine.' The thought suddenly occurred to him that James Meredith's two per cent might become important after all.

'So who are his near relatives?'

'His mother, and he has an older brother called Alfredo who I believe has been running the family business and estates since his father became ill.'

'Does he have any other family?'

'There's a younger sister called Francesca. I suppose she's about twenty-one or so by now. She and Toni were very close, but I didn't see much of her. I don't know how she'll react to his death.'

The inspector finished his fifth page and laboriously prepared his next sheet. While he wrote painstakingly, Ben's mind ranged back to his last visit to the Villa Cimbrone. He had only occasionally seen the wilful young girl with the vitriolic temper whom Toni seemed to view with a tolerant smile. In the way of Italian families she had been kept well out of Ben's way, except for the family gatherings at the dinner table.

Somehow he had gained the impression that Francesca did not approve of him. Perhaps she blamed Ben for the fact that Toni spent so much of his life away from home, either in London or travelling around Italy in search of wines. The two weeks which Toni had spent in hospital recovering from his climbing accident would not have helped to soften her attitude.

Ben reflected morosely that it was more than likely she would consider him to blame in some way for Toni's death. He fervently hoped that he wouldn't be anywhere near when the terrible news was broken to her.

'His mother?' Paisley was gazing at him intently.

'I spoke to her very little. She had no English and my Italian is rudimentary to say the least. Alfredo is married to a woman called Sylvia whom I've only met a couple of times.'

'Which part of Italy does his family come from?'

'Southern Italy – near Naples.'

The policeman rubbed his chin as he looked at him. 'Right, now let's come to the events of this evening. At what time did you return to your flat?'

'It was quite early. I think it must have been soon after ten when I paid off the taxi.'

'Did you notice anything unusual before you went in? Were there any lights on? Did you hear any unexpected noises? Were there any doors or windows open?'

Ben considered carefully. 'I don't remember anything. You can't see the office door from the street, so I probably wouldn't have seen if there was a light on in there.' He thought for a while, and then hurried on, 'I do remember that all the lights were off when I let myself into the shop. I suppose that's why they knocked over the display stand which alerted me.' He shuddered. 'Otherwise I might not have found Toni's body until the morning.'

'Did you check the communicating door to the shop before you went up to your flat?'

'No. I didn't think of it.' Ben didn't mention the fact that he had been concentrating on the prospect of deflowering Mollie.

'But it was definitely locked when you tried to open it after hearing the noise?'

'That's right. It took me a few seconds to find the keys and get it unlocked.'

Paisley wanted to get the details right. 'You actually tried it before you got out your keys, and it was definitely locked.'

'Yes,' agreed Ben. 'Yes, I'm sure it was.'

'OK. Now tell me what you saw as soon as you opened the door.'

'Well, nothing at first. It was too dark. But as soon as I turned on the light I saw the display unit knocked over. Then I saw the outside door was open a little way.'

The inspector led him through the subsequent events up to the point where he telephoned the police. Ben once again apologized for touching the body, but Paisley shrugged it away as being of no importance. He seemed to have less interest in the body than in the objects surrounding it.

As he prepared the next page of the statement (the eighth by Ben's reckoning) he asked, 'Now Mr Cartwright, can you think of anybody who might have wanted to kill Mr Cimbrone – anyone at all?'

'Nobody,' said Ben after long, hard consideration.

'Perhaps there's someone he upset or harmed, possibly in Italy. They do seem to have some strange ideas over there – all those vendettas and things.' The inspector shook his head doubtfully. 'Do you know of anybody in Italy who might have had a reason to kill your partner?'

'No!' Then Ben's thoughts returned, unbidden, to the events of two years ago which he'd been trying to forget ever since.

'Mr Cartwright?' Paisley was watching him closely.

Ben sighed. 'Well, there was something. But I don't see how it could have led to this.'

'Please tell me about it and leave me to decide the relevance.'

'Very well.' He took a deep breath. 'About two years ago I was invited to have a holiday with Toni and his family at their villa on the coast near Naples. While I was there I met his brother-in-law, Carlo. In conversation I was unwise enough to say that I had done some rock-climbing. It turned out that Carlo's passion was climbing and so he arranged for himself, Toni and me to climb a very demanding cliff-face in the Apennines.'

Ben paused, feeling again the shudder of fear that had crept up his spine and set his hair on end. He forced himself to continue. 'The climb went disastrously wrong. Carlo was leading, Toni was second and I was bringing up the rear. Carlo slipped and fell. He took Toni part way with him but I managed to save him. However, I couldn't do anything for Carlo and he died. That's all really.'

He was aware that the policeman was watching him closely, looking for his weaknesses. 'Was your partner blamed for the accident?' he asked.

'Toni? No! The Italian inquest said Carlo' death was their equivalent of misadventure. There was never any suggestion that Toni was to blame in any way.'

It was different for Ben. Toni had told him that there had been dark mutterings about Ben's failure to save Carlo, who was an important man in the area – mutterings which Toni claimed to have silenced. Nevertheless, Ben was left with the uncomfortable thought that his partner might have been sacrificed trying to protect him.

After a long pause, the inspector said, 'I can't see that this unfortunate accident can have led to the victim being treated in this atrocious way. Is there anything else you can tell me about your partner's past?'

'I don't think so.'

'Nobody else who might have a reason to hate him? I would remind you that this murder was a particularly nasty one with signs of torture before he was killed.'

Ben thought again but shook his head once more.

'Nobody he upset badly among your business contacts?'

'He was a most charming person. Everybody liked him.'

'What about your employees – or some of your suppliers? Are any of them likely to have a reason to want to take revenge against him or the company?'

'I can't think of anyone. We've had a few changes of staff in the last couple of years, but I don't think we've ever treated anyone unfairly. Anyway, Toni didn't deal with that side of the business: I'd be the target for a disaffected employee.'

The inspector wore a puzzled frown. 'He never gave you any idea that he had any problems. Were you close enough for him to have confided in you?'

'I believe we were. But he never mentioned anything like that.' Ben scratched his forehead.

The inspector sniffed. 'In any case the Italian angles would not be my responsibility. Well, I think that's the lot for now. Is there anything else you want to tell me?'

'I don't think so.'

'Anything it might be useful for me to know?'

Ben shook his head.

'If something else occurs to you later, I can be contacted at Charing Cross police station. Here's my card.' He placed it on the table in front of the young man. 'Now then – this is your statement as I've written it down. I want you to read this right through to make sure it's correct, then sign every page in the space at the bottom to confirm that it is a true record of what you said. Take as long as you like. Make sure there are no mistakes. The document might have to be used in court one day.'

The inspector pushed the small sheaf of papers across the table to him. 'Once that's complete, I hope that I shan't need to trouble you again. But I might need to come back to you if something else comes up as a result of our investigations.' He shook his head. 'Frankly, I don't think we'll get very far on this one. I think the coroner will pass a verdict of "killed unlawfully by persons unknown".'

'Now then.' He stood up. 'I want a chat with Mr Kirkpatrick while you're signing the statement. Call me when you've finished. Then you can go upstairs to your bed.'

Half an hour later Ben had seen the police off the premises. The body had been removed to the morgue. The bloodstained items had been bundled up and taken away for evidence and a receipt had been handed to him. He had been advised that victim support counselling would be offered to him in the morning – would he please be polite to them?

He checked once again that the locks were set and the alarms switched back on. Then he turned off the lights and made his way up to his flat. He reflected sadly on the destruction of his hopes earlier in the evening. Would Mollie ever be willing to come back to his flat with him again? He somehow doubted it.

He sighed as he put his hand in his pocket and felt the little metal emblem nestling there. He realized that he had forgotten to tell Inspector Paisley about it. He shrugged dismissively. It would have to wait until the morning. He couldn't see the importance of ringing up the man now to tell him about some little piece of metal which probably had nothing to do with Toni's death in any case.

He would show it to Inspector Paisley when he saw him next.

- 3 -

Ben arrived at his solicitor's office at 12.35 p.m. the next day. He was feeling slightly tense from shock, shortage of sleep and several hours' frantic activity trying to get the business ready to re-open. In the end they made it – just after eleven o'clock – only two hours late.

Peggy, his middle-aged secretary, was still tidying the office. He was confident that she would have everything cleared away and running smoothly by the end of the day. The rest of the staff were all working as usual. Of course they had been shocked when they heard about Toni's death, but they hadn't known him very well because he was away travelling most of the time. He seldom spent long in the shop during working hours. Perhaps that made it easier for them.

His solicitor had telephoned at 11.30.

'Hello, Benjamin.' James Meredith always called him Benjamin. 'It's James here. I thought I should ring you to tell you how desperately sorry I was to hear about Toni's death.'

'That's kind of you.'

'It must be a terrible shock for you. He was such a nice fellow. You'll be devastated to be left on your own so suddenly. It must be a great loss to the business.'

'Yes, it is, but we'll get over it. Don't worry about that'

'Well, I'm here to help in times like these.' Ben could hear the man's oily smile at the other end of the line. 'Why don't you come and have lunch with me? We might be able to sort a few things out.'

'It's a bit difficult this morning, James. We're still trying to get the shop organized and I don't feel I should leave—'

'What I want to see you about is important, Benjamin. I think we should discuss it straight away.'

'What do you mean?'

'I can't explain over the phone. I suggest we have a relaxed conversation face to face. I'll book us a table at the Hyde Park.'

That made Ben gulp. Lunch was going to set James back well over a hundred pounds. He wouldn't do that unless there was something important at the end of it.

'All right, James. I'll be there.' Ben didn't like the sound of this at all. He supposed there were quite a lot of things which would need to be sorted out when a partner died suddenly, but he couldn't understand the desperate urgency.

'Can you be at my office at half past twelve? We can have a little chat before going out for lunch.'

'Very well, James. I'll see you at twelve-thirty.'

'Fine.' There was a sharp click and the dialling tone whirred in his ear.

Ben put down the phone thoughtfully. Something was worrying him about that call. It wasn't James's smugness – he always sounded like that – but something was wrong and Ben couldn't put his finger on it.

It was only later that he began to wonder how James had heard about Toni's death so quickly.

As soon as he walked in, Ben was shown straight into James's office by the glamorous secretary. She was yet another in the series which James seemed to regard as an essential part of a solicitor's office. This little foible had always amused Ben because the man seemed so staid in other ways.

The office was unusually quiet today. James came forward to greet him with his hand outstretched and his head on one side in the characteristic attitude he adopted with his clients.

'Hello, Benjamin. What a terrible business this is.'

Ben had never felt quite comfortable in conversation with James. The cultured accent bred at Harrow and Oxford always seemed a little false to him. However, his father had used Merediths for many years and had held a high opinion of them. Ben felt a little guilty for condemning a man for such artificial reasons.

James ushered him to a comfortable chair near the window which looked down on to one of the courtyards in the Inner Temple. From here he could see the strolling lawyers enjoying the autumn sun.

'A small sherry as an aperitif?'

'Please.' Ben watched the secretary as she poured the sherry. He was sure she was aware of his observation. She displayed plenty of cleavage as she bent to put the glass on the coffee table beside him. Why was he getting this treatment?

Ben resolutely turned his attention to the sherry which was a good Amontillado and none too small. He took a draught, at the same time warning himself to stay alert.

'It's all right, Stephanie,' said James to the glamour bird. 'You can go to lunch. I'll drop the latch when we go out'

He rested his elbows on the desk, put the tips of his fingers together and regarded the young man seriously. 'Well, Benjamin, have you considered what you should do now?'

Ben shook his head. 'I hadn't really got as far as thinking about it. The police didn't leave till after one last night and I was up at seven to get the shop ready to open this morning.' He shrugged at James's raised eyebrows. 'Well, the staff were available; the police had no objections. There didn't seem to be any reason to stay closed. It might have inconvenienced our customers if we hadn't opened as usual.' Somehow the excuses appeared a bit lame when they were spelled out.

But James seemed to agree. 'Quite right. Quite right' He nodded emphatically. 'You always did have a sound head on your shoulders. I remember your father had no fears about you taking over the business.' He smiled in a paternal way. 'In fact, it's about the business that I wished to speak to you. You may feel it's a little premature but – well, as you indicated just now, life has to go on.'

What was all this was leading up to? James seemed to be taking a long time to get to the point. The man hesitated, almost as though he was waiting before he plunged in. Ben realized that the solicitor was worried about something. At last he continued.

'Benjamin, I have been asked to have a word with you. The Cimbrone family has been in touch with me. In short, they wish to acquire your shareholding in Cartwright Cimbrone. They are willing to offer you five hundred and forty thousand pounds for your stake in the business. You realize that is a very handsome offer without them even looking at the books.' He paused dramatically. 'What do you say?'

Ben sat in stunned silence for a few seconds. Then the anger burst out. 'Well, *they* haven't lost much time. I only e-mailed Alfredo the news of Toni's death at eight o'clock this morning. I haven't even received an acknowledgement yet.' He looked at James suspiciously. 'You rang me at eleven-thirty. How did this all happen so quickly?'

The solicitor spread his arms wide in innocence. 'As you know, the business world is a small place these days. I don't ask questions. I just carry out instructions.' However, he didn't manage to look Ben in the eye.

'But, even so. . . . Why do they suddenly come out with an offer like this? It sounds as though they're more worried about the future of the business than they are about Toni's death.'

James smiled obsequiously. 'The Cimbrone family obviously believes in moving quickly. I suppose they feel they must protect their interests.'

'What do you mean? I'm perfectly capable of running the British end. I've done it for long enough.' He paused as he thought about it for the first time. 'I suppose that now I could do with someone new in Italy, but that end is their responsibility.'

'All right. All right,' James soothed. 'You can't blame them for taking a constructive attitude.'

'Constructive attitude? That's rubbish! They've been doing very well out of Toni and me. He told me himself that their exports have increased dramatically since we started promoting their wines in Britain.'

'Perhaps they want to take the whole business a further step forward. You haven't got a lot of working capital for expansion, have you?'

So was that the reason for the offer? Ben knew that shortage of cash was his weakness.

James leaned forward persuasively. 'What do you say to their offer? It seems very good to me.'

'I don't know about that. It doesn't sound much of a return for the forty years which my father put into the business and my own last eight years.'

'It's way above the face value of the shares. You could never realize that much money from any other source.'

'Come off it, James. You know we could have screwed that big brewery for a lot more than the eight pounds a share which they offered us last year if we had been interested in selling at that time.'

'I'm not sure that I understand your terminology,' said James stuffily. 'In any case, you couldn't sell without the agreement of a majority of the shareholders. Cartwright Cimbrone is a close company. That stops you from selling your shares independently.'

'The point is, James, that nine months ago Toni and I both agreed that we wouldn't think of selling. We decided that the future prospects were too good. Why should I change my mind now?'

'For the very reason that the future of the company has changed with Toni's death. The Cimbrone family might stop supplies to you if you carried on trading on your own.'

'Let them,' Ben burst out. 'There are plenty of sources of wholesale wine. They'd be the losers if they tried to pull a trick like that.'

'But can't you see the benefits of this offer to you personally, Benjamin?' James was almost pounding. the desk in his anxious enthusiasm. 'This is where the future is.'

'That's rubbish, James. The future is with me. Just give me one good reason why I should hand the Cimbrone family my hard-won business for them to mess around with.'

'Surely you can see that they want to control their outlets.'

'Well, they damned well can't control this one. Let them set up their own organization if they want to have control of it. I'm not afraid of competition from them.'

James sighed. 'Don't get so upset, Benjamin. It's no good trying to fight them. They already own a big slice of your business. They can frustrate you any way you turn. There's no future in that for you or for anyone else.'

'All right.' Ben took a deep breath and tried to get a grip on himself. 'I know I'm going to have to reach some sort of financial arrangement with them, but I want to remain in the wine trade. I don't know any other kind of work.'

'Oh, I don't think you need to worry about that,' said James. 'There's more to this offer than just the money. They want to give you a job as well.' He waved his hands vaguely. 'Of course, I think they intend to appoint a general manager from Italy. But they're looking for growth. They want to expand into the provinces, open new outlets, make the whole thing a much bigger operation. There's even the possibility of a subsidiary in America. I believe they were thinking of offering you the job of sales manager for the whole of this country.'

'They seem to have done a lot of thinking since this morning,' said Ben suspiciously.

James ignored him. 'It would be a better salary than you get now. You could choose your own car, within reason. There'd be a generous expense allowance, non-contributory pension – everything like that.'

Ben exploded. 'Can't you get it into your head, James? I don't want to be a bloody salesman. I've been running my own business for eight years. Would you go back to being a solicitor's clerk just because someone gave you a rise and a fancy car?'

'That's hardly a sensible comparison,' said James huffily.

'Well, you can tell them that I'm damn well not going to be bought out. I want to go on just the way I am. I may be small; I may even be less efficient than a big company, but at least it's all mine.' He poked his finger at the other man. 'And you can also tell them that I don't think much of them for raising this matter even before Toni's been buried. Good God, it almost seems as though they were planning this before he died. A fine family he must have. I bet it's that bitch who's married to Alfredo. I could tell she didn't like me. But to do it the very day after he dies—' He shook his head. 'Well, I just don't know.'

'Oh, come now, serious matters like this can't be allowed to drag on for a long time. I would think this is just what Toni would have wanted.'

A terrible thought struck Ben but he rejected it instantly. 'If you're trying to suggest that Toni was a party to all this, I'm afraid I just won't accept that. He and I had the best possible working relationship. He never gave me any indication that his long-term aim was to hand over control to his family in Italy.'

'Don't be so sensitive, Benjamin. Toni was firstly a Cimbrone. He would obviously consider his family's wishes above all others.'

'But he would never have been persuaded into something like this.'

'How can you be so sure? His views may not always have coincided with yours.'

Ben shook his head. 'No,' he said with finality, 'you can tell them there's nothing doing.'

The solicitor cleared his throat and looked down at his hands which were now laid flat on the desk in front of him. 'I'm afraid you may not have much choice,' he said.

'What do you mean?' Ben felt his breath go short. Was there a hidden agenda here?

The man opened his mouth and closed it again. He seemed to be searching for the right words to explain his comment. Ben had no intention of letting him off the hook.

'Exactly what *do* you mean, James?' he asked grimly. There was long pause and he almost shouted. 'Come on, man, explain yourself.'

After a while Meredith spoke again. 'You will recall, Benjamin, when we set up this company, that it was decided that you and Toni would not hold half the shares each.' He swallowed nervously. 'This was arranged in order to avoid the company being caught in an impasse if you disagreed over policy. It was agreed that two per cent of the shares would be held in trust and that the voting rights for those shares would rest with the trustees.'

'Yes. That was your suggestion, and we could both see the sense in it. In fact the matter never arose because we always talked through any disagreements and sorted them out without any need to involve the trustees.'

'You are also aware,' continued James, 'that I am at present the sole trustee. You know also that I get no benefit from these shares myself. I am charged, under the rules of the trust, to use the voting powers – call it the casting vote if you wish – in the best interests of the business and therefore of all the shareholders.'

'What are you getting at, James? Those arrangements were to sort out problems between Toni and me. They are irrelevant now he is dead'

James shook his head. 'That is not correct. I have checked the exact wording of the trust document. As I thought, the trust does not terminate on the death of one of the other shareholders.' He pushed a sheaf of papers across the desk. 'You can look yourself, if you wish.'

'So what does that mean?'

The solicitor at last looked up at him and Ben could see there was naked fear in his eyes. What he couldn't understand was whether Meredith was afraid of him, or of something else.

'I have decided, in the best interests of all the shareholders, that the Cimbrone offer should be accepted. I have agreed that the trust should sell its two per cent of shares to them and should then be wound up.'

Ben was aghast 'Do you mean to say that you can sell up to one of the shareholders without the agreement of the other?'

'The trustees have that power, but are only entitled to exercise it in the event of the death of one of the main shareholders.'

'I remember that, but the intention of that clause was to allow Toni or me to keep control if one of us died so that the survivor could carry on the business.'

'I'm afraid,' said James with a twisted smile on his face, 'the trust document does not mention that intention. So I have acted in accordance with the literal meaning of Clause forty-seven. It is all perfectly legal. I have sold out to the company which controls the business interests of the Cimbrone family in Italy. I understand Toni's shares will also be sold to them. It is that company which has made you the offer I told you about just now. I urge you to accept. In my opinion it is the only way in which your business can survive.'

'And if I don't?'

Meredith shook his head at Ben. 'The Italians will hold effective control without your shares. They can do what they like. However, they agreed with me that you should not lose out in any way as a result of the new arrangement.' He smirked. 'I should like you to know that I insisted that a fair offer was made to you before I agreed to sell. I think you would be most foolish to throw it back in their faces.'

Ben switched his attack. 'Why do you have so little faith in me, James? I've been doing a good job, haven't I? Is this the way to repay the trust which my father and I have put in you over the years?'

'I must remind you again, Benjamin' – the solicitor's face was grey but he puffed himself up as he spoke – 'that Toni Cimbrone also placed his trust in me. That trust has been transferred to his heirs. I feel I have a duty to you all. I believe that I can best discharge that duty by making the decision I have.'

'That's rubbish, James. My God! There must be a way of fighting this. How can it be legal to hand the whole lot over to some people who have had nothing to do with it before and have never contributed anything to it? It's only the money which talks. I suppose if I came along with a better offer for the shares, you'd accept that, would you, and damn the others?'

'Can you arrange a better offer?'

'I – well – perhaps.'

Could he go back to the brewery? Would they still be interested?

And would they let him stay in control?

'I would have to know before four o'clock this afternoon so as to countermand my acceptance.'

Ben had to be realistic. He had no chance of arranging anything in that time. In any case, he suspected the brewery would give him no more freedom than the Cimbrone family. He knew that either way he was beaten.

'You know damned well that I can't sort out anything that quickly. I'd need at least a week.'

James leaned forward, trying to be persuasive. 'Benjamin, if you go home and think about it,. I'm certain you'll agree on reflection that this is the best course for all of us. I'm confident that the Cimbrones would hold their offer open for a little while so as to give you time to consider the matter fully. Take a few days off. You can leave the business under someone else's care, can't you? Talk to another firm of solicitors, if you wish. I have no objection to you showing them this copy of the agreement. But I do urge you to accept as soon as possible and take the package they are offering. It will open up a new and challenging future for you. Just think what you could do with five hundred and forty thousand pounds. You could get a new flat of your own. And you'd have a better-paid job than you have now. It would be an eight-hour day instead of all the hours you work at present In fact, I don't understand how you can even think of turning it down.'

Ben hated him. It was all so bloody neat. James was such a damned smooth operator. But he wasn't comfortable in this role. Ben was absolutely sure by now that there was something suspicious happening.

'And what about you, James? What do you get out of all this?'

'Nothing at all. I've already told you that the terms of the trust ensure that there is no benefit to the trustees.' He leaned back in his chair. 'Perhaps I'll have some small amount of relief from worry.'

'Come now, James, are you telling the truth? Surely the Cimbroni must be giving some sort of reward to their hatchet man. There must be something in it for you. What about the reorganization of the business? The new expansion will mean that there's lots of work for a British lawyer. No doubt there'll be other suckers to disinherit along the way.'

Meredith drew himself up pompously. 'You had better not repeat anything like that outside this room, Benjamin. Comments like that are actionable.'

'But you don't deny it.'

'I think your suggestions are beneath contempt'

'And I think your offer is beneath contempt,' Ben leapt to his feet 'You can tell your new backers that they've got a fight on their hands. The only way they're going to get rid of me is the same way that they removed Toni.'

Shaking with almost uncontrollable rage, Ben swung round and strode out of the office. He heard nothing of the solicitor's shouted reply as he ran down the stairs and out into the hushed bustle of the lunchtime Inner Temple.

- 4 -

Ben caught the 8.30 flight the next morning from Gatwick to Naples. It was one of those dismal October days which make you dread the long winter ahead. But Ben didn't notice the weather. His thoughts were elsewhere.

After he had left James Meredith's office the previous day he had walked around London for more than as hour. In his preoccupation with the row with his solicitor and the problems about the business, he was scarcely aware of the route he was taking. It was a long time before the rage subsided and he began to think in logical terms which didn't involve beating Meredith to a pulp or placing a bomb in the Villa Cimbrone.

It was obvious that the solicitor's support had somehow been bought by the Italians. Ben could see no other logical reason for his decision to hand over the business to them. It didn't make commercial sense. James was fully aware that the company had been built up to its present level largely by Ben's efforts. Something else must have persuaded him.

However, Ben was determined to fight to retain the company. He knew that he could run it by himself. It was operating efficiently and profitably. From what he had seen of them, the Cimbroni weren't likely to do any better. In fact, Alfredo was going to have his hands full just coping with their estates in Italy after the recent death of his father. He couldn't understand why they were now so intent on grabbing the business for themselves. It wasn't likely to increase their sales to Britain. They had never shown any interest in the London end before. Meredith had somehow tried to suggest that they had been hatching plans with Toni over a long period. But that didn't make sense unless they knew that Toni was likely to be murdered. And that raised a whole new set of unthinkable thoughts.

In any case, Ben had trusted his ex-partner. Something else must have happened to make them change their attitude. He wanted to know what that was – and he wanted them to change things back again.

As his mind started to operate on a more reasonable level he began to regret his outburst of temper to James Meredith. Maybe he was unwise to reject the offer so bluntly. There were other more subtle ways of fighting to keep control. On reflection, he decided he should send an e-mail to his solicitor that afternoon, apologizing for his outburst and saying he intended to give the Cimbroni a considered decision in a few days. By this means he hoped to gain some time so that he could sort out his relationship with Toni's family.

Meanwhile one thing was clear. He had to get an immediate and firm grip on the business – one which the Cimbroni would find difficult to shake off. Now that the company was known particularly for its Italian wines, it would be important to try to maintain supplies. He had stocks to keep him going for at least three months until the current year's vintage came through. He was fairly confident that he could continue the purchasing side from the point which Toni had reached before his death. But he would have to be prepared to buy his wines from the shippers, instead of direct through the Cimbroni company. He had all the paperwork, addresses and contacts. Later he might decide to appoint an agent in Italy if he could find the right man.

He hoped that cash would not be an immediate problem. He and Toni had both been sole signatories on cheques since they often didn't see each other for some weeks. In practice there was only one cheque book which Ben held in the office. So nearly all payments were made by him. The two of them used to meet approximately once a month when they went through the cash book and Ben accounted to Toni for the sums he had paid out.

So that afternoon Ben called in to the bank. They appeared to know nothing of any impending changes in the ownership of the company and Ben didn't advise them otherwise. He purchased a draft on the Bank of Naples for £20,000 made out to himself. His explanation was that he needed the cash for the purchase of wine stocks on a forthcoming visit to Italy. He could redeem it later for cash and pay the money into his personal account if the need arose. Just over £10,000 was still left in the account for day-to-day expenses and salaries. He would be back before the end of the month to pay the staff. Overdraft facilities existed with a limit of £50,000 if he should need them. He assuaged any feelings of guilt by promising himself that the money would only be used for the good of the company.

The premises were more of a problem. The seventy-year lease had been transferred into the name of the new company. He recognized that it was one of the areas where he might be vulnerable. He decided to write to the landlords informing them of Toni's death and assuring them that there was to be no change in the company's direction and policies. He signed the letter as managing director. That should at least delay any legal moves to try to take over the premises during his absence.

He decided to take Peggy into his confidence. She was very loyal. When he told her about his interview with the solicitor she was horrified that the Cimbroni could behave in this way. She agreed to help while he was in Italy. He arranged with her that all cheques in future were to be made out to Mr B. Cartwright. These and the cash takings were to be paid into his personal account. Credit-card sales were to be discontinued at present. Customers were to be told that it was due to financial reorganization following his partner's death. He signed a letter of instruction to Peggy covering these arrangements. That should protect her in the event of any subsequent legal proceedings.

Then he telephoned the airport and booked his seat on the next flight to Naples. He had decided that the only course open to him was to confront the Cimbrone family at their home. There he would do his best to persuade them to change their minds. Otherwise he was prepared to threaten them with a long, difficult battle in the British courts if they wanted to oust him. That ought to dampen their ardour for the takeover.

At the last minute he decided he ought to telephone Inspector Paisley to check he had no objection to Ben going to Naples. The policeman only asked for his mobile phone number, in case he wanted an answer to any unexpected questions. He told Ben that police inquiries were still at any early stage. In fact, he seemed almost to have lost interest in the case.

*

Ben settled himself into the gangway seat and took out his paper. But he found he wasn't reading the words. His mind was racing ahead to his meeting with Alfredo. Language would be a problem. He didn't think that Alfredo's English was very good. Probably it was similar to Ben's Italian. Perhaps they could find someone to act as an interpreter.

Suddenly his paper was pushed to one side and he found his nose was only a few inches from a spectacular cleavage. The bursting brassiere was a deep pink with maroon embroidery. The blouse, which was a lighter pink, was made of a kind of rough silk and didn't seem to have any buttons to hold it together. The throat above the splendid chest was long and white and seemed to go on forever. Above it the full red lips were smiling tolerantly.

'Excuse me, could I get to my seat?'

The voice was deep and throaty; the accent East Coast American. The question was full of amusement.

Ben pulled himself upright in the confined space. He was covered in confusion. 'I-I'm sorry. I was deep in my paper.'

'So was I,' she chuckled.

She squeezed herself past, apparently in imminent danger of bursting out of her tight clothes. As he breathed in to give her more room he swallowed a lungful of a deep, rich scent more suitable for evening wear. He helped her to settle into her seat, put her bag in the overhead locker, found the end of her seat belt for her, playing the perfect English gentleman. Of course she was the sort of woman whom every man would want to help.

Then it was time for them to strap themselves in while the aircraft taxied out for take-off. Busy with his thoughts, Ben didn't notice that his neighbour had fallen silent.

The aircraft turned on to the runway and rolled to a halt as the engines were run up to full power. Then there came the crescendo of furious noise, the lurching rush along the tarmac, and the sudden swooping sensation that seemed to leave the stomach behind as the nose came up and the aircraft took off.

He watched out of the window as they climbed into the low cloud and found themselves wrapped around with cotton wool. It was then that he became aware that his hand was being gripped with a passionate strength. Long fingernails were digging into the flesh of his wrist. He turned to look at the woman next to him and was surprised to see that her face was a deathly white and her eyes were closed. For a moment he wondered about calling a stewardess.

'Are you all right?'

The blue eyes opened and gazed at him. They were dark with fear. The pale lips were slightly parted. The stomach was drawn in and the splendid chest was rising and falling tremulously. 'Wouldn't you think, the thousands of miles that I've flown, that I'd be used to it by now?' she whispered. 'But every take-off still terrifies me.'

'Do you think a drink might help you relax?'

She smiled hesitantly. 'Why, thank you. A Scotch would go down very well.'

At that moment they broke through the heavy shroud of cumulus masking southern England into a brilliant pink and blue world. The sun burst into the cabin, putting colour into the drab faces. As far as one could see out of the windows on each side was a magnificent cloudscape stretching away like some massive, boiling sea which had been frozen into inactivity.

Ben's eyes strayed back to his companion and he smiled. 'If you'll release me for a few seconds I'll call a stewardess and see what they've got.'

She dropped his hand as if it had been red hot. 'I'm sorry. I hadn't even noticed what I was doing.' She looked down at his wrist and picked it up again, massaging it like a bruised apple. 'Oh, look what I've done to you with my nails. I'm so sorry. What must you think of me?'

'Don't apologize. It hardly hurts at all,' said Ben gallantly. 'I'm very pleased to have been of service.'

He was rewarded by another smile and a little shake of the blonde curls. 'You English, you're so polite.'

That was the beginning of what Ben decided was a most enjoyable flight. His companion began to relax when she had a drink in her hand. The colour came back into her cheeks. He discovered that Donna Carter was a ready talker. He soon heard about her job in New York as an advertising executive and her love of travel. She had been all over the world and 'done' Europe on several ocacasions.

'If's the best way I can think of spending my alimony.'

'You've been married?' Ben thought she didn't look old enough to have finished a whole marriage.

'Uh-huh. My ex was called Joseph A. Carter, Junior – the creep. It lasted fourteen months and three days. He was a bastard. Each day of those fourteen months I promised myself I'd take him for every cent I could grab.' She smiled at him rather bitterly. 'I reckon I'm now costing him at least the profits of a small oil well every year.'

Ben kept quiet on this topic. The morality seemed a little strange, but then this was the first time he'd had such a frank conversation with a woman about her marriage. Soon the talk passed on to other things. As they drank and chatted together Ben forgot all about the problems facing him in Italy and those waiting for him at home when he returned.

By the time a late breakfast was served by the stewardess, Donna was back to her former cheerful self as she told him what society was like in New York. She exchanged her bacon for one of his tomatoes. She was enthusiastic about English breakfasts.

As the flight and the friendship progressed she began to coax him into talking about himself and his life in England. 'London is my favourite city after New York,' she said. 'So much always seems to be happening there.'

Almost without his own volition, Ben found he was discussing his business problems and the reason for his flight to Naples. He told her of his determination to fight every way he knew to retain his hold on the business,

'You've done just the right thing,' she agreed. 'You go straight in and confront them. Don't you let them force you out.'

She nodded at him earnestly. 'Have you noticed how your problems start to get smaller once you face up to them? I always say that to myself. That's how I got rid of Joseph Carter. He was pleased to see the back of me at any price by the time I'd finished with him.'

Ben sipped his coffee in acquiescence.

'I'll be disappointed if you don't come away from Naples with their full backing.' Donna waved her plastic knife at him to emphasize her point 'You're a young guy. All they really want to know is that you're going to stand up and fight for your business. Once they can see that they're not going to walk off with all the money you've earned for them in the last few years, they'll soon step into line.'

Ben was a bit shocked to realize that he'd divulged rather more than he'd intended of his own none-too-legal plans to this warm, garrulous American. Luckily she already seemed to be a whole-hearted admirer of his aims.

He was enjoying Donna's company so much that he was suddenly surprised to find the three-hour flight was nearing its end. A disembodied message from the pilot informed him they were starting their descent. Then he noticed a change in the engine note and the angle of the aircraft tilted forward. He glanced out of the window and saw they were coming in over the sea to start their approach to Naples Airport.

The voice came over the intercom. 'Will you fasten your seat-belts please, ladies and gentlemen? There may be some turbulence on our approach to Naples associated with an increase in activity of the volcano Solfatara. There is nothing for you to worry about. We will be landing at Naples in just under five minutes where the ground temperature is twenty-three degrees. We hope you enjoy your visit.' The voice was cut off with a hollow click.

There was a sudden increase in vibration as the aircraft throttled back. The previously smooth flight was replaced by a pitching and yawing motion as they descended into the disturbed air above the land. The aircraft banked as the pilot lined up for the approach. Ben noticed that the grey, worried look had come back into Donna's face.

'Don't worry,' he tried to reassure her. 'It will be over in a few minutes. There's nothing at all for you to worry about.'

She gave him a bleak smile. 'Everyone tells me that each time. Next thing you'll tell me to relax. Everybody does, but it never seems to help.'

'Do you want my hand again? Try and see if you can draw blood this time.'

He was rewarded by a real smile as she took it.

'I've been hoping you were going to ask before,' said Ben. 'I was willing to donate it for the whole flight if it would help.'

Donna raised her eyes to the roof. 'Now he tells me!' Then she suddenly shut her mouth as the aircraft dropped like a stone into an air pocket and the engine note rose sharply.

She said nothing more for the next few minutes as the aircraft weaved its irregular way down the approach path and over the threshold of the runway, but all the time she gripped his hand tightly. Then came the final sharp descent, the bump of the wheels on to terra firma, the wild roar of the engines and the violent braking as the pilot applied reverse thrust. Ben hardly noticed the aircraft's motion. He was too busy enjoying the sensation of having his hand squeezed tight against Donna's soft, full bosom.

When he looked at her, he noticed her pale complexion once again. Her eyes were tightly closed and her lips pressed together in a hard line. He suddenly realized that she was quite a bit older than he had previously assumed. However it made her no less attractive to him.

It was only when they had rolled to a halt outside the terminal and the engine note had died away, that she finally opened her eyes and exhaled a deep breath. But she still kept a tight hold of his hand and Ben made no attempt to remove it. He felt a quickening of his pulse as she gazed at him with her eyes bright blue again. However there now seemed to be a shortage of words in comparison to the way in which they had flowed so freely from her before. This fear of flying seemed to strip away the mask of maturity and turn her back into a vulnerable girl. Ben found himself feeling a lot more affectionate towards her than he should.

As he helped her from her seat, he was almost sure she purposely leaned against him as she slid past and preceded him down the gangway. Ben felt the bachelor in him stirring. At the exit door she paused and waited for him. He placed an arm firmly about her waist and helped her down the steps. As they walked across the concrete to the arrivals door he carried her bag and she linked her arm through his. They seemed almost like a couple going on holiday together.

He said, 'Well, you may not have enjoyed your flight very much, but it's been a lot of fun for me.'

'It's the best flight I've had in a long time.' When she looked up at him, her face had a kind of half-smile but her eyes were serious. That look set him wondering just a little. Then she winked, the veneer of fun back on again. 'I'll have to see if the alimony will run to hiring an escort in future.'

Ben tried to match her bantering tone. 'If you're going back to London in a few days' time I'd be willing to do the return trip for free.'

'Hey, I hope you're not going to wait until we return to hold my hand again. I think you ought at least to give me the chance to buy you dinner one evening to say thank you.'

'How could I refuse an offer like that?' Ben stood back and held the door open for her.

'That's OK then. I'll give you the name and number of my hotel while we're waiting for the bags.'

As they stood by the conveyor she gave him her card with her New York address on it (in case he ever went that way) and wrote down the name of her hotel and the phone number. They were standing very close together. He could sometimes feel her hair tickling his cheek and smell the slight scent still clinging to her. But he was sure that neither of them believed they would actually meet again.

He tried to take a firm grip of his thoughts. He was here for the purpose of conducting important business – the *most* important business of his life. He really must concentrate on the matter in hand. He didn't have time for a casual flirtation, did he? But where was the harm in having some pleasure at the same time as he was working?

Just then Donna called out, 'Hey, there's my bag,' and the moment passed.

She rushed off across the baggage hall to get it. Then Ben saw his own suitcase come out on the other side and he went to collect it. But the crowds were thick around the conveyor and it took him several minutes to extricate himself and his bag from the mêlée. When he finally turned round to look for Donna, she was nowhere to be seen. Why had she suddenly disappeared?

He went to where he had last seen her, but her case had disappeared and so had she. He spent a couple of minutes looking around the arrivals hall but he couldn't find her. So, with a little shrug, he gave up. It was probably more sensible that way. Perhaps he would have an opportunity to ring her after he had been to the Villa Cimbrone. Philosophically he made for the exit.

As he reached the door a small Italian came over to him. 'Signor Cartwright?'

Ben nodded, surprised. He hadn't realized that anyone but Peggy was aware that he would be here.

The swarthy little man beckoned. 'Come. I have car.'

'How on earth did you know who I was?'

The fellow didn't seem to understand. He grabbed Ben's arm. 'Car this way.'

'Are you – from Cimbroni' He felt slightly ridiculous talking this pidgin English.

'*Si. Si.*' The Italian nodded furiously. He grabbed the case from Ben's unprotesting grip and set off across the road towards the car-park. Ben had to hurry to keep up with him. He could already feel the heat raising prickles under his shirt.

The man made for the far corner of the large car park in front of the airport building. He had a small Fiat parked there. He stood Ben's case on end on the front seat. Then he opened the back door for his passenger before he scurried round and jumped into the driving seat. Ben scarcely had time to get in and close the door before the car was off with a violent jerk and a haze of blue exhaust.

They weaved through the car park and on to the exit road which led past the terminal building. As they passed the main doors he saw Donna come out. A tall, good-looking man held her case in one hand and her left elbow in the other. Ben was convinced she saw him as his car went past, but she showed no sign of having recognized him.

Oh well, he thought to himself as he peered at her out of the rear window, I suppose I shouldn't be surprised that it didn't take her long to find a new escort.

A few seconds later the little car swung into a roundabout and she was hidden from view. Why did he have the feeling that she had been keeping clear of him and yet watching him leave at the same time?

- 5 -

The Fiat pulled out of the airport entrance and was immediately embroiled in the Naples midday traffic jam. The driver didn't take the ring road where the traffic at least appeared to be moving, even though it was nose to tail at thirty miles an hour. Instead they crossed straight over at the junction and dived into the city itself. They were soon in a long broad street full of noise and action.

It was Ben's first experience of Naples traffic which was like nowhere else on earth that he had ever seen before. Drivers were constantly pulling out, turning off, crossing over, making U-turns, stopping for chats with friends or arguments with other drivers. They didn't bother to give any indication of their intentions. Between the cars and vans hurtled innumerable scooters and mopeds, driven by young and old. None of the riders appeared to have heard of safety helmets. Some had old ladies sitting side-saddle on the pillion and carrying massive shopping baskets on their laps. Others had livestock in cages. From this activity rose a cacophany of sound made up of revving engines, screaming drivers and a bewildering variety of horns. The pitiless sun beat down into this narrow canyon of babel through a haze of petrol vapour and pollution. The whole experience was exhausting.

It was a relief when the driver turned off the main street into one of the narrow, shady side streets. Here the tall flats towered above them, their balconies seeming almost to meet above their heads. Shutters were closed against the noise and dust of the street. Lines of washing criss-crossed between the balconies like strings of tatty bunting.

The Fiat speeded up. It weaved between the scattered, parked cars, bouncing over rubbish and debris and disturbing urchins playing in the gutters. In this way they made irregular but better progress. The little Italian driver certainly seemed to know his way around Naples. He swung from right to left and back again through the network of narrow streets, plunging across main thoroughfares and threading his way round small piazzas until Ben was utterly bewildered and had lost all sense of direction. In the end he just sat back to observe the motley collection of humanity which peopled the worst slums of Western Europe.

Some of the impressions remained vivid long after he had returned to London. In one of the main streets he watched people stepping uncaringly over the body of an old woman with a small dog seated by her head. No one seemed to bother whether she was alive or dead. Wherever they went there were emaciated animals with ribs showing through their fur, picking around the heaps of rubbish or squabbling over scraps of food. It was common to see adults urinating in the gutters. Flat dwellers threw bowls of fluid into the streets from upstairs balconies. Everywhere was rubbish and filth and detritus.

Ben scarcely noticed as the car turned into another short, dingy street lined with the same high buildings either side. About halfway along it suddenly came to a halt. The little man jumped out and ran round to the other side of the car. He opened Ben's door.

'You get out here,' he commanded in a none-too-friendly tone.

He opened the front door, took out Ben's case and stood it in the road, slamming the car door behind it.

'What's this?' asked Ben, emerging into the heat and the smells. 'This isn't Posillipo.'

The Italian was already getting back into the driver's seat. 'You wait here,' he repeated.

He shut his door, let the car into gear and accelerated away with what seemed like a desperate urgency. Ben's still open door banged against his case, sending it flying into the gutter, before it rebounded shut. The Fiat raced off and squealed round the corner at the end of the street on two wheels.

As the roar of the engine dwindled away to nothing an almost tangible silence settled on the street, broken only by the distant sounds of the city seeping round the corners. Here there were no happy noises of children skylarking. Somewhere near at hand a solitary dog barked, lazily but frequently, like a creaking sign swinging in the wind.

Ben walked over and rescued his case from the gutter. Mystified by his sudden abandonment, he looked around him. This street was hardly more than a wide alleyway. On both sides the buildings were like many others in the area. They were four or five storeys high with narrow metal balconies projecting from the upper floors. The shutters were closed tight to bar the entrance of the slanting rays of the sun.

There was a solitary old car parked against a wall towards the far end of the alley. As far as he could see it was empty. There was no sign in the whole street of any person and no other feature to relieve the monotony, save the usual piles of rubbish. It seemed as though this place had been forgotten by humanity.

Why had he been abandoned here? What was he supposed to be waiting for? Ben thought it was an odd sort of a place to arrange a meeting. Perhaps the other car was actually waiting for him. The driver might have fallen asleep in the heat. It seemed an unlikely prospect, since the vehicle was old and tatty. But it was worth a try.

He picked up his case and started down the street in the direction of the car. As he did so two men, who had previously been out of sight, moved out of the shadow of a doorway near the vehicle and began to walk towards him. They were big, tough-looking men, dressed in dark clothes. One had sunglasses on. Their step was slow and purposeful and their arms hung free by their sides as though ready for action. Ben felt the hair rise on the back of his neck.

He had heard about the multitude of petty criminals who were supposed to people the poor quarters of Naples, taking advantage of foolish tourists who strayed from the safe main streets. He decided to try the other way.

He turned round and started to retrace his steps. He remembered that the road they had come from was wider than this one. A couple of hundred yards to the left along that street was one of the main boulevards which they had crossed in the little car.

A quick glance behind told him that the men had quickened their pace. Ben began to hurry. Perhaps they would simply turn out to be the carriers of a message from the Cimbroni. However he preferred to receive it where there were other people around.

It was then that a third man came round the corner in front of him. Although the fellow was twenty yards away, Ben picked him out clearly. He was dressed in a suit made of a black, shiny material. He was hunched forward and the jacket seemed to rest on the back of his shoulders. It had narrow lapels which framed a black T-shirt. His greasy hair was slicked close to his head. His trousers were tight to his legs and his shoes had pointed toes. The American term 'hood' floated into Ben's mind.

The man halted and his hand came out of his pocket. Ben's heart seemed to stop as he saw the man was holding a knife. The man waved the knife in front of him, daring him to come any closer. Ben halted. He didn't want to end up like Toni's grotesquely murdered body in the office in London.

There was a shout behind him and the two men broke into a run. That galvanized Ben into activity. With a desperate urgency he leaped for the nearest door in the wall to his left. Luckily it opened as he turned the handle. He pushed inside and slammed the door behind him. In the gloom he could see a flight of stairs straight ahead. He went up these three at a time, fear giving his feet a nimble sureness. At the top he turned right and tried the door facing him. It was locked.

He heard the front door crash open and the light flooded in again. As quietly as possible he dashed along the landing and up the next flight of stairs. This time the door on the right opened. Breathing heavily, he stepped inside, still carrying his suitcase in his left hand.

Ben found he was in a dark parlour filled with massive, ornate furniture which left little floor space. A great lace-covered table filled the centre of the room. On the opposite wall was a large oval mirror which was partly obscured by yellowing drapes. In a corner to the right was a small shrine with a candle which flickered in front of a painting of the Virgin Mary. He turned back and closed the door, slipping home the iron bolt near the floor for extra security. Perhaps, if he kept quiet, they might not find him.

But that hope was short-lived. As he straightened up he was startled by a scream from behind him. Ben spun round. He saw a short, plump, middle-aged woman in a black dress advancing on him from the door at the back of the room. Suddenly she rushed at him with her hands raised and her voice babbling excited Italian. But at the same moment there came a violent shaking of the door behind him and she froze into immobility. There was a crash as someone applied a shoulder to the door.

Ben edged round the table towards a pair of narrow double doors which he had noticed leading towards the front of the house. As he did so there was another crash and the door burst open. The slick Italian stepped into the room followed by the other two. He held out his left hand – the one without the knife. It was a shock to hear him speak in broken English. That meant that he obviously knew who Ben was.

'Pliss. You give me the mock.'

'What?'

'We know you have it.'

He stepped forward a pace and Ben backed closer to the double doors.

'You do not go.'

When Ben continued to retreat things started to happen quickly. With hardly a pause the hood raised his right arm and threw the knife straight at him. Ben's automatic reaction was to jerk up his case to protect himself and the knife buried itself up to the hilt in its top with a dull thud. More astonished than frightened, Ben reached down and caught hold of the flat wooden handle. He pulled and the knife came out with a hollow creak. He found himself looking at a smooth-sided little implement with a blade no longer than the handle. It was surprisingly heavy. He felt an inconsequential feeling of regret about the damage it would have done to his clothes. Grasping the little knife firmly, he raised his eyes and the blade to the Italians. They paused, uncertain of his intentions.

The woman let out a loud wail. Without even looking at her, the hood hit her across the face with the flat of his hand. She toppled back against the wall and slid slowly down until she was sitting on the floor. Her eyes were wide with terror and her mouth had dropped open to reveal an ugly row of yellowed teeth.

The hood started to move round the table towards him. One of the toughs followed him and his mate went the other way. Ben decided it was time to get out. Cautiously, he backed through the swing doors behind him, making threatening gestures at them with the knife. He glanced to left and right. The room he entered had a high ceiling. There was a large bed in one corner which was half covered with an untidy heap of cushions. A variety of heavy furniture stood against the walls. But on the other side of the room was a pair of double French windows which were standing open. Full-length shutters were closed across the windows to keep out the heat.

With a sudden rush Ben let the doors swing closed and made for the shutters. They clattered open and he found himself on a small balcony which had a metal railing about three feet high. A couple of straggly pot plants stood to the left. Ben made for the other end, looking down to the street as he went. It was at least twenty feet below. That was a long way to fall without injury. There was nobody down there to whom he could appeal for help.

The swing doors banged open behind him and made his decision for him. As the Italians burst on to the balcony Ben hurled his damaged case at them and had the satisfaction of seeing all three of them go down in a heap of jumbled arms and legs. Without further hesitation he made for the balcony rail.

A washing line hung across the street to a balcony on the other side. He grabbed it and slashed at it with the knife. Most of the strands of the rope parted but at least two remained. However, he was already hurdling the rail, dropping the knife as he went, and grabbing the washing line with both hands. He frantically began to pull himself across the street hand over hand on the rope, half-sliding as it sagged.

He had only gone three or four feet when the last two strands parted with a twang and he found himself hurtling through the air. With a desperate yell he twisted his body, let go of the rope and landed feet first in a heap of garbage. It was probably that which saved him from breaking an ankle. He overbalanced, fell flat on his back, and the wind was knocked out of him with a whoosh. As he looked up at the balcony the three Italian heads appeared side by side, peering down at him. The next moment they were gone and Ben recovered his sense of urgency.

Somewhat shakily he got to his feet, stumbled down the alleyway and out into the street beyond. Gasping for breath, he ran as fast as his shocked body would allow him towards the main road where he hoped he might find safety.

Suddenly a little Alfa burst out of the traffic at the end of the street and started towards him. It screamed to a halt not five yards away, and there at the wheel was Donna, gesticulating furiously. Overwhelmed with relief, Ben scrabbled at the passenger door handle as she leaned over to open it.

He almost fell into the seat, pulling the door shut behind him, and gasped, 'For Christ's sake, get out of here as fast as you can. There are three men after me with a knife.'

Donna needed no further urging. With a violent lurch and a squeal of tyres she accelerated down the road, while Ben collapsed back into his seat, breathless and speechless. His last view of that place was of the three Italians rushing out of the side street and leaping for safety as the little car bore down on them at a dangerous pace.

Donna drove through the centre of Naples like a woman possessed. Ben had never seen such driving. She seemed completely fearless, both for herself and for the car. Pedestrians and animals leapt aside; other cars swerved out of her way or screamed to a halt; the drivers took one look at her smiling face and low *décolletage* and made way for her with a grin and a touch of the fingertips to the lips.

As soon as he had regained his breath Ben asked the question which had occupied his mind for the last few minutes. 'How on earth did you come to be in that street at that very moment?'

'I was looking for you, of course.' She glanced at him sideways and grinned. Ben noticed a young man take a huge step backwards to avoid premature disablement as she rushed past. 'Listen my friend, no one runs out on me. I was all set to offer you a lift. Next thing I see you running off with some little Italian. I didn't much like the look of him.'

Ben pulled a face. 'When I came back with my case, you'd disappeared. I looked everywhere for you.'

'I'd only gone to collect my hire-car. It didn't take me more than five minutes.' She tossed her curls. 'You didn't wait long.'

He knew she wasn't telling him the whole truth, but he decided now was the time to be humble. 'I'm sorry,' he said. 'I thought you'd forgotten all about me.'

'What, and give up holding your hand for the whole flight back? Besides, that driver seemed a nasty piece of work.'

'You should have seen his mates. They'd give you bad dreams at night.'

Donna nearly took six inches off the front end of an expensive sports car as they burst out of a side street into one of the main thoroughfares. 'It sounds as though you've run foul of the local mafia. This must be the sort of thing these dodgy Italians try on new arrivals to make a few euros.'

'But why do they have to choose me? Do I look like a soft touch?'

She gave one of her throaty chuckles. 'Benjamin – you certainly do.'

'I suppose it was lucky I had you to keep an eye on me.'

'I tell you it was a hell of a job trying to keep up with you. That little Italian knows how to drive. I thought I'd lost you a couple of streets back when our scruffy friend nipped across a main road and I had a bit of a dispute with a taxi driver. These blokes are worse than they are in New York.'

'Thank God you chose the right turning,' said Ben. 'I reckon you saved my life.'

Donna smiled. 'You're welcome. It seems fair recompense for what you did for me on the plane.'

'It's my turn to buy the dinner now. I'm the one who's in your debt.'

She winked at him as she swung. into a gap that seemed half the size of the car. Her manoeuvre was accompanied by a fanfare of horns. 'I've got some ideas about that,' she said.

A thought suddenly struck Ben. 'Here – I left my case behind with all my clothes in it.'

'How on earth did you do that?'

'Well, one of them threw a knife at me and it hit the case instead of me. Then, when they chased after me, I threw the suitcase at them to slow them down so that I could get away.' Ben gave Donna a graphic description of his tangle with the Italians and his means of escape.

'Wow!' she exhaled when he had finished. 'You certainly had a narrow squeak.'

'But now I've lost all my clothes and everything, else,' he lamented. I remember now that I forgot my briefcase and left it in the little car. I've got nothing except what I'm wearing.'

'What about. your passport?'

Ben felt in his inside pocket. 'Yes, that's still there – and my wallet. So at least I can get some money. I'll have to buy new clothes This lot stink.'

'You do smell a bit like a rubbish bin,' agreed Donna, wrinkling. up her pretty nose. 'The first thing you need is a shower and a clean up. That's where we're going now.'

The car shot out into a large piazza with a grand statue in the middle. Donna cut straight across four rows of traffic at a crazy angle. She nearly executed a young policeman as he leapt on to his traffic island for safety. Then she screamed into the magnificent entrance arch of the Hotel Excelsior. A porter rushed forward to open the car door for her and offered his hand to help her out. Ben could almost see the man drooling over her curvaceous body as she emerged from the car. She smiled at him devastatingly, handed him the car keys and addressed him in fluent Italian. Bowing low, the man hurried to the boot and extracted several large cases. Ben wondered where on earth they had come from.

'This way, Benjamin.' Donna swept into the reception hall followed by the porter, staggering under the load of her baggage. Ben trailed behind, almost unnoticed and feeling a poor third.

Donna turned to him. 'You leave all this to me,' she said. 'I'll sort out something for you. Let me have your passport.'

Ben carefully stood among her cases, trying to shield his stained trousers from any prying eyes. He hoped they were not too worried about strong smells in this hotel. However most people appeared to be much more interested in La Signora Donna Carter who seemed to have taken centre stage in the life of the Hoel Excelsior.

He looked round. There on the shelf beside him was the early edition of the Naples evening paper. In the centre of the front page was a large photograph of a blasted, lunar landscape with jets of smoke and steam rising from it. SOLFATARA ERUPTA blazed the headline. The article below seemed to be a description of the new activity in the volcano which had been semi-dormant for centuries. However it was now becoming active again. Ben was able to make out that thousands of people were being moved from the city of Pozzuoli which was built all round the volcano. The city centre, the old town around the harbour and the suburbs near the crater itself were now prohibited areas. Police patrols arrested anyone found inside the barricades.

Donna finished chatting up the reception clerk and came over to him. 'Here you are. I've arranged everything. All you need to do is sign this registration slip. Any squiggle will do.'

Ben put his illegible signature where Donna indicated and she took it back to the desk. Then she returned, took his arm, and shepherded him to the lift. He carried one of her cases and the porter trailed behind with the others. She pressed the button for the tenth floor.

In the lift she pressed a ten euro note into his hand. 'I think its better for *you* to hand over the tip,' she murmured. 'These Italians are sticklers for doing things the right way.'

'I haven't much cash with me,' said Ben. 'I really need to get to a bank.'

'There's one just round the corner but it doesn't open till four. We can go later.'

Ben thought she seemed to know her way around Naples pretty well. Just then the lift stopped and Donna led the way along a thickly carpeted corridor.

'It's just down here on the right.'

'Have you been here before?'

'This is my fifth visit.'

Donna stopped outside room 1008. She inserted the key and opened the door. Ben looked past her into a beautiful room with a large double bed. But what most caught his eye was the complete wall of windows on the far side of the room. They opened on to a balcony which provided the most magnificent views across the Bay of Naples.

Ben followed the porter into the room. 'Wow,' he said. 'I hope mine isn't as expensive as this.'

'This is yours,' said Donna over her shoulder.

He gulped and she grinned at him. 'Aw, don't worry. Joseph Carter's paying.'

'Really?'

'Uh-huh. Shouldn't you tip the porter?'

'What? Oh.' Recalled to his duty, Ben handed over the ten euro note. The man bent low as he took it 'Grazie, Signor Carter.'

'Pardon?' Ben watched the door close behind the man then turned to face Donna who winked at him.

'It's a little secret between me and the man on reception. I reckon it's the first generous act that Carter Junior has done in the whole of his life, and he doesn't even know about it'

She crossed to the bed, unzipping her skirt as she went and letting it drop round her ankles. She slid off her blouse and tossed it on the bed. Then she reached behind her back to undo her bra.

'I sure am looking forward to that shower,' she said.

Ben hastily went to check that the lock was secure on the bedroom door. When he turned back, Donna was coming towards him. Her naked body was an uplifting sight to a weary man who'd been chased round Naples for the last couple of hours.

She laughed at the expression on his face, walked right up to him and poked him in the chest. 'Are you coming for a shower or not?' As he reached out to touch her she spun away and added, 'And don't forget to stick your clothes outside the door for room service. I don't want to share my bed with a tramp.'

Ben. stood, as if in a trance, and watched her buttocks undulate into the bathroom. Then he hastily started to take off his trousers.

- 6 -

The wall along the front of the Villa Cimbrone was at least ten feet high. It was old and crumbling, with a spectacular growth of weeds sprouting from the parapet. Nevertheless it would be hazardous to try to climb over it. In the centre the stonework to the once splendid old gateway was sadly deteriorated. Only the large iron-bound gates were freshly painted and the hinges newly oiled.

Ben pulled at the large brass knob set in the right hand gatepost. It started a bell jangling somewhere in the distance. But gradually the noise died away and only the silence returned. He looked around. The dusty road was deserted, hemmed in along both sides by similar high walls. The only difference was that most of the others were in better condition.

Donna had dropped him at the main road. She hadn't seemed too keen about testing the springs of the little Alfa over the rough potholes of the side road that led to the villa. So Ben had left her there. He was carrying his brand new briefcase which contained all his worldly possessions – a sponge bag and the change of clothes he had purchased that morning. He had walked round to the driver's door to say goodbye.

' 'Bye.' Donna's words were bright, but her voice was more husky than he remembered it before. 'Don't forget to ring me soon.'

That was to remind him that he was also carrying the brand-new mobile phone which she had insisted he buy, 'So that I don't lose you so easily next time'.

'Thanks for everything,' he said.

'Tell me when you see me next.' She tried to wink but her lashes stuck together and she had to rub her eye with her forefinger.

Ben leaned in at the window to give her an inadequate peck on the cheek. He was rewarded by a view down the front of her loose cotton dress which nearly extended to her navel. With a quick, 'Goodbye, then', he turned and walked off down the gravelly road trying to concentrate on the task ahead. After a few seconds he heard the Alfa rev up and pull away.

It was now late afternoon but the sun was still beating down mercilessly. There was very little shade and no breeze in the roadway. Ben could feel himself beginning to perspire freely. He put down his new briefcase, took off the jacket of his dry-cleaned suit and slung it over his shoulder. Then he yanked again at the bell-pull and started the mad jangling going once more. The day, which had started so well, was beginning to run downhill.

They had been very late getting up that morning. In fact it had been well after ten before they had rung for breakfast to be served in the room.

'A man has to keep his strength up,' Donna reminded him, looking enticing in a see-through negligée.

The waiter had shown no surprise at the undressed condition of the guests. After eating, it had been another two hours before they finally got up and showered and dressed – Ben in his freshly laundered clothes. He calculated that they hadn't left the bed for nearly twenty hours.

They had caught the bank just before it closed for siesta. Donna had half-charmed and half-bullied the little bank clerk into setting up a new account for Ben, into which he paid his draft. Then she persuaded the man to let him cash a cheque for ˇ1,000 without waiting for clearance. Actually she'd asked for two.

With the money in his wallet, they went shopping and Donna took great delight in helping him to choose a new outfit. Ben had an uncomfortable feeling that she was trying to make him look like something off a Miami beach. Then it was back to the hotel for another love-making session. So, by the time they had lingered over a light lunch on the balcony and the inevitable further wrestle on the bed, it was nearly four o'clock. He had dressed in his dry-cleaned suit and shoes to look more formal. By then it was getting late to call on the Cimbrone family.

*

Ben returned his attention to the doorbell. The people here didn't seem in a hurry to reply. But he had no intention of leaving without his interview with Alfredo. Impatiently he jerked at the pull-handle again. Almost immediately a small door in the main gate opened and an old retainer poked his head out nervously.

'*Signor?*'

'*Desidero parla a Alfredo, per favore.*' Ben had tried to work out the Italian while he waited.

'Eh?' The dark, wizened little face took on a puzzled expression.

'*Signor Alfredo Cimbrone,*' repeated Ben, loudly and slowly.

'Hah,' said the old man, shrugging expressively. 'No strangers today please.' And he began to close the gate.

Ben caught hold of the knob to stop him. It was obvious that much had changed since he last came to visit this house, but he was sure that old Emilio still recognized him.

'Mr Cimbrone *will* see me,' said Ben, trying to sound confident. 'I'm his business partner. Tell him that Ben Cartwright has arrived from England.'

He fished in his jacket pocket for a business card. His hand fastened over something hard and square and metallic. He drew it out and looked at it. It was the metal emblem he had found near Toni's body on the night that he was murdered. How strange that it should have remained in his possession since then and had even survived the hotel laundry.

His thoughts returned to the present 'Just a minute. I have—'

Then he stopped. For he had seen that Emilio's face was contorted with fear. The old man seemed to have just received an awful shock. His eyes were wide with terror. Ben didn't know what had happened to him.

'*Si, signor. Si, signor.* I am very sorry.'

There was a rattle at the back of the door as he made haste to let Ben in and, in no time at all, it was swung open for him to enter. Surprised by the sudden change in the man's attitude, Ben stepped over the coaming into the shaded courtyard and looked around him.

There was a clatter behind him as the door was closed and locked. The next second Emilio was beside him, plucking at his sleeve.

'*Si, signor*. Please to come this way.' The little man led him across the paved courtyard, where abundant dumps of moss and weeds had forced their way between the cracked and broken stones. The rose bed in the centre was a tangle of weeds. When he looked up at the front of the house, Ben could see that most of the windows were closed and shuttered. The paintwork was dirty and peeling, the gutters choked and leaking. The place showed every sign of severe neglect.

Why, Ben wondered, had it been allowed to deteriorate like this in the last couple of years? He realized that the Italians weren't as house-proud as the British, but Toni had been interested in the upkeep of their property in England. Why hadn't he done more for his ancestral home?

They went up the steps and through the large front door beneath the crumbling portico. He noticed that its stained-glass fanlight was cracked and dirty. The hall was dark and cool, but it appeared unkempt. There was thick dust lying on the furniture as though no one cleaned it any more. Emilio led him down a side corridor on the left and into a small sitting room. He pulled the dust covers from a settee and motioned for him to sit down.

Mumbling something about Signor Alfredo, the little man closed the door behind him, leaving Ben on his own. He looked round the shrouded room. The whole place gave the impression that it was no longer lived in, with the furniture covered in sheets and a pall of dust everywhere. The room was lit by a pair of tall French doors which would open on to the sun-drenched terrace above the garden. The late afternoon sun was streaming straight in through the windows and Ben found it stiflingly hot. He felt in urgent need of fresh air.

The doors squeaked protestingly as he put his weight into turning the handle. When he pushed them open the air outside was scarcely any cooler than that in the room, but at least it was fresher and less dusty. Ben noticed that one of the shutters outside the window stood half open and jammed, while the other was missing altogether. Through the opening Ben had a fair view of the garden. His eyes took in the terrace where some of the weeds were three feet high. As far as he could see the rest of the garden was a complete jungle of undergrowth. Once again the general dilapidation seemed to indicate that no one was caring for the place. Things had certainly got a lot worse since he was here more than two years ago.

He couldn't understand it. He knew that Papa Cimbrone had been ill for a long time, but Alfredo was young and active. He assumed there was no shortage of money. Toni had told him that the Cimbrone exports of wine had never been better. Yet the whole place had been allowed to run down. It was as though there was no longer anybody who loved this once beautiful old house.

While he was musing by the open window, Ben suddenly became aware of a conversation going on somewhere nearby. In fact it sounded more like an argument. It was dominated by a woman's high-pitched staccato voice. He could imagine the furious, gesticulating hands; the lips drawn back to expose the teeth; the dark, angry eyes. A man answered her in low, dull tones as if sullenly apologetic. There was also a third voice which interjected from time to time with a strange, almost nasal twang. It was low enough in pitch to be a man's, yet it had the modulation of a woman.

Intrigued by this unknown dispute, Ben took a careful step through the doorway and on to the terrace. The aspect from here was approximately south-west. In the afternoon sun the light-coloured, peeling stucco and the stone paving seemed to intensify the heat and the brightness. Coming from the shady room, it took Ben a few seconds before he could see clearly. Then he noticed a pair of shutters which stood open only three windows from where he stood. He took a few further, fascinated steps towards the argument, regretting his poor knowledge of Italian.

Just at that second a man came through the window on to the terrace. Although Ben hadn't seen him for two years, he instantly recognized Alfredo, now head of the Cimbrone family. But it appeared that recent events had taken their toll on his health. In that time he seemed to have aged considerably. His dark hair was shot through with grey. His once smooth face was creased and fringed with deep, sagging jowls. His shoulders had slumped and he had developed a loose pot-belly. Although he must have been no more than forty years old he looked nearer sixty.

Alfredo could not have missed seeing Ben, but he barely seemed to apprehend him. The man's eyes were unfocused, his step and direction unsure. It was as though he was bent on some vague quest which shut out all other thoughts. Perhaps his mind was still dwelling on the row behind him, now snuffed out by his precipitate departure.

The next second a tall, proud beauty of a woman stepped on to the terrace with unhurried tread. She was dressed in cream riding breeches and a high-necked white blouse which was pulled in to a tiny waist by a broad black leather belt. Her raven hair was drawn into a bun at the back of her head, revealing high cheekbones topped by dark sloe-shaped eyes. Her nose was long and straight and slightly spatulate at the tip. Her beauty was only marred by her thin, compressed lips which gave her face a disapproving look. He recognized her as Sylvia, Alfredo's wife.

She halted in the doorway, eyeing Ben with undisguised suspicion. Behind her he sensed there was another person. But whoever it was kept out of sight. It was as though there was some evil presence hovering over her shoulder.

Shaking off that disturbing thought, Ben stepped forward and held out his hand. 'Alfredo, it is so long since I last saw you. I am so sorry about Toni. It will have been as big a shock to you as it was to me.'

Alfredo took his hand limply and murmured something which Ben didn't understand. It didn't seem to be a reaction to Ben's words. Perhaps he didn't have enough English to understand what he was saying.

It was the woman who spoke first. 'You are Signor Cartwright.' It was a statement without warmth.

'Good afternoon, Sylvia,' said Ben with a slight inclination of the head.

She spoke again in Italian to Alfredo. Her voice was sharp and interrogative. Alfredo replied with a shrug of the shoulders as though disclaiming responsibility. Sylvia looked again at Ben. She spoke English with a slight American accent 'How did you come to be here?'

Ben was puzzled. 'Well, by air, of course. I caught the eight-thirty flight from Gatwick.' He declined to mention that it was yesterday's flight.

'No. How did you get *here*?' Her arms swept around her. 'Here in the house.'

'Ah, I see what you mean. I knocked on the gate. Emilio recognized me. I have been here before.'

She made another short comment in Italian to Alfredo who didn't react.

Ben said, 'Didn't you get my e-mail saying I was coming?'

There was a short hesitation, as though she was trying to decide what would be the best response. Then she nodded.

'I was very sorry to be the bearer of such terrible news.'

She said '*Si*' almost so quietly as to be inaudible. Then she turned to Alfredo and said something further. He heard the word terrible being repeated.

Toni's brother bowed and nodded at him and said, '*Si* – terrible, terrible.'

Oh, my God, thought Ben. His English is even worse than my Italian. Our negotiations are going to be totally reliant on this woman. But he said to her, 'Would you tell Signor Alfredo that I have heard about his offer for the shares in my company. I have come to talk to him about that.'

She nodded but paused for a moment before she spoke to her husband. Was there now a wary look in her eyes? She said a few words in Italian and Alfredo nodded.

Sylvia turned back to him. 'It is not possible. I am sorry but he cannot speak to you now.

'I know it's a bad time to discuss these things, but is very urgent. It should not take Alfredo very much time.'

'No. No, it cannot be done. Not today.'

Ben took a deep breath. 'Signora Cimbrone, this affects the whole future of my company. It is very important to all of us. I have travelled all this way so that this matter may be cleared up. Surely Alfredo will at least spare a few minutes to discuss it with me.'

'I am sorry, *signor*.' Her smile was like ice. 'Today we have other very important things which are happening. We cannot spare any time today.'

'Then tomorrow. I could come tomorrow morning.'

Sylvia spoke again in rapid Italian to her husband who made a slight movement of his head. Ben could not tell whether it was a nod or a shake. She turned back to him. 'Very well. It shall be tomorrow morning.'

'Thank you,' he said. 'At what time shall I call?'

Again there was a rapid exchange of Italian before she replied, 'Be here at noon.' Ben bowed in acquiescence. He had a nasty feeling that no one would be at the Villa Cimbrone when he returned the next day.

He resolved that he would be outside at 6 a.m. even if that raised objections from Donna.

'Thank you, *signora*.' He advanced and took her hand. 'I will not keep you any longer.'

Some impulse made him bend and kiss her fingers. As he straightened up he saw that she was watching him with an appraising, almost a speculative look. Ben wondered whether there might be a way through her armour-plating after all. He turned to Alfredo and extended his hand. After the slightest hesitation, Alfredo shook it limply. Ben made for the door and Sylvia began to follow him.

At that moment a lovely young woman came on to the terrace. For a second her face lit up in one of the most beautiful smiles Ben had ever seen. It instantly swept away any lingering thoughts of Sylvia.

'Hello. It is Signor Cartwright, is it not?'

Ben suddenly realized that this vision of beauty, who seemed to speak such excellent English, was Francesca – Toni's younger sister. She had changed out of all recognition from the haughty but skinny schoolgirl of two years ago. Now she was a mature and delightful woman. He most admired the way she was coping with her beloved brother's recent death.

'Hello, Francesca,' he said awkwardly. 'I'm so sorry about Toni.'

Her face clouded for an instant, then cleared again. 'Never mind,' she said 'I hope that I shall see him very soon.'

Sylvia came up behind him. 'Today is Francesca's betrothal.' There was a warning note in her voice and her hand gripped his elbow with extraordinary strength.

So that was it! The realization suddenly struck him that they hadn't yet told Francesca anything about Toni's death. Perhaps they were trying not to spoil her special day. His opinion of Sylvia improved a little. But he felt a sense of disappointment that Francesca was to be married off when she was still so young.

'Really?' he said. 'Who is the lucky man?' His voice didn't seem to be his own.

'Why, my brother Dino, of course.' Sylvia released his arm. 'Their marriage will further cement our two families together.'

Ben looked from one woman to the other. Neither seemed to be taking any pleasure from the conversation, for possibly different reasons. With Papa Cimbrone and Toni's deaths hanging over them, it must seem a pretty joyless future for the whole family.

'Well – er – congratulations,' mumbled Ben.

Francesca nodded brightly. 'Are you coming tonight?'

'Signor Cartwright is just leaving us,' Sylvia broke in. 'He would not wish to intrude upon a family occasion.'

'Oh, but he is very close to the family,' said the girl. 'He is Toni's business partner and friend. He will be representing Toni. He will be able to tell us all about what Toni is doing at the moment.'

When Ben looked at Francesca he saw that for some reason her eyes seemed to be pleading with him. Those eyes exercised a strange grip on his mind. He found himself saying, 'I would be very pleased to attend if it does not cause any inconvenience.'

'It is impossible! I cannot find room at the table at this late stage.' Sylvia almost stamped her foot. 'Besides, what would Father Paoli say? You are not a Catholic, are you, Signor Cartwright?'

Francesca tossed her head impatiently. 'Do not be so old-fashioned, Sylvia. I am sure that Father Paoli would not mind if I wished it. Anyway he always loved Toni. He, too, would wish to hear about his life in England.'

'But everything is arranged—'

'Please, Sylvia, I wish him to come.' She switched her appeal to Ben. 'Will you not do this one little thing for me?'

He looked again at Sylvia. The woman said something under her breath in Italian. Then after a pause she inclined her head. 'Very well,' she said quietly, but Ben did not like the look in her eyes.

'He can stay in Toni's room.' Francesca spoke almost gaily. 'I am sure it is ready because we never quite know when he will next turn up.'

'No. I will prepare a room in the guest wing.' Sylvia turned to Ben. 'But please, Signor Cartwright, I would ask you to remain in your room until seven o'clock this evening, because a lot of arrangements have to be made and everyone is very busy.'

'I understand,' said Ben.

'I will send Emilio in a few minutes to show you to your room. Do you have everything you need for your toilet?'

'It's all in my briefcase.'

'Dinner will begin at seven o'clock. Please be prepared. Emilio will collect you when everything is ready.' Sylvia crossed to the doorway through which she had come on to the terrace. 'Come now, Francesca, we have much to do.' Taking the girl's elbow she guided her back into the house and Alfredo followed dutifully at their heels. Ben noticed that he was not permitted to meet brother Dino.

- 7 -

Emilio came for him a few minutes after seven. The moment Ben reached the dining-room, he could sense there was tension in the air. People seemed to be sitting or standing in isolation, rather than chattering in groups. There was none of the cheerful conversation and laughter which one would have expected before a joyous event such as a betrothal.

There were only eight people in the room, including a young maid who was standing by a drinks trolley in front of the fireplace. Near the head of the decorated dining table was Alfredo. He was in stilted conversation with a couple who were standing about two paces away from him, as if he were infectious. During the whole evening Ben was never introduced to either of them. He presumed them to be relatives of Sylvia and Dino; they hardly seemed to be friends of Alfredo.

In the corner, a little shrine had been set up and beside it stood the person whom Ben assumed to be Father Paoli. He was a plump little man dressed in a shiny black, high-collared shirt under a grey jacket. He seemed nervous and ill-at-ease, seldom talking unless in response to a comment from someone else. Standing near him, but completely ignoring him, was a slim young man with a dark olive skin and rather flashy good looks. Ben decided that this must be Dino. The fellow's face was set in a supercilious sneer most of the time. He only seemed to find any pleasure in the world when he was inspecting a part of himself or his apparel. Ben found himself beginning to feel sorry for Francesca.

As he entered, Sylvia moved away from Dino's side and came to meet him. But there was no smile of welcome on her face, no indication that she had been in his room only half an hour before, wearing that revealing green dress which matched her eyes.

Of course, then she had wanted his assistance.

'Signor Cartwright?'

Her voice had startled him into an awkward half-sitting position on the bed. It was as though her entry had been completely silent. Or had he dropped off to sleep as he studied the ceiling and wondered about the strange position circumstances had landed him in?

'Signor Cartwright. I wish to have a few words with you.'

She came close to the bed and he could smell her scent, a strange mixture of a heavy evening perfume and – was it incense? Her raven hair was tied on top of her head in a mass of curls and she was wearing a dark-green dress with a low décolletage which was tightly moulded to her figure. Her bosom was just at the level of his eyes and Ben noticed it was much fuller than it had seemed this afternoon. Her eyes almost seemed to match the colour of her dress. He wondered how an extraordinary woman like Sylvia could be married to such a dullard as Alfredo.

She paused for a moment. as though choosing her words with care. 'Signor Cartwright – can I call you Benjamin?'

'I'd prefer Ben.'

'All right – Ben.' She paused. 'You say you wish to discuss the business in London with us.'

'Can you speak for Alfredo and his mother?'

'Truly.' Her lips were smiling but the look in her eyes was calculating. 'You perhaps do not understand that in Italy the family is everything.'

'You mean that you will discuss it with Alfredo and Mama for me?'

She shook her head. 'I will discuss it with my father. He is Mancino Vitelli. He is the head of the Vitelli. Here we give him the title of *capofamiglia*.' Her smile broadened. 'You would perhaps call him the godfather.'

Ben felt his spine tingle. 'Is he also the godfather of the Cimbroni?'

'Truly. Now he is. With the death of his own father, Alfredo accepts that Mancino is the head of both families.'

This disclosure was starting to explain a lot of things. Ben couldn't help feeling it was a worrying development. What were the aims of this Mancino Vitelli. Why might he want to gain control of Cartwright

Cimbrone in London? Would Ben be able to negotiate with him?

Sylvia was watching him closely. 'I am Mancino's only daughter.' She tossed her head. 'You might say I am his favourite. So I may be able to help you if you wish to speak with him. I can probably speak to him for you. But you will need to discuss it fully with me. You will need to tell me exactly what you want.' Her eyes were half-closed but they were watching him closely. 'We may be able to – how do you say – fit our plans together.'

Looking into those hypnotic eyes Ben found himself replying, 'I understand.'

'But I cannot discuss it with you tonight. You are coming here tomorrow at noon. There will be nobody here but me. We will discuss it fully then.'

'Very well.' He felt a crawling sensation in his stomach as he thought about the next day. He didn't know what he was letting himself in for. However he knew he had to do it if he wanted to save his company.

'Also, Ben, I wish to warn you about Francesca. For some time she has been very difficult. You see – she was upset by her father's death. Of course we all were – but Francesca more than the others. She is still a very young girl and doesn't know her own mind.'

Ben moistened his lips. He felt like asking why a girl who apparently didn't know her own mind was being betrothed. But he knew the old-fashioned ways of the southern Italians, so he said nothing.

'For that reason I do not wish to tell her yet of her brother's tragic death.' He fancied the shadow of insincerity flickered across her eyes, but he couldn't be sure. 'I will find a way to tell her about it in the future when she is ready to react properly. I ask you not to say a word of it to her tonight.'

'I wouldn't dream of it.'

'It is not good that you are joining us this evening.'

'I'm sorry,' Ben admitted. 'I didn't know what to say to her.'

'Well, what is done is done. You will understand that I did not wish to upset her again. But I would ask you to keep very quiet and not to take any part in the ceremony, unless it is at my request. It is a very important ceremony to us. It is something which the families have been planning for years.'

'I promise only to speak when I am spoken to.'

'Please do not attempt to talk to Francesca on any matter. I understand her and the difficult period she is going through at the moment. I do not wish her to be further upset by some thoughtless comment.' She rested a hand on his shoulder. 'Do you promise me this?'

'Very well.' Ben found himself looking into the almost mesmerizing depths of those green eyes. His shoulder seemed to have an electric tingle running through it.

'It is a pity you did not come a few days later. I would have been able to make you so much more welcome. But perhaps there will be time later.' Now her eyes reminded him of a contented cat. Her hand slid off his shoulder and, with no more than the gentlest rustle, she was gone, leaving him with a pounding heart.

Ben even wondered afterwards whether he had dreamed the whole thing.

Behind him there was a muted click as old Emilio softly closed the door to the dining-room. The little sound seemed to increase his feeling of isolation. Ben felt acutely embarrassed at blundering into a strange family ceremony where nobody wanted him to be. Desperately he searched the room, but he could not see Francesca, who at least might have welcomed him with a smile.

'Will you have a drink, Signor Cartwright?' asked Sylvia, her eyes now cold and distant. Had she actually been in his room only half an hour ago?

'Later, thank you. First I should like to have a word with Signora Cimbrone.'

She gave him a warning look. 'Please be brief and do not mention Toni. She understands very little these days.' She returned to her station beside her brother.

Hesitantly, Ben approached Toni's mama. The old lady was sitting in a large upright chair near the window with her back half towards the rest of the company. He was even more shocked by her deterioration than he had been by that of Alfredo. When he had last seen her she had aged, but he could tell that she had once been a splendid woman. Toni had told him that she had been the centre of power in the family, occupying the position of the traditional matriarch. Now she seemed to have become very old and bowed, broken by the tragedies which had swept over her.

Ben thought she resembled nothing so much as a great old, shapeless cushion thrust into the chair and sagging in the middle. She was dressed all in black linen with her white hands projecting from the centre of the large bundle at awkward angles, twisted and gnarled like driftwood on a beach. A piece of black lace was pinned to her nicotine-stained hair, as if left there by a casual gust of wind. Beneath it, her face was startlingly white with the grey lips scarred across it. But the age and the sorrow couldn't completely obscure the dark, gimlet eyes which seemed to open straight into the back of her mind. In them he could detect a gleam of hatred and despair at the unknown people who were destroying her family.

He reached forward and held her hand. He gathered together the best he could of his halting Italian. 'Mi dispiace, Mama,' he murmured. 'Mi dispiace per Papa. Mi dispiace per Toni.'

For a second her eyes fluttered up to meet his and she gripped his hand with surprising strength. She looked as though she was going to say something of importance to him.

But, after a long pause, all she whispered was 'Oh-oh, grazie.' Then her gaze fell to her lap again and she was once more immersed in her private grief.

Ben crouched beside her wondering whether to say more – wondering how to say more to her. He felt he should not get up too soon and move away. However he was saved by the arrival of Francesca. All eyes swivelled away from him and alighted on her with relief as she swept into the room.

She was attired as though for a summer party, in a dress of a variety of shades of green and blue. The top was loose and light and with a surprisingly low-cut neckline for a young girl who was about to become betrothed. The skirt flared out from the waist and licked around her calves as she walked. Ben thought that she brought sunshine into the dismal dining-room. Like all the others, he couldn't tear his eyes away from her.

He was surprised that she hadn't dressed herself in something more demure to suit the occasion. And from his covert glance at the faces of the other people in the room, Ben judged that their conservative values had been profoundly shocked by her irreverent clothing. He heard a sharp intake of breath from Mama. He also noticed that the priest's mouth had dropped wide open.

Sylvia quickly crossed the room and spoke to her urgently in a low voice. The girl tossed her head. Although Ben couldn't hear her reply it was obvious that she was refusing to comply with the other woman's request. Sylvia's next comment had more of a pleading note to it, but Francesca pointedly turned away. Ben thought what a handful she must be.

The next moment her eyes alighted on him and she came across the room to greet him. Ben had a nasty feeling that Francesca had decided to make use of his unexpected arrival to divert herself at his expense. There was a little forced smile on her face but her eyes were upset and angry.

'Thank you for coming, Benjamin. I want you to tell me all about London and what life there is like with Toni,' she said in an overloud voice.

Oh, my God, thought Ben. What do I do now?

Fortunately Sylvia came to his rescue. 'That will have to wait until later. Now that we are all here we will start the meal. Francesca, you are to sit at the head of the table to the right of Father Paoli.'

Ben gratefully concentrated on finding his place. He was squashed into a position on the far side between Mama and Sylvia. Dino was on Father Paoli's left and next to Sylvia. Alfredo was at the foot of the table and the couple with the unknown name was seated opposite him.

The next hour held little pleasure for Ben. Sylvia addressed no more than the odd formal comment to him regarding the food. On his other side Mama seemed to be completely unaware of any of the other persons present. She sat hunched over her plate and ate negligible amounts of the food given to her.

The meal consisted of a seemingly interminable string of small dishes, mostly consisting of pasta or vegetables. The latter were normally eaten cold, shaken in oil and vinegar. Occasionally there were other individual dishes of highly spiced fish or very chewy, half cooked meat. Fortunately, it appeared to be perfectly acceptable that one should only eat as much as one wished of each dish, leaving the remainder to be collected by the maid before the next small offering was served. Only the middle-aged couple and Father Paoli seemed anxious to finish up everything that they were given.

The meal was a subdued affair with very little conversation, and what there was, of course, took place in Italian. So Ben tried to occupy his time by studying the personalities around the table as betrayed by their eating habits. He noticed that the priest stuffed the food into his mouth with a frantic enthusiasm, seldom leaving any on the plate, as though afraid that the succour was about to be spirited away from him at any second. All the while his shifty eyes ranged restlessly round the table like an intruding bluebottle – hovering, yet never quite alighting.

Ben could hardly observe Dino without leaning too far forward. He only noticed that the man appeared to peck at his food with the quick yet savage action of a hawk, almost seeming to flick the morsels from the plate to his mouth. He ignored all the others around the table, Francesca included. But occasionally he addressed brief comments to Sylvia in his harsh, sharp monotone. Ben was now quite sure that his was the third, unseen voice he had heard in the argument that afternoon.

Francesca picked over her food with indifference, normally keeping her eyes lowered. Occasionally, she flashed a glance at. Ben. If he returned the look she would flush and hastily drop her eyes again. He wondered if she had also had a warning from Sylvia. Ben found it difficult to keep his eyes off her face. He thought her colouring was delightful. Her hair was dark, yet fine and glossy. Her skin seemed unusually pale and creamy for an Italian, but she had a blush on her cheeks like a ripe peach.

The couple who were opposite him said little, even to each other, but they ate much. It seemed to Ben that the meal was being treated by them as a sort of reward for services rendered. Maybe they were independent witnesses to the main event of the evening – the betrothal. Ben wondered just what kind of event that was going to be.

His attention moved on to Alfredo. Seated at the foot of the table he appeared to be detached from what was going on. There was a strange dilation to the pupils of his eyes which puzzled Ben. It almost seemed as if he was suffering from some kind of shock to his system. He seldom spoke, occasionally addressing a comment to the lady on either side of him, but hardly ever receiving a response. All in all, Ben concluded that there was little atmosphere of celebration around the table.

Finally, after more than a dozen courses had been served, consumed and cleared away, everything seemed to be ready. The maid brushed the crumbs from the cloth with a silver brush and pan. At a nod from Sylvia, the priest rose and went to the shrine in the corner of the room. Item by item he removed the candles, the statue of the Madonna, the box containing the communion bread and wine, and the cross, leaving only the pedestal standing in front of the shrine. He arranged these items in front of his seat at the head of the table and remained standing in front of his chair.

Then he turned to Francesca and spoke some words to her. She replied in a strange, almost sulky tone. He asked her a further question and she said, 'No!' At that Sylvia made a sharp comment in which Ben could make out the name of Alfredo. Francesca almost shouted back at her. It seemed that things were not going well. In a few minutes everyone seemed to be on their feet and talking except Mama and Ben.

Francesca turned and appealed to him. 'Signor Cartwright, it is the custom for the girl on such an occasion to have an adviser who should counsel her on what her replies mean for the future. Normally that adviser is the girl's father, but since Papa is no longer with us, the others wish me to choose Alfredo. However I wish to choose you. Are you willing to be my adviser?'

'Signor Cartwright is not even a Catholic,' Sylvia cut in. 'He would not wish to intrude into a family matter.'

'Well, I *would* have chosen Toni to be my adviser, but he cannot be here.' She turned back to Ben. 'You are his best friend. He has always spoken very well of you. Are you not willing to advise me what you think he might have said to me?'

Ben was aghast. 'But I don't know what sort of advice Toni would give to you. I never had a young sister. I wouldn't even understand the questions which you will be asked.'

'I will translate for you. My English is very good.'

'This is foolish.' Sylvia addressed Ben direct. 'You cannot possibly know what is best for Francesca and for the families. Only Alfredo can know what is the proper advice to give.'

Ben was inclined to agree with her. 'Francesca, I can't tell you what you should do without knowing what your long-term intentions are. Wouldn't it be better to take your advice from Alfredo?'

'Alfredo doesn't know how to give advice.' For some strange reason she seemed to resent her older brother's involvement. 'Alfredo does not even know what he wants for himself.'

'Please do not talk like that,' Sylvia burst in. 'It is you, Francesca, who does not know your own mind. At one time you are in favour of the betrothal and at another you turn against it.'

Francesca ignored her. 'Will you help me, Ben, or will you not? I don't know what Toni will say when I tell him that you refused to come to the aid of his younger sister.'

'I will not allow Signor Cartwright to become involved,' said Sylvia. 'How can you humiliate us in this way, Francesca? You must behave properly if the betrothal is to proceed.'

'I want nobody's help but Signor Cartwright's. What is wrong about choosing my own adviser? Most girls in my position do it nowadays.'

'If your father was alive he would make these decisions for you. He would never allow you to hand over the family's honour to some stranger.'

'If my father were alive I would be able to rely on him giving me advice which I could trust.' Francesca's voice was very low and Ben judged that she was near to tears, but she wasn't going to give in.

Sylvia burst into a torrent of noisy Italian. As though this had released the floodgates, all the others, who had previously remained in shocked silence, joined in. Only Alfredo said nothing – whether from embarrassment or indifference, Ben could not tell. Meanwhile Francesca sat obdurately biting her lower lip and staring down at her hands which were placed on the table. She refused even to respond to their shouting. At last Ben could stand it no more. He rose to his feet and held up his right hand.

'Quiet please,' he shouted. 'Please listen to me.'

Gradually the noise died away.

He turned to Sylvia. 'Surely there must be a way of resolving this. Will you permit me to take Francesca into another room and talk to her for a few minutes to try to convince her?'

'That is impossible.' Sylvia's eyes flashed fire at him. 'In Italy we do not allow a young maiden to be alone in a room with a man without an escort.'

Ben indicated the middle-aged woman across the table from him. 'You could ask this lady to escort us in order to see that no incorrect behaviour occurs.'

Sylvia tossed her head. 'She does not know any English. She would not know what you are saying.'

'If that matters, you could come yourself.'

'No,' said Francesca sharply.

Sylvia ignored her. 'I am afraid it is out of the question. There is no time for that now.' Francesca stood up. Her chest was rising and falling with emotion. 'Then the ceremony may proceed without me.' She turned and rushed from the room.

Once again consternation broke out and they all except Mama seemed to be on their feet, talking loudly. Ben gained the impression, from the glances cast in his direction, that they were holding him to blame for Francesca's behaviour. He had to admit that she seemed to be a very wilful girl. It was obvious that this sudden objection of hers was spoiling some long-standing arrangement between the two families. Perhaps the reason for it, as Sylvia had suggested, was that she was overcome by the recent tragedy of her father's death.

Sylvia turned to him. 'Signor Cartwright,' she said coldly, 'I must ask you to leave us. You will understand that we have some very important matters to discuss.'

'Of course.' Ben rose with relief.

'I will show you to your room.'

She preserved a frigid silence as she preceded him up the cool marble staircase to the second floor, through the door into the north wing, and along the dark corridor to his room. Ben felt. like a naughty little boy being sent to bed. His thoughts returned to the consternation around the table below.

Everybody had been very upset that the betrothal plans had been thwarted – everyone except Francesca and himself.

- 8 -

Ben awoke some time in the middle of the night. He didn't know at first what had disturbed him. All he knew was that he was suddenly and sharply alert. He raised his head in the pitch-blackness and tried to make out the objects around him without success. An ominous silence hung in the air. The darkness was almost tangible. It seemed so quiet that at first he had the feeling he had gone deaf. Then he heard something creak and his body froze.

What was it? It seemed to come from the direction of the door. He strained his eyes to try to detect anything that moved. Above the beating of his heart he fancied he heard the faintest click followed by a slight rustle. He felt as though the pattern of the darkness was changing. Then the realization dawned upon him. The bedroom door was opening very slowly.

After a few moments the door inched closed again. A shadow moved away from the corner of the room and cautiously approached the bed. Ben could make it out more clearly now. He braced himself for the expected attack. Still there was no sound. The strange thought flitted through his mind that this man was a superb cat burglar.

He suddenly realized that the fellow was now only about three feet away. He fancied he could even hear the faint sound of breathing. At any moment now the attack would come. He tried to prepare himself for rapid movement. It was going to be difficult, hampered as he was by bedclothes. He decided on a bit of play-acting. With a big sigh he rolled over on to his left side so that he was facing the attacker. As he did so, he dragged the quilt with him. Luckily it wasn't tucked in and it pulled clear behind him. With the covers held in front of him like a shield, he suddenly leapt at the burglar.

The trick worked. The fellow wasn't expecting the attack and he went down under a heap of bedding. Ben landed heavily on top of him. For a few minutes there was a furious struggle as he tried to get a grip on the wriggling body. The man was quite small but surprisingly agile. If it hadn't been for the element of surprise and being swamped by the bedclothes, he would probably have got clean away. At last he gave in, lying gasping and half-asphyxiated under the quilt, and with Ben sitting astride him with his knees firmly gripping the panting body.

Ben looked round. Now he had a problem. He tried to measure the position of the bedside light in the darkness. To reach it he would have to give up his position of superiority. As far as he could tell the man didn't have a weapon or else he had dropped it in the struggle. Ben decided he would have to try another surprise move and hope his luck. held. He felt around in the quilt until he found the top of the man's head. Then he suddenly grasped a handful of the fellow's thick hair and leapt to his feet, pulling the poor chap with him towards the head of the bed. The next second his other hand reached the switch. Light flooded the room.

There was squeal of anguish from his attacker and Ben let go the hair. In front of him knelt Francesca. She was dressed in nothing but a thin black sweater and trousers. There were lightweight slippers on her feet. Her face was scarlet from lack of oxygen and contorted with pain.

'*Mama mia,*' she gasped, rubbing her scalp.

'Good God! What on earth are you doing here?'

'Please – please turn out the light' There were tears springing into her eyes.

'What do you mean?'

'Turn the light out' Her voice had a new asperity. 'You will give me away. I have sat up half the night waiting for a chance to slip away. It has taken me more than an hour to get here. I do not want you to raise the alarm.'

'I'm sorry.' Ben reached up and switched off the light. The room was again plunged into darkness.

'Thank you.' But she didn't sound grateful.

Ben grinned to himself. 'I'm sorry if I hurt you. You should have said something when you opened the door.'

'I didn't know you were awake. You made no sound.'

'You didn't make a lot yourself. I think it was that which wakened me.'

There was a pause while this was digested. Then Francesca spoke again. 'Here. Come and hold my hand so that I know where you are. We will sit on the bed while we talk. It is important that I speak to you, but we must be very quiet.'

Her hand was like ice. He could feel her body trembling, whether from cold or exertion he wasn't sure. 'Why have you come here?' he whispered.

'I will tell you. When I saw you this afternoon I knew you were the answer to my prayers. If you had not come, I would have been forced to go through with the betrothal to Dino. I did not know how to get out of it until you came. Within a year I should have been married to him.' Ben felt her shudder.

'I assumed that was what you wanted.'

'What – that snake?' He was shocked by the scorn in her voice. 'I have never wanted to marry him. I hate him and his whole family.'

'Then why did you agree to the betrothal.'

She gripped his hand violently. 'I did not agree. You do not understand what it is like in Italy. This betrothal was something that was arranged between the families many years ago. Dino is the last son of the Vitelli. All the other branches of their family have died out. They decided it was important that he should have the right wife. I was never consulted.'

'I didn't know that sort of thing still happened.'

'It happens very much among the big families in southern Italy.'

Ben shook his head. 'But I don't understand why it had to be you who was chosen to be Dino's wife.'

'For that you need to know our family history. You see, for many years the Cimbroni and the Vitelli were sworn enemies. They had hated each other through many generations. Then our fathers came together and vowed friendship to each other – I do not know why. These marriages were arranged to cement the new friendship – first Alfredo and Sylvia, then Carlo and me.' He felt her shrug. 'But you know what happened to Carlo, so I had to make do with Dino – the snake of the family.'

'Well,' said Ben doubtfully, 'I suppose it's no good going through with it if you don't like each other. I should have thought that your family would have understood that.'

'It is not only that. This so-called friendship between the families has not been between equals. The Vitelli now have hold of everything. How do you say that?'

'Do you mean a takeover?'

'That is it. The Vitelli have taken over. They have decided everything. They have all the money. They have all the control. We can do nothing. Since my father's illness we do not even usually live in this house.'

'Where do you live?'

'We stay in part of the Vitellis' huge great town house in Naples. It is like a prison. We were only allowed to return here for Papa's funeral and for the ceremony of the betrothal, which traditionally should take place in the future bride's home.' She sighed. 'You see the state that the place is in. Usually there is nobody here except old Emilio and his wife.'

'Ah, so that explains it. I must say it seemed very different from when I was here two years ago.' Ben frowned. 'But why do you allow this to happen?'

'It has happened very slowly – very cleverly. I think that perhaps my father had begun to see what was happening. But he had become ill and weak. And then—' Her voice broke. 'Then he died before he could do anything about it.'

There was a silence. Ben searched for something to say but failed.

Francesca started again. 'Alfredo is no good any more. Once he seemed more like a man. But now he is so weak that he is like clay in Sylvia's hands. She decides everything for him. He just does as she says. I think that if it were not for Mama they would sell the villa here and destroy the last of the symbols of the Cimbrone.

'I was surprised that the place had become so run down. Toni was so proud of it. I was surprised to find that he had let it happen.' Ben suddenly realized that he had spoken of his friend in the past tense.

Fortunately, Francesca didn't seem to notice. 'That is right. I hoped, when Papa died, that Toni would come back and take over. Toni is still strong. I want to tell you that you must let him come back here from London. We need him. He will fight them. Toni will not let them take over. Will you make him come back?'

Ben felt his heart turn to lead. Someone had to tell her very soon what had happened to her brother. But he knew it would destroy her when they did. She had placed all her hope and faith in Toni. Who would there be for her to turn to, now that both her father and her brother were dead?

'I wanted to talk to him about it when he came for the funeral,' she sniffed. 'But he hardly stayed at all. He came only to the ceremony. I was not able to speak to him on my own. It always seemed that Sylvia was watching us. Within a few hours he was gone again. He told me that he had some very important things he must do but that he would be back.'

Her voice was very plaintive. 'But I have not seen him since then. He knew about the betrothal. I am sure that he would not have missed it unless something awful had happened. I thought when you turned up that you might have come instead of him. But you brought me no message from him. Were you sent by Toni?'

'No,' said Ben, pleased that she couldn't see his face.

'Have you come to take me to him? I have written to him to say that I wish to leave this place. Is that why you are here?'

'No. I'm not here for that.'

'Then why are you here?'

'Well. . . .' Ben knew he would have to tell her about what had happened to her brother. But how did he start to find the words?

'Please tell me. I don't understand why you won't tell me anything.' And when he still remained silent, 'There is something wrong, isn't there? Has something happened to him? Is he ill or hurt?'

Ben gazed into the blackness. He couldn't keep it from her any longer without telling downright lies. It seemed that there was no way that he was going to be able to avoid being the person to wreck her life and her hopes. Desperately, he searched for a way to break it to her without hurting her too badly.

The oppressive darkness was creeping in on him on all sides. Now that she had stopped talking, the silence had settled like a great thick eiderdown all around them. It seemed to be softly roaring in his ears, like the rush of a waterfall which has been near for so long that the sound has ceased to intrude. Something at the back of his mind was urging him that this noisy silence was important. Then suddenly he felt the hair begin to rise on the back of his neck. For he had realized what it was.

Ben leapt off the bed and rushed to open the door. Once he was in the corridor he could hear the ominous crackling and smell the smoke.

'Turn on the light,' he shouted. 'The place is on fire.'

Nothing happened. Ben rushed back to the bedside table and switched the lamp on. Francesca was sitting there as though dazed.

'Hurry up,' he shouted.

He crossed to the wardrobe. As quickly as he could he pulled on his trousers over his shorts and slipped his bare feet into the shoes. He got out his jacket. As he put it on he checked that his wallet and passport were still in the inside pocket. When he turned back to Francesca she was still sitting on the bed. Her eyes seemed to be glazed.

'For God's sake get moving.'

'He's dead, isn't he?'

He grabbed her hand and dragged her behind him to the door. 'We've got to get out quickly, Francesca. The fire's got quite a hold. This old place will go up like a torch.' He looked at her more carefully. 'What's the matter? Don't you understand?'

She was hanging back, holding on to the door handle with all her strength. Her eyes stared fixedly at some wisps of smoke which were starting to filter under the door facing them across the corridor. It seemed to paralyse her.

'Francesca!' he yelled. 'We've got to make a run for it.'

Still she didn't respond. Her body had gone rigid, frozen with fear. Her eyes were big and black and staring. Her mouth was wide open as though emitting a silent scream. She seemed completely frozen into immobility. He had to go for help for her.

Ben let go her hand and stepped out into the corridor. He could see that smoke was seeping under some of the other doors and starting to gather below the ceiling. He turned left and made for the door at the end of the corridor which led to the main house. He caught hold of the stiff old brass handle, turned it and pulled. But the door didn't move. He applied both hands and his full weight to the door without any effect. He looked down at the lock and gave the door a violent rattle. It yielded a fraction then came up against something hard. It was then he knew that someone had bolted it from the other side. As a result they were locked into this wing of the building and the whole thing was about to burst into flames.

Behind him he heard Francesca coughing. She was now clinging to the door with both hands and he could see that the smoke around her was getting thicker. He would have to try to get her out through a window. They were on the second floor. It would be necessary to fashion some sort of a rope from the sheets on the bed. He didn't know how she would respond to being made to climb out of a window. Could he persuade her to go down it if he went first?

However, two steps into the bedroom made him realize that there was no chance of them getting out that way. The fire, which had obviously broken out on the floor below, was much worse now. The room was full of black, choking smoke and he could see hungry flames darting through gaps in the floorboards. Even as he watched, they suddenly burst out in front of the window. With a great gush of fire the heavy curtains seemed to evaporate into the air and there was a tinkling of glass as the window shattered in its frame.

Ben was deflected by a renewed fit of coughing from the girl and he turned back to her. 'Francesca, you must get moving,' he shouted urgently.

He took her arm with the intention of getting her into the corridor. But her whole body was locked rigid. He tried to drag her hands from the door handle which she was grasping with frantic strength. She was clinging to it as though it was her lifeline. What on earth could he do with her?

The next second the centre of the bedroom floor exploded in a mass of flame. It was that which saved her. For the first time her eyes opened wide and focused on the fire. She let out a piercing scream and threw herself at him.

'Come on. This way.' He dragged her into the corridor, half-stumbling and half running, and pulled the bedroom door shut behind him.

He tried the other door facing them, but it was locked. He looked around. Conditions in the corridor had significantly worsened in the half-minute or so while they had been in the bedroom. Looking towards the house it didn't seem too bad, although the smoke was now too dense to see the bolted door. However when he looked the other way his heart nearly failed him. The floor seemed to glow and bulge as he watched. Smoke was seeping through gaps in the boards. It looked as though the whole place was about to erupt.

'What is at that end?' he asked, taking in a lungful of smoke.

'The back steps,' Francesca gasped. She seemed to have woken up. 'That is the way I came in. I knew where the key was.'

'So the door is unlocked?'

'Yes.'

'Then we'd better hurry. Run as fast as you can for the door. Keep to the side of the corridor.'

He pushed her in front of him and they set off. But they had gone no more than a few paces when a rush of flame burst through in the centre. Francesca immediately stopped, her limbs once more rigid with terror. Ben hesitated for only a fraction of a second. He swept the petrified girl into his arms and tried to sprint through the swirling smoke and flames. To his tired brain he didn't seem to be moving. His feet were like lead. His progress was desperately slow and the door seemed to creep closer.

Half the distance was covered – three-quarters. Another gush of flame burst through the floor just beside him. Only five paces to go – three – two. Then suddenly the floor seemed to collapse below him and he was falling.

As he hurtled forward he tried to roll into a ball to protect his precious burden. The next second he crashed into the door and blackness descended upon him.

- 9 -

Ben realized later that he had probably only passed out for a short time. The next thing that he became aware of was that he was lying on cold stone and that his shoulder hurt like hell. However there was also the compensation of having soft, black hair brushing his forehead and the touch of a gentle pair of lips on his cheek.

He opened his eyes and found he was gazing up into Francesca's beautiful face. It seemed to be haloed by the light in the ceiling. Had the fiery young woman turned into an angel? Was she an emissary of heaven? But her eyes were troubled. Ben was touched by the fact that she looked genuinely worried about him.

'Oh, thank God,' she gasped, as she saw him open his eyes and his few seconds of pleasure were at an end as she jumped up. 'Quick! We must get out of the building before the fire burns down the door.'

Ben dragged himself reluctantly to his feet. His right shoulder hurt enough to have been dislocated by the recent fall and he found it was difficult to do anything with his arm. Francesca helped him up, all attention to his comfort. Now they were away from the fire she seemed to have recovered her strength.

Clinging to each other, they stumbled down the four flights of stone steps to the ground floor. They pulled the great oak door open and at last they were out into the cool night and running for safety. As they breathed in the pure fresh air they had to stop. Then they both began to cough. It built up slowly and agonizingly as the smoke came out of their lungs. There was nothing they could do to stop it. They couldn't even find the breath to talk or the strength to help each other.

At last the coughing died away and Ben turned back to look at the house. Francesca too was gazing with a terrible fascination at the fire which was now bursting out of the roof of the wing of the villa where they had recently been fighting for their lives. The windows of the top storey were great torches of flame – glass and frames gone in the searing heat. Elsewhere in the house the lights were on and voices were shouting. In the distance he could hear the braying sirens of the fire engines which betrayed that someone had at least been awake to raise the alarm.

'Was I the only one sleeping in that wing?' asked Ben.

'Yes. That used to be the guest wing. It is hardly ever used these days.'

The thought which had been nagging at the back of his mind suddenly came to the surface. 'Then someone was trying to kill me,' he said, in as matter-of-fact a tone as he could muster.

'What do you mean?'

'Someone locked the door between the corridor and the main house. If you hadn't let yourself in by the back steps, we wouldn't have been able to escape. Of course, they didn't know about you – so you would have been an unfortunate accident.'

There was a long silence. At last Francesca said, 'I wondered why Sylvia did not put you in Toni's room.'

Ben paused for thought. 'Who do you think would find me such a nuisance that they would want to kill me?'

'Who? Well – Sylvia, of course.'

'Sylvia? You surely aren't serious?'

'Of course I am. She is like a viper. She would not be afraid to kill you if you got in her way.'

'But why on earth should she want to kill me?'

Francesca shrugged. 'I do not know. But she will have a reason. I think perhaps she fears something about you. She was watching you very carefully this evening. There is something about you that she does not like. When she knows she has failed she will try again.'

'I can't believe that Sylvia is a cold-blooded murderer. She seems so—' Ben was remembering the suggestive comments she had made to him when she came to his bedroom. He shook his head. 'I'm sure she has no need to go around killing people.'

Francesca laughed flatly. 'I see her charms have also had their effect on you. But you do not understand her. She will not kill you herself. She will arrange for someone else to do that and then sound quite regretful afterwards.'

Ben suddenly felt an urge to leave this place and get as far away as he could from the dangers it presented. His whole plan in coming to Italy seemed to have been completely destroyed. He had expected to be having long and perhaps difficult negotiations with Alfredo. Instead he seemed to be in danger from some sinister family organization about which he knew nothing. He was beginning to wonder if the mishap which had occurred just after he landed at Naples airport had really been the accident which he had assumed until now. He decided it was time he returned Francesca to her family and removed himself from danger.

But before he could tell her this, the cacophony of sound from the approaching emergency services burst fully upon them. All of a sudden there were men with hoses running everywhere. Very soon streams of water were playing on to the roof from all directions.

'Come on,' said Francesca. 'We must go.'

'You can leave me. Go and find Alfredo so that he won't worry about you. Don't tell them anything about me. The family will think you were woken up by the fire. That will explain why you're dressed like that.'

'What are you going to do?'

Ben grinned sheepishly. 'I think I'll go somewhere where I'll be made a bit more welcome.'

'Then I will come with you.' Francesca folded her arms in a gesture of finality.

'You can't do that. You're the only daughter of a high-class family. Your place is with them. You can't go walking around the streets of Naples at night on your own.'

She gave him a pitying look. 'You sound just like my parents. Besides, I will not be alone. I will be with you. My family will have to accept that.'

'I think I've got some sympathy with them,' he muttered.

'Well you may think what you wish, but I am not staying here,' said Francesca firmly.

'Where will you go?'

'I know a place which will do very well for the two of us,' she said. 'We will be safe there for a few days. I will show you the way.'

Ben shook his head. 'You can't leave your family without a word.

They will be worried about you. You must go back to them while you can. You will be quite safe with them.'

'Ben, will you please listen to me?' Francesca gazed straight into his eyes from a few inches away. He could almost feel the extraordinary energy coursing through her body. 'This is my one chance to escape from the Vitelli. If I stay I shall never again have any freedom. Do you understand this? I want to get away now. I will not walk back into the prison which they are making for me. If you will not help me I shall have to go by myself.'

In. the face of her intense passion Ben found himself silent. What could he do with her? The most sensible thing would be to step back and let her make her own way. He suspected that she was going to drag him into all sorts of problems. But could he just turn away and leave a young, vulnerable girl on her own?

'Ben, will you please help me?' Now her voice was soft, caressing, wonderfully pleading.

He found his resolve weakening. 'Well, OK. But I think that you should at least tell them what you are doing.'

'I will write them a letter and post it to them tonight. Will that satisfy you?'

Ben sighed. 'I suppose so.'

'That's it, then.' She seemed almost gay. 'I think perhaps we should leave before someone starts to look for us.'

They set off round the perimeter of the garden, keeping as deep in the shadows as they could. Nobody paid them any attention at all. Any noise they made was masked by the noise of the fire. They reached a small door in the front wall which was half-hidden amongst the luxuriant vegetation. It could be opened from the inside and they let themselves out into the roadway without any trouble.

Their route passed close outside the main gates. Looking in, they could see that the driveway and turning circle in front of the house were filled with emergency vehicles. A number of other people were standing expectantly outside the gates. Ben paused to watch. He saw firemen climbing up ladders and smashing windows in the half-gutted wing to help the hoses reach the seat of the fire. He wondered whether they had been warned and would be searching to try and find his incinerated body.

He noticed that a little knot of people was standing a few yards away from the front door. He was sure they included Alfredo, Sylvia and Dino but it was too far away to pick out the expressions on their faces. Ben suggested they ought to go and reassure them, but Francesca would not hear of it.

'We must get away while we can. They will find out soon enough that we have gone. Then they will be after us.'

Once away from the gates they began to run towards the main road. But they had only gone fifty yards or so when Francesca slowed down. It seemed as though the nervous energy which had driven her this far had gone out of her and she was flagging. Ben realized that she wasn't going to get very far without help. He began to work his damaged shoulder to try to prevent the muscles from stiffening up. They were both inadequately dressed and Ben's trousers had been partly burned by the fire. Francesca was trying to hobble along the unmade road in thin slippers. Now he regretted not thinking about bringing the new mobile phone which had been left on the table beside the bed to be consumed by the fire.

'How far is it to Naples?' Ben asked.

'I'm not sure. Perhaps about five kilometres.'

'We'll never make it. You're just about done in and I can't carry you with this shoulder.'

Francesca was adamant. 'I am not going back. Nothing will make me return to that house while the Vitelli control it.'

'Where else can we go?'

'We will go to Toni's flat,' she said triumphantly. 'Only he and I know about the place. I know where he hides the key. I have told no one else about it. I have some clothes there, so I will be able to dress properly.'

'Toni never mentioned a flat to me. I would have thought he would at least have given me the address. Where is it?'

'It is in Naples – quite near the city centre. He has only rented it since last year.'

'I suppose it's more convenient than staying at the Villa Cimbrone.'

'More convenient!' Francesca snorted. 'It has nothing to do with convenience. Toni hates the Vitelli as much as I do. He wanted somewhere which they could not control.'

By now they had reached the main road and set off in the direction of Naples.

'If it's near the city centre, how will we get there? You can't walk that far.'

'I know,' she said triumphantly, 'we shall get a lift.' She immediately stepped out into the road to flag down an approaching car.

Before he could protest a little Alfa pulled into the side and a head of blonde curls leaned out of the window. 'Hi there,' said a jaunty American accent. 'I know you're not going to believe this, but I was just coming to look for you. I guessed you might be in trouble.'

'Donna,' laughed Ben. 'Why is it that you keep turning up when I've lost most of my clothes?'

'Benjamin, you know it's just your body that I want.' She leaned across to open the passenger door. 'Well, who's the lady?'

Ben brought Francesca forward and introduced her. To his astonishment she immediately climbed into the front passenger seat as though it was a taxi she had ordered. She seemed not in the least embarrassed by her skimpy attire.

'Will you please take us to the centre of Naples,' she asked, as though expecting to be obeyed. 'I will direct you to the flat of my brother.'

Open-mouthed, Ben climbed into the back seat and watched as an unusually silent Donna did as she was instructed.

Toni's flat was on the fourth floor of a fairly old block in a quiet quarter not far off the Posillipo road. While Donna stayed with the car they climbed the stairs without exciting any interest. They stopped outside an anonymous door. It still struck Ben as incongruous that his friend, who had always appeared to be so close to the rest of the family, should have kept a place like this very near to his home. He understood that there must have been some special purpose in it. In fact he was beginning to wonder whether Toni had been living some kind of double life about which he knew nothing. Francesca instructed him to reach up to the centre of the moulded architrave above the doorway. Sure enough the key was there.

'Not very original,' said Ben. 'Anyone who wanted to gain admission wouldn't have had to search very hard to find it. It was lucky that no one knew about Toni's little bolt-hole.'

Ben turned the key in the lock and swung the door open. He reached inside, felt for the light switch and turned it on. What he saw made him gasp. The flat was little more than a large bed-sitting room. But the place was a complete and utter shambles. Obviously someone else had known about Toni's secret hideaway and had very thoroughly broken the place up.

The furniture had been tumbled over and smashed. Any contents of cupboards and drawers had been pulled out of their containers and tossed on to the floor. The mattress of the bed which stood against one wall had been slashed open with great long cuts down the centre and around the seams. There was a large built-in wardrobe on one wall which stood open. All the clothes which it had contained had been ripped from their hangers and now formed a heap, half in the bottom of the cupboard and half on the floor. Even Toni's climbing gear, which must have been stacked in the bottom of the wardrobe, had been pulled out and tossed to one side. It was clear that someone had searched the place very thoroughly. It reminded Ben uncomfortably of his own office on the night when they had found Toni's body. Fortunately, there was no gruesome figure on the floor this time.

Francesca took one look through the doorway at the devastation and burst into tears. 'Oh, what will Toni say!' she exclaimed. 'What terrible things thieves are!'

Ben kept grimly silent. He didn't think this comprehensive damage was the work of mere thieves. For a start there was no sign of forced entry. The door was undamaged and the glass in the window wasn't broken. This needed thinking about. He took Francesca's arm, shepherded her into the room and closed the door behind them.

'It won't be any good us trying to stay here. Somebody knows about this flat already. Just find your clothes and we'll go.'

She looked at him uncertainly. He noticed that the young lady, who had looked so assured and self-confident a quarter of an hour ago, had suddenly been deflated. She seemed again like a defenceless little girl. He couldn't help admitting that he liked her better this way. He patted her on the shoulder.

'Come on. Let's get on with it.'

She nodded and got to work. While she searched through the jumble in the bottom of the wardrobe, Ben went into the kitchen. Here there was a similar scene. All the cupboard doors were open. Crockery had been carelessly thrown on to the floor and now lay in smashed heaps. The drawers had been pulled out and upturned. Even the fridge was standing with the door wide open and the compressor still running. He lifted out a carton of milk and sniffed it cautiously. The smell of rancid cheese assailed his nostrils. The refrigerator had obviously been open for several days.

Ben replaced the carton and pushed the door shut with his elbow. Then he went to the bathroom. Here at least there wasn't the same mess. There had been no cupboard to empty on to the floor. One look round its clinical tiled walls would have told the searchers that there was nothing worth wasting their time on. The only reminder of Toni was a container of shaving soap with a fresh razor lying beside it. On a sudden impulse, Ben put them in his jacket pocket. They might come in useful later before he could get to the shops to re-equip himself.

He went back into the main room. Francesca had now pulled on a grey roll-neck sweater and jeans. She had found a pair of light canvas shoes for her feet. Although she still looked pale, she seemed to have recovered her composure.

'Come on,' said Ben. 'There's no point in staying here. I expect Donna can arrange a room for you at the hotel. She seems to be able to organize anything.'

Francesca didn't reply, but she followed him out of the flat. Ben locked the door and pocketed the key. He had no intention of letting anyone else get in to the place by the easy route. Then he took the girl's elbow and shepherded her down the stairs.

Donna took them straight up to her magnificent room at the hotel. Francesca was very quiet as her eyes took in the modern splendour. She sat on the bed and looked up at Ben as if waiting for a lead.

'Hadn't you better get some sleep?' he asked.

She shook her head. 'I could not sleep now.'

'You'll feel better as soon as the shock has worn off,' said Donna. 'I'll go and find my friend Marco and get him to arrange a room for you.' She looked purposefully at Ben. 'I think you ought to tell this girl the facts. She ought to know what really happened. It has to come out sooner or later.' She turned back to the door. 'I'll see you as soon as I have made the arrangements.'

Ben saw that Francesca was looking up at him. 'What does she mean?'

Oh hell, thought Ben, Donna's dropped me right in it. But instead he asked, 'Do you know who might have done all that damage in Toni's flat?'

'I have no idea. He told me that I was the only other person who knew about it. Just wait till he sees it.'

Ben sat down on the bed beside the girl. 'Francesca, when did you last see Toni?'

'Let me see.' She put her hand to her forehead. 'It must have been five – no – six days ago.'

'What did he say to you when he left?'

'Only that he was going to be away for a few days.'

'He didn't say where he was going?'

'No.'

'Did he say that he was going back to England?'

'Oh, he wasn't returning to England.' Francesca was emphatic. 'He would have said goodbye properly if he was leaving Italy.'

'But he gave you no idea of what he was planning to do?'

'He would not say anything to me.' She plucked at his sleeve. 'Why? What is the matter? Is he all right? What did that woman mean when she spoke to you just now?'

He spoke almost to himself. 'What I don't understand is why they didn't tell you anything.'

'Ben!' She pulled him round to face her. 'What are you saying? You mustn't treat me like a child. Everyone treats me like a child. No one will tell me anything.'

'I suppose they didn't know *how* to tell you.'

'It's Toni, isn't it? Something has happened to him. I have felt this for several days. Please, Ben. You must tell me the truth.'

'Francesca, there's no gentle way to say this.' Ben tried to keep his voice as calm as possible. 'Toni is dead. Alfredo should have told you before.'

He stopped, appalled by the look on her face. It looked like some haggard mask with the eyes staring at him, black and fathomless. It wasn't a look of shock or sorrow. Her face was a picture of pure hatred.

'I knew it,' she whispered, hardly seeming to move her lips. 'What happened to him?'

Ben swallowed. 'I – I found him dead in our office in London. That was when I came home late on Tuesday night. I e-mailed Alfredo on Wednesday morning. But, Francesca, somehow the family knew about it before they got my message.'

'Yes,' she breathed. 'Yes, they did. Alfredo could not look at me on Tuesday. Now I know why that is. It is because he knows who killed Toni. For the last week he has been keeping out of my way. It is because he was afraid I would trap him and get the truth out of him.'

She seemed to be talking to herself. Ben couldn't understand why she was so unmoved. Why were there no tears? He had expected her to be overcome with emotion, to attack him, to blame him for what had happened. But he was not ready for this inhuman coldness. Ben almost wondered whether she had understood him fully.

'Francesca—' he started.

'It is all right, Ben. I also believe 1 know who did this. And when I am sure I shall be revenged. I may only be a woman, but I know how to hate. I will see that those who have done this will pay for it.'

He was horrified to hear such words coming from the mouth of a young girl. 'Francesca! You're shocked. You don't know what you're saying.'

She ignored his comments. 'What about you? Why did you come all this way to Italy? It was not just to tell me about what had happened to Toni.'

'Well – no. There *was* something else as well.'

'What was that?'

Ben watched her carefully. Now she sounded as though she was having a chat over afternoon tea. He didn't like her change of mood at all. He felt as though he was sitting on the edge of a volcano which was about to erupt.

He tried to pick his words carefully. 'Your family – the Cimbroni – they want to buy me out of the business and take it over themselves. I came to see Alfredo about it. I wanted to see if I could get him to change his mind.'

'Buy you out of the business?'

'Yes. That is the business which Toni and I have built up in London. You see, they now own his shares.'

'I see. But Toni would not have liked them to buy you out.'

Ben looked at her sharply. 'I don't think so. That is what I told them. But I have not been able to talk to Alfredo.'

'It is no good to talk to Alfredo. He is like a baby in Sylvia's hands.'

'I thought that he would be in charge now that your father has died?'

'He is in charge of nothing,' said Francesca, her eyes alive again and sparkling dangerously. 'He will never be in charge. It is Sylvia who is in charge. And behind her it is Mancino Vitelli who decides everything. It is the Vitelli who you must convince.'

'Who is this Mancino Vitelli?'

'He is the father of Sylvia and Dino – and once of Carlo. He thinks he will soon become my father-in-law. Then he will have all of us in his hands.' There was no mistaking the bitterness in her voice.

Ben was silent for a moment, digesting this latest information. It sounded as though there was more beneath the surface than he had previously realized. He didn't like the sound of it at all. But he was deeply involved. He could not turn back now.

'How do I get to see this Mancino Vitelli?' he asked.

'I will take you to see him. He will have to see me. He must tell me just what has happened. You will come with me and he will see us both and answer our questions.' Francesca's body was arched forward. Her eyes were blazing with a quite incredible intensity. 'Then, when he has answered us . . . I will kill him.'

Ben's mouth dropped open.. He was lost for words. Was she serious? What on earth was she talking about?

She looked up and laughed in his face. 'I have often thought about how I would do it. The Cimbroni must have their revenge. Somebody must kill him. And I am the only one who is left to do it. I am not frightened. There is nothing that they can do to me now. They cannot take anything more away from me.'

Ben raised his hand to comfort her, but she sprang away from him, as wary as a stray cat.

'Francesca,' he said, 'you are overwrought. You are shocked by what I have told you.' Indeed at any moment he expected her to break down in tears – for the shock to recede enough to let her grief break through.

'Do not try to change my mind, Ben. I am the only one left to do it And he will not fear to let me near him. He will think I am only a woman.'

'You are tired,' said Ben. 'Why don't you rest? Try to get some sleep. You'll see things differently in the morning.'

To his surprise she nodded, suddenly compliant. 'I *am* tired,' she admitted.

With a sigh of relief, Ben stood up. 'Here, lie on this bed for a while.

You can move to the other room when Donna comes back.' He pulled back the covers as she stood up and kicked off her shoes. Then she lay down and he draped the bedclothes over her.

'Ben, please,' she asked, 'I do not wish to be alone just at this moment. I sometimes frighten myself when I am alone. Will you stay with me?'

He nodded and smiled. 'OK. I'll stay.'

'Right here in the bed?'

'If you like.' Obediently he took off his shoes and got in beside her, fully clothed.

She snuggled up to him like a tousle-headed child. 'Will you put your arms round me? Toni used to put his arms round me to comfort me when I was upset.'

So he put his arms round her and she settled her head on his shoulder. Within a few minutes her breathing had settled into an even rhythm. But Ben could not find any comfort. His mind was turning over what she had told him about Sylvia's father. If Francesca was right, it sounded as though that man was the key to all this. However he didn't share her casual belief that they could just go to his house and demand to see him and negotiate with him – particularly if she was going to carry on with her declared intent of trying to kill him.

He was puzzled by Francesca and her strange variations in behaviour. At one time she seemed to be a proud, beautiful, self-possessed woman. The next moment she could be as wild as a tiger. Then suddenly she would become as small and vulnerable as an upset little girl. She was certainly a handful.

Donna returned a quarter of an hour later. Despite the fact that it was the middle of the night, she had succeeded in finding another room. But by now Francesca was in a deep, untroubled sleep.

'Ssh.' He put his finger to his lips as Donna told him about her success.

'What are you going to do with her?' she demanded – but softly.

'I can't move her now,' Ben whispered. 'She's only just gone off to sleep and she said she doesn't want to be on her own.'

'What do you mean? Am I getting kicked out of my own bed by some chit of a girl?' Donna was starting to get angry.

'Shush. She's very upset tonight.'

'Don't you shush me. I'm upset too.' Her voice was starting to rise, but a groan and a restless movement from Francesca made her lower it again. 'Are you just going to lie there and let her cuddle up to you all night?'

'What else *can* I do?'

She shook her head. 'I suppose I'll have to take the other room. Tonight's ruined anyway. This isn't at all the way I'd planned it.'

She rustled round as she collected her things. Then she switched off the light and departed with a grumpy, 'I'll be back first thing in the morning.'

Ben peered down at the beautiful sleeping face on his chest. He couldn't really see her expression in the first of the morning light which was starting to seep through the curtains, but he was nearly sure that a beatific smile had taken over the sleeping features.

- 10 -

The sun beat down out of a cloudless sky, searching out every nook and cranny of ancient Pompeii with a pitiless attention to detail. The old paving stones of the Forum seemed to vibrate with the heat. Ben rested his hand lightly on the railing round one of the plinths and instantly whipped it away again as the heat sizzled his skin.

Where the hell is she? he demanded silently for at least the fifth time in the last half-hour. Francesca was over forty-five minutes late. Two o'clock she had said. Now it was fast approaching three. Of course, Donna had made it worse by dropping him at half past one, just in case the girl should be early. That meant he had now been hanging around for an hour and a quarter.

Ben surveyed the crowds of weary, perspiring sightseers with a jaundiced eye. Normally, he would have found the scene full of interest, but not today. Somehow he had known since he first woke up that it was going to be one of those frustrating days. It had taken him hours to get to sleep last night, partly because of the pain in his shoulder and partly through trying not to wriggle too much and therefore waken Francesca. Then, when he had finally dropped off, he had slept too long and too heavily. By the time he was properly awake the sun was already streaming through the window and across the satin covers on the bed. The ornate ceiling above his head was reflecting a bright pink from the tiled terrace and the long, translucent net curtains fluttered drowsily in the breeze coming through the open windows.

Somehow it was the soft hush of the air-conditioning that reminded him of the scene the night before and brought him back to full wakefulness. Then he realized he was still lying in bed half-dressed.

The feeling of dirt and perspiration, the stiff ache in his shoulder, the unpleasant taste in his mouth, the articles of clothing scattered about – those things he had expected. But something else was wrong. Where was Francesca? He hadn't heard her get up. He had no idea what she was doing. He felt he was responsible for her in some way.

He became aware of an urgent desire to urinate. No doubt she was occupying the bathroom – just where he wanted to go. She had probably recently lowered herself into a long, hot bath and would stay there for at least the next half an hour. Well, he would see about that.

He forced himself to get up. It was a slow business. He was still stiff and weary from his cramped, uncomfortable sleep. He worked his shoulder, massaging the bruised muscles. At least it appeared that nothing was seriously damaged in that area.

He hardly noticed his ruined trousers flapping around his legs as he crossed to the window and pulled the patio door wide open. He stepped out on to the balcony and into the mid-morning heat. Floating up from below came the soft mixture of street and waterfront sounds, the rumbling noise of industry from around the bay. One of the *aliscafi* bound for Capri was just heading out of the harbour. It suddenly began to speed up as he watched, lifting itself out of the water on to its hydrofoils. A few seconds later the dull boom of its engines echoed round the high buildings which crowded the waterfront.

His sense of bodily discomfort returned. Francesca would have to hurry up. Ben left the balcony and crossed to the bathroom. He tapped on the door but there was no reply. He called out 'Francesca' without receiving any response. When he opened the door it was dark inside. He even switched on the light for the specific foolish reason of checking that it was empty. For a few moments he felt more relief than anxiety at her absence. But, as he washed his face, his mind began to function at last. What had happened to her? He left the bathroom and crossed to the bedroom door, swung it open and collided with Donna as she bounced in, looking as lively as a kitten despite her crumpled dress.

'Oh that was nice,' she said, as he let go of her.

'Have you seen Francesca?'

'Of course not. She was with you. Did you have a good night together?'

Ben ignored the sarcasm. 'She's gone.'

'Oh dear,' said Donna cheerfully, 'what *can* have happened to her?'

'I don't know,' he complained. 'When I woke up she wasn't there.'

'Run out on you, has she? I tell you, Ben, you're going to have trouble with that one.'

He scowled. 'Will you be serious? What do you think has happened to her? I do think she ought to have said something to me before she left. She's not used to looking after herself. She won't have any money or anything.'

Donna walked over to the bedside table and picked up a piece of paper which was lying there. She read it and passed it to him. 'Why aren't men born with common sense?' she asked.

The note was quite short. It said: *Dear Ben. I have phoned Alfredo. There is something I must do very urgently. I will meet you in the Forum at Pompeii at two o'clock. Love Francesca. P.S. I have taken ˇ200 from your wallet.*

When Ben looked up Donna was cocking an amused eyebrow at him. 'I reckon that girl can look after herself a lot better than you think. Never mind, at least you seem to have her love.'

'What the hell do we do now?'

'Well,' she said, 'we've got more than four hours before I drop you at Pompeii. I want first go in the shower.'

Ben thought that Donna seemed somewhat distracted when she dropped him outside the Porto Ercolano. As usual, she had driven the ten miles from Naples like a maniac, following a route of her own invention which seemed to consist mainly of a variety of bumpy, dusty side roads. Just when Ben thought they were completely lost, they came round a corner and screamed to a halt beside the entrance kiosk. He noticed also that she only spared him a light peck on the cheek as she leaned across to open the door for him. Perhaps she was still upset about last night. However he grinned to himself when he remembered how forgiving she had been this morning after the shower.

'Ring me when you want to be picked up. Take care.' And she was off in her usual cloud of dust almost before he had time to close the door.

Women were strange things, Ben reflected. One minute they were all over you and the next they treated you as if you'd got the plague.

He looked round the open area in front of the gates, taking in the several sales kiosks. The day was hot and bright. So the first thing he did was buy a lightweight hat with a green eye-shield. It didn't go very well with his third new outfit in the last two days, but at least it stopped him having a headache. Then he paid his admission fee and another ten euros for a map and guide in English.

'Attach yourself to a group of sightseers,' Donna had said. 'One man walking round on his own sticks out like a sore thumb.'

Ben wasn't sure how Donna knew about things like that. There seemed to be a lot of surprising sides to her personality. It was also strange how she kept turning up when he was in trouble. Did she have some sort of private radar system? He didn't have an answer to that, so he shrugged to himself and leaned against the wall outside the Villa of Mysteries. He decided he would study his map and wait for a suitable group of tourists to come along.

Five minutes later a party of Germans straggled by. They seemed on none-too-friendly terms with each other. A few overweight ladies trailed along behind the guide, pink with perspiration as they tried to make conversation. The rest strolled individually or in small groups, sometimes chatting among themselves. Ben thought it odd that so many of them insisted on wearing dark suits and carrying plastic mackintoshes – even in this heat. They obviously couldn't have looked out of their hotel bedroom windows before they started out that morning.

Nobody seemed to notice when he tagged along with them as they made their way up the Street of Tombs, where the monuments still contrived to look grim and forbidding, even in the flattening heat of the Italian afternoon. They arrived at the Forum a little before two. Since then Ben had done one complete circuit of the huge square with the uncaring Germans. When they trudged off in the direction of the Stabian Baths, he transferred his allegiance to a large crowd of Japanese, most of whom seemed to be dressed in a similar way to himself. All he had to do was sag a little at the knees to be perfectly disguised.

But how long was this going to go on for? By now he was definitely getting fed up. He looked again at his watch as he stood on the edge of the group by the foot of the steps leading up to the Temple of Jupiter. It was five to three. Where the hell had Francesca got to?

The Forum was a big place and there were several hundred people scattered around it at the moment. He decided to survey each segment of the square carefully to see whether he could pick her out. So he stepped up on to the surround of one of the column plinths in order to get an extra bit of height. His eyes worked their way methodically down the left-hand side in the dancing heat. Then they swept across the far end and started up the colonnade on the right.

Suddenly he saw something which made him stiffen. Standing by one of the columns near the far corner was a man he thought he recognized. In fact he was almost sure it was the hood who had tried to knife him in Naples two days before. With a sick feeling in his stomach he looked again more carefully at the other corners of the Forum. Sure enough he spotted one of the gangsters almost opposite him halfway down the square. He'd missed the man on his previous search.

After another careful look around he finally located the third man near the corner to his right. The bloke was no more than fifteen yards away. They seemed to have placed themselves at vantage points where they could watch the crowd. Ben acknowledged that he may have begun to develop a persecution complex, but there was no doubt in his mind that they were looking for him. In fact it seemed incredible that none of them had spotted him so far. Perhaps it was the hat.

If he had been sensible and remained with his group of Japanese when they moved away from the Forum, it is likely that Ben would have escaped detection altogether. However his nerves were on edge by now. He was convinced that Francesca wasn't coming and was beginning to wonder whether she had lured him here to draw him into a trap. He felt alone and under threat. He wanted to get away as quickly as possible.

Cursing the girl for landing him with this problem, he bent and checked his map. He wanted to get out of Pompeii by the nearest exit which led away from his three pursuers. He decided that his best route would be to make for the Porta Nola. Just outside the gate was a station on the Circumvesuviana, the small gauge railway which ran round the bay from Naples to Sorrento. From there he would be able to get a train back to the city. Francesca would have to come to find him at the hotel if she still wished to.

Thus set on a course of action, Ben decided to creep away from the Japanese group as quickly as he could, while at the same time keeping an eye open for the other three. However, just as he got to the corner of the square, disaster struck.

His mistake was to pay too much attention to the three gangsters and not enough to his own route. Suddenly his foot caught the corner of the stall of one of the souvenir sellers. Before he could take avoiding action, he had knocked the post away from the remainder of the structure. It may have been a particularly rickety stall or he may just have been unlucky, but his horrified gaze saw the whole stall sway and crash to the ground, spilling cheap souvenirs everywhere. The next second he was assaulted by a large Italian matron roaring for revenge. He stepped back, tripped over something behind him, and fell flat on his back. His hat flew off as he landed.

Although he immediately jumped to his feet and apologized and tried to placate the woman, the damage was done. A crowd immediately started to gather. People seemed to be pouring torrents of abuse on him in various foreign languages from all sides. As he looked round, he saw that the nearest of the toughs was already walking purposefully towards him. Ben decided that now was the time to get out.

He side-stepped the stallholder and ran. He was not alone. From the shouts behind, it sounded as though at least fifty of them were chasing him. He made straight for the nearest exit from the Forum. This proved to be a narrow, unevenly paved street lined on both sides with half-ruined houses. Twenty yards along he turned sharp left up a side street, and after another fifteen yards he went right again to try and throw off the pursuers. Five yards ahead of him the road was barred with a sign saying *Pericolo – Entrata Divieta*.

For a second Ben hesitated. Then he realized what it was. He had read that the earthquakes of a few years before had caused extensive damage to the ruins and that a large part of the ancient city had not yet been repaired and made safe for visitors. Ben decided that the least of the two dangers to which he was exposed lay ahead of him. He hurdled the barrier, ran a further twenty yards down the street, ducked through a crumbling gateway and into one of the damaged buildings. He went through the entrance, across the atrium and came into what had once been a little garden, now overgrown and half-submerged in collapsed walls. There he stopped to listen for sounds of pursuit. But, except for a few shouts in the distance, he could hear nothing.

He got out his map again to check roughly where he was. He still appeared to be heading in the general direction of the Porta Nola. He had no idea whether he would be able to get out that way, but he preferred the prospect of scrambling over some mounds of rubble to facing the three crooks behind him. The thought occurred to him that perhaps he'd find some men working on the ruins, although there had been no sign of that sort of thing so far. He would just have to try to keep clear of them if he came across anyone like that.

Ben put his map in his pocket and cautiously made his way out of the back doorway into another narrow street. There was no one in sight but he moved off cautiously. He often changed direction and frequently checked over his shoulder to see if he was being followed. He kept as close as he could to the shady side of the street, although he had to make frequent detours to avoid the piles of rubble from collapsed buildings. The earthquakes certainly seemed to have caused major devastation to this part of the already ruined city. What remained of roofs and walls had fallen in many places. Lintels and door surrounds had tumbled to the ground. Pavements had cracked and tilted. Everywhere weeds and creepers were starting to cover the rubble. The whole place seemed like a giant bombsite.

Ben kept up a steady pace, perspiring freely in the hot afternoon sun. He thought that he must be getting somewhere near the gateway by now. A few minutes later he rounded a corner and saw the old city wall ahead. It was about twelve feet high at this point with a rough, irregular top, punctuated by occasional bushes. Getting on to it would be no problem, because it had collapsed on the ancient city side in several places. However Ben wanted to be extra careful now that he was close to his destination. Once on top of the wall he would be exposed to any searchers. He half climbed one of the piles of rubble until he could raise his head cautiously above the top of the excavations. He looked round carefully.

At first he saw nothing. But then his care was repaid, for he picked out one of the gangsters walking along the edge of the field just above the limit of the excavations and looking down into the ruins. The man was obviously trying to spot anyone who might be moving about below him. Ben couldn't see where his two mates were.

Keeping his head down, he decided to look for a less exposed place to cross the wall. Sure enough, about twenty yards away there was a small clump of olive trees protruding over the top. He reckoned there was a good chance of him crossing unseen at that point. So he dropped down and made for the spot. The wall here was in better repair. But the uneven brickwork provided plenty of holds for an experienced climber. Ben could have wished for a better pair of shoes than the dainty ones with pointed toes which Donna had chosen for him. However, it only meant that he had to transfer more of the load to his hands.

He edged cautiously on to the top of the wall, keeping his body low behind the weeds. The urge to look round to check on his pursuers was almost overwhelming, but Ben had read somewhere that the sunlight landing on a white face is a surer giveaway than slow, careful movement. Taking a deep breath he crept out of the undergrowth and slid under the overhanging olives, expecting to hear a shout at any second. However, luck seemed to be with him. He raised himself to a crouch in the protecting shade and looked back. The man had his back turned at this moment, so now was the time to move.

There was a low barbed-wire fence along the outside of the wall and the drop here was nearly twenty feet, but it presented no real obstacle. Ben chose to go down one of the sinewy but slippery olive trunks. Keeping his weight wide to increase his hold he quickly shinned down to the ground. At last he felt safe. He moved round the clump of olives and found himself face to face with one of the people who had been searching for him.

'*Oh, mama mia*!' The girl burst into a string of grateful Italian.

Ben was feeling hot and irritable and persecuted. Francesca looked cool and refreshed and beautiful in a bright green dress of some light, filmy material which he guessed she had bought with some of his ˇ 200. It only served to increase his annoyance.

'Where the hell have you been?' he demanded. 'You should have met me more than an hour ago.'

She spread her hands in an expansive apologetic gesture. 'I know. I am sorry. I was already later than I thought. But then I found that I did not have enough money left to buy a ticket to get into the *scavi*. I was just trying to find a way in.' She raised her eyes to his. 'And what were you doing here? This is a forbidden area.'

'I'll tell you what I was doing. I was being chased by three murderous Italian gangsters. I notice that you were conveniently nowhere to be seen when they were after me.'

'What do you mean? I don't know anything about any gangsters.'

'Don't you?' He shrugged. 'Well, it's no good arguing about it here. We'd better get out of this area while we can. Have you any idea how we can get away?'

Francesca pointed. As if by magic an electric train was approaching the station a couple of hundred yards away. With only a second's pause they ran for it.

'You can buy tickets on the train,' she panted. 'That is – if you have the money. I have none left.'

He didn't have the breath to ask how she had got through ˜ 200 since this morning. It was a silly question anyway.

Safely seated on the train opposite Francesca as it drew out of the station, and with no sign of his pursuers, Ben recovered his sense of righteous indignation. 'That was a hell of a fix that you nearly got me into back there.'

'That *I* got you into? Ben, what are you talking about?'

'Those three men who had the Forum staked out – looking for me.'

'What men? What is the matter with you?'

'The matter with me is that ever since I arrived in Italy I seem to have been chased by criminals armed with knives,' said Ben sarcastically. 'I wondered whether you or your family might have anything to do with it.'

Her eyes widened. 'With knives? Were they trying to kill you?'

'I didn't hang around long enough to find out. Perhaps the dear little chaps just wanted to trim my nails for me.'

'But you do not think that I know anything about that?'

'Well, how did they know where to look for me?'

'They did not know from me! I have told no one but' – she faltered for a second – 'but Alfredo.'

'Alfredo! Why did you tell Alfredo? Perhaps you *wanted* him to spread my whereabouts all around the Bay of Naples.'

Francesca looked so upset that he instantly felt sorry for what he had said.

'I do not think Alfredo would have told anybody. I believe I can trust him even though he cannot help me. And,' she countered, 'what about *your* friend Donna? I'm sure she knows just where you are.'

'It was Donna who brought me to Pompeii.'

'Then she is the one who led them to you.'

'Donna? How could she do that? She doesn't know anyone in Italy.'

Francesca snorted. 'Huh. She knows a lot more than she tells you, that one. Don't you think it funny that she turns up at the Villa Cimbrone in the middle of the night when there is a fire? Then – *poof* – she finds hotel rooms after everyone has gone to sleep.'

'You are forgetting,' said Ben, 'that she has helped you a lot. And two days ago she just happened to save my life.'

'Oh, she only wants you to keep her bed warm.' And when he looked shocked, she added, 'I could tell that by the look on her face.'

'I don't think there's any point in you talking about things that you know nothing about.'

'You think I know nothing of love? You wait until I am ready and then I will show you all about love.'

Francesca's eyes were flashing. Her breath was coming quickly. Ben was stunned by her beauty. He didn't know what to say to her. At that moment the train plunged into a tunnel and total blackness descended upon them. Suddenly Ben felt a hand grip the hair on the nape of his neck and warm, trembling lips were pressed against his. She gently rocked her head back and forth in a most provocative way. Almost as a natural reaction he reached out for her, but she had already moved out of reach. The next second the train burst out into the startling, bright sunlight again and there she was, seated across the carriage from him, with her cheeks just a little bit pinker and her eyes lit by the ghost of a smile.

Ben was lost for words. After a few seconds he turned to look out of the window. His eyes were skimming over the bright blue of the bay below him, but his thoughts were in turmoil. The next second there was a rustle and her head was close to his again.

'I am sorry, Benjamin. Do not be angry with me. I was trying to find out how to get help in our quest against the Vitelli.'

Ben hesitated. He wasn't sure he wanted his attempts to retain his business to be coupled with Francesca's declared aim of being revenged against Toni's killers.

'Will you forgive me?' she pleaded.

He swallowed. 'Was it Alfredo you went to see this morning?'

'Yes.'

'I thought you said he was useless.'

She pouted. 'So he is if you want him to take any action against the Vitelli. But he knows many things about them that I don't know – things that have been kept from me.'

'What things?'

'I wanted to find out why the Vitelli are involved with the Cimbroni. Why do they have a hold over us? Why are they so powerful?'

'So what did he tell you?'

'At first he would tell me nothing. I think he was trying to pretend that his wife is not an evil snake. But then I told him that the Vitelli had killed Toni and that they had burned down the guest wing to try to kill you last night. He said he didn't believe it, of course, but I think he was shocked and he could see that it might be true.'

'So what did he say?'

'He says he knows very little himself. But he has told me who we should go to who will tell us all about what happened many years ago. I believe it is that which has led to what is happening now.'

'So who is it?'

She looked at him seriously. 'Did Toni ever tell you about our grandpapa? For many years he has lived on Capri in seclusion. But when we had problems Toni went to see him and he has often been able to help.' She sat back on the seat and stretched her arms above her head. 'That is where we are going.'

'We're going to Capri now?'

'Uh-huh. It is called the island of dreams.'

'How do we get there?'

'It won't take us long. This train takes us to Sorrento. We will get the *aliscafi* from there. Do you have enough money?'

Ben pulled out his wallet and checked. 'Just over three hundred euros. Will that be enough, or should I go to the bank? What are you planning to buy other than a couple of tickets for Capri?'

She laughed. 'That will be more than enough.'

'Good.' He nodded. 'So, how old is this grandfather of yours?'

'I don't know. He just seems to have been around forever and now he cannot see any more. But he is very clever – very sensible. In my family we have always gone to ask his advice about important matters.' She looked out of the window across the bay as the train began its descent into Sorrento. 'He lives in a little villa high above the sea. I think you will like it there.'

Ben watched her surreptitiously as she gazed into the distance, lost in her own reverie. He thought it was remarkable that she seemed to have got over the shock of learning about her brother's death. But he couldn't help wondering how on earth her grandfather was going to be able to help him with his own problems.

- 11 -

Ben was kept waiting in an austere sitting room in her grandfather's house while Francesca went and explained their presence to the old man. After about ten minutes she returned and led him out of the back door of the little villa and along a shady gravel path overhung by orange and lemon trees. Ben could see the green fruit which were starting to ripen.

The path terminated in a small paved loggia which was open on three sides, but with a low balustrade. The view from this point was one of the most spectacular which Ben had ever seen. As far as he could tell they were at a point several hundred feet directly above the sea and looking approximately north towards Ischia and Naples, although the land could only be vaguely discerned through the brown, early evening mist.

Seated in a creaking old basket chair in front of this magnificent view and with his back half-turned to their approach was a frail, bent old man with long, snowy white hair, his face and hands like brown, wrinkled parchment. A woollen rug was wrapped around his knees despite the warmth of the evening.

Francesca ran forward and crouched beside him. 'Grandpapa, this is Ben. He has been a very good friend of Toni for seven years.'

The old man turned his face towards him and Ben noticed the pale, unfocused eyes. He was struck by the irony of the blind old man sitting in front of this splendid view of which he could see nothing.

The girl beckoned and Ben moved forward. 'How do you do,' he said, rather formally. But he took hold of the offered hand and shook it warmly.

'You are welcome,' said the old man in a pale, reedy voice. 'It is nice to hear English spoken again. Will you please take a seat?'

Ben looked around but could only see a single, rather rickety, upright chair. He looked at Francesca who nodded and settled herself on a footstool by her grandfather's feet. So Ben collected the shaky chair and sat down near the balustrade.

'Do you like my view?' asked the old man, as though reading his thoughts.

'It's unbelievable.'

'I have lived here for twenty years. I have not seen the view at all for three years. And before that I was not able to see it properly for another five years. But when I sit here and feel the breeze on my face, I can remember it all just the way it was. I can hear the sounds of the *motoscafi* going to the Grotta Azzura and the screams of the petrels along the cliff-edge and I can see them as brightly in my mind as if they were in front of my eyes. Do you understand?'

'Yes, I think I do,' Ben agreed.

'I remember things very well,' said the old man. 'I sometimes think that it is the only thing that my body can now do properly.' When Ben stayed silent, he went on, 'I also remember many things which I do not wish to have on my memory. But a person cannot choose. I think it is about some of those unspoken things that you wish to speak to me.'

'Yes,' said Ben. 'I'm sorry if it disturbs you.'

'Oh, it is not your fault. Perhaps it is my fault for trying to run away from them many years ago. Perhaps I should have faced up to them then, as you are now doing.'

Ben wasn't quite sure what Francesca had told him. It began to sound as though she had cast him in the role of St George slaying the dragon. Ben wished he only had half her optimism – and half her innocence.

'Francesca said to me that you were the one who found the body of Toni,' said the old man.

'Yes.'

'The police do not know why he was murdered?'

'No. Whoever it was who killed him had ransacked our office. It seemed as if they were looking for something.'

A ghost of a smile crossed the old face. 'But you do not know what.'

'I was hoping that you might be able to help me with that,' said Ben.

'You did not find anything yourself after they had gone?'

'No.' Then he remembered. 'Well, I – I found one little thing. But I don't think its important.'

The old man was leaning forward, his sightless eyes intent on Ben's face. 'Tell me what you found and I will tell you if it is important.'

Ben's hand strayed to his jacket pocket where it fingered the badge he had picked up from beside the murdered man. 'It was something that fell out of Toni's hand when I – when I moved the body. It was a small metal object.'

'Describe it to me.'

He pulled out the piece of metal and looked at it. 'I have it here. It is just over an inch – about three centimetres square, but less than half a centimetre thick. It is made of a heavy grey metal.'

'Yes. And what is on it?'

'There is a picture of a black dog held by a chain and with blood dripping from its jaws.'

'Ah.' The old man's voice was so quiet that Ben found it difficult to make out the words. 'That is the Wolf of Hades.'

'What is the Wolf of Hades?'

'That is the hound which, the myths say, guards the entrance to hell. You must understand that here in the south we have our own version of the old myths. A lot of strange things are supposed to have happened here. We are a very superstitious people. You will have heard of the Greek myth of the Sirens?'

'I believe so.'

'That occurred on this very island. And we have our own explanations for a lot of things. There is an area to the west of Naples called the Campi Phlegraei which means the fields of fire. It was called that by the Greeks because there was so much volcanic activity there in ancient times. And there is a place in the Campi Phlegraei which the ancient peoples believed was the entrance to Hell. Even the Romans believed this. It was probably a kind of large volcanic hole from which hot air and gases emerged, but it must have been much greater than the usual fumaroles.' He paused for a moment. 'The hole which is left is more than a kilometre across. Now it has filled with water and is called Lake Avernus. This is where the old myths say the Wolf of Hades has his lair. It is said that he goes out into the world as far as his chain will allow him, and that he consumes the unwary souls who come too close to the gateway to Hell.

'I see.'

'But what you do not see, my friend, is what this has to do with the death of Toni. It is this which leads me to the Vitelli. However, before I tell you about them I must first tell you some more about Toni. You see, he came to see me six days ago.'

That made Ben pay close attention. He could see that Francesca's gaze was also fastened on the old man's face.

'Yes, Toni also asked me about the Vitelli, and I told him what I am going to tell you now. It was the first time that he had heard it.' The old man sighed and shook his head. 'When I was a boy I learned these things at my father's knee. In the new world my people have become civilized, but they have also grown weak.'

Ben looked at Francesca. She shook her head slightly as if to indicate that she didn't understand what he was talking about.

The old voice wandered on. 'And from what Toni told me, I think he had found out some things about the Vitelli and Cimbrone families. He would not tell me exactly what it was. But what I told him made his mind up.'

'The Vitelli are the family of Alfredo's wife, are they not?' asked Ben, somewhat unnecessarily.

'That is so.' The old man smiled bleakly. 'More's the pity.'

'So Toni had found out something about them?'

'That is right.'

'But you don't know just what it was?'

'I'm afraid I do not. Toni said it was best that I did not know, in case the Vitelli came here looking for information.'

'Have they?'

He shook his head. 'I told Toni they would not come. They at least have some respect for my age.'

'What was he going to do about the Vitelli?'

'He said he was investigating them. He had found out many interesting things. He was staying at a secret address in Naples to avoid suspicion. He did not say where that was either.'

'We've been to that address,' said Ben. 'Somebody else had got there before us. The place had been smashed up.'

'So it was discovered,' muttered the old man. 'I was afraid he would not be able to keep it a secret.'

There was a long pause. Grandpapa seemed to be musing to

himself. At last Ben could stand it no longer.

'There was something you were going to tell us about the Vitelli,' he prompted gently.

The old man jerked up from his reverie. 'Ah, yes. Yes – that is very important.'

There was another long pause while he collected his thoughts. At last he began. 'To understand what I am going to say, you must go back a very long way. You have to realize that since the decline of the Roman Empire, Italy has been a collection of separate states. Sometimes they were independent. Sometimes they were the subjects of other nations like the Austrian Empire. But never until about six generations ago was the whole of Italy combined together as one nation. And even now the government in Rome does not have the same power in the land as the British Parliament does in London.'

He paused and Ben wondered whether his mind had wandered again. But suddenly he returned to his story.

'In a country like this the powerful, the high-born and the very rich often behaved as if they were above the law. It was not unusual for them to run their own part of the country in the way *they* wished rather than in the way the government would have wished. This was especially so when the government was weak and was often changing.' He spread his hands in the Italian gesture. 'I understand that in the north the state is thought to be more important. But down here in the south it is often the person who is more important than the state.'

He paused and looked down at Francesca. 'This talking tires my throat. Will you get me a glass of orange, my dear?'

She jumped to her feet and hurried to do as he asked. As she went up the path, the old man leaned forward, suddenly imbued with a new sense of urgency.

'There are some things that I want to tell you that I do not wish the girl to hear.' He shrugged. 'No doubt she will hear it herself one day – perhaps from you. But maybe not quite yet, eh?'

He settled back in his chair. 'I will try to be brief. Once the Vitelli were one of the greatest families in southern Italy. They owned much land, many vineyards, several palazzi. They were merchants and they were traders. They were nobles in the kingdom of Naples. But so much power in the hands of so few people and with so little control did the worst for them.

'I believe you say in England that power corrupts.' He smiled at Ben. 'Well, that was true of the Vitelli. But there developed in the family a schism. There were two ways of thinking. The older brother said that the Vitelli should become the biggest and the most powerful family in the whole of Italy. Maybe they would even become the kings one day. The younger said that they were already rich and powerful enough and that they should care for their people and do good things in the world and bring benefits to Italy by industry and by trade. These two ways of thought were led by two brothers who in the end quarrelled totally. The father, an ignoble fiend called Alphonso Vitelli, decided in favour of the elder brother. The younger one was expelled from the family. He left with some of his supporters and said that he would never again call himself by the Vitelli name. So he took the name of the house where he went to live, and thus was born the Cimbrone family. That younger brother was my own great-grandfather.'

He paused to let his words sink in. Ben gazed out over the bay, but his mind was dwelling on this tale of 150 years ago.

'The Cimbroni were now very weak,' continued the old man. 'The Vitelli lost no opportunity to destroy their prosperity. Most of their friends and supporters fell away and returned to the Vitelli, or they were eliminated. But Angelo Cimbrone was a wise and sensible man. He slowly built up the Cimbroni by trade and by industry as he had said that he would. He always dealt fairly with all men and he passed instructions to his sons and his other supporters that they were to do the same. Gradually the Cimbroni once more became a power in the land and the Vitelli suffered as a result. That continued until the 1920s when Mussolini, whom we knew in Italy as *Il Duce*, came to power. Some people were pleased that Italy was once again ruled by a powerful and ruthless dictator. Some families became strong supporters of *Il Duce* in return for the rewards of power. One of these families was the Vitelli.'

The old man wiped a tear away from his cheek. It seemed he still felt the memory of those days very keenly. 'My father would not side with *Il Duce*, and certainly not with the Vitelli. He was imprisoned on some charge. I do not know that it was ordered by the Vitelli, but I suspect it. After five years he died in prison. That was not long before his fiftieth birthday.' A kind of pleading note seemed to have come into his voice as he continued.

111

'At that time I was a young man. Francesca's papa was only a few years old. I had a lot of difficulty just trying to stop the whole of our business from being swept away. For a time it seemed likely that our lands would be given to the Vitelli through some ancient claim. I was prepared to do anything to stop that. So I agreed to give them tribute.'

'What does that mean?' asked Ben.

'I agreed to pay them money each year in return for immunity from prosecution. It was to be a portion of our income but there was a minimum amount per year. I was young and foolish when I signed the agreement I realized too late that I had saddled my family with a burden which would keep them poor even when we should have had riches. But what was I to do?'

He continued bitterly, 'I know now that I was weak and cowardly. There came a time a few years ago when the wine crop failed and we could not afford to pay the tribute for that year. When the Vitelli came to me and said that they were willing to bury our old differences and once more become friends, I had no choice but to agree. Of course there were conditions. We had to acknowledge their superiority and follow their instructions in certain business dealings. We were to agree to the uniting of the two families by a number of marriages. But for me it seemed to present a way out of our troubles. I thought it was a way that I could protect my family from any more suffering. And for more than fifty years the tribute and the killings stopped.' He breathed in deeply and his sightless eyes dropped to his feet 'But now it seems that the killing is back.'

He sat forward with a sudden urgency. 'I know now that I was wrong. There is no other way but to fight them. The Vitelli are the kind of people who will take advantage of another person's humanity and treat it as a weakness. They must be defeated. That is the only way to protect all the other ordinary people.'

He slumped back in his basket-chair as though exhausted by the telling of the story. Ben was worried for a moment that it had all been too much for him and had caused him to become ill. But just at that moment Francesca returned with a tray bearing three glasses and a jug filled with orange juice and crushed ice. She filled one for her grandfather and he gratefully took it from her, drank a long draught and set it down on the balustrade with a precision born of long practice. Thus refreshed, Grandpapa Cimbrone continued his tale while the other two sipped at their delicious drinks.

'I was telling your friend,' he said to Francesca, 'that Alfredo's marriage to Mancino's girl was a mistake. The Vitelli have not changed. Now they will not rest until they have ruined and destroyed the Cimbrone family by whatever means they are able to use.'

His granddaughter remained silent, but her eyes had acquired a dangerous glint.

'You will want to know,' continued the old man, 'what the connection is between the Vitelli and the Wolf of Hades. Well, my children, the answer is simple. The estates of the Vitelli used to cover a large part of the Campi Phlegraei including Lake Avernus. In the past the *signors* of the Vitelli claimed to have the protection of the beast which they said they cared for. Perhaps it is a tale that would raise no more than a smile nowadays. But in the past it was a good way of ensuring the obedience of the superstitious peasantry, for they would always be afraid of having their souls thrown to the Devil by the Vitelli.'

He paused and took another drink from the tall glass which was encrusted with dew. Ben remembered the awe with which he had been treated by old Emilio when he mistakenly showed him the metal emblem, but he decided to say nothing for now, as the old man continued his story.

'The Vitelli therefore came to adopt the Wolf of Hades as their badge – what you call a coat of arms in England. It is many years since I went to the Villa Rafallo, which is the summer home of the Vitelli, but you will have been there recently, Francesca?'

'That is right, Grandpapa – only two weeks ago.'

'Did you notice the carved coat of arms in the stonework above the doorway?'

She shook her head. 'No, I didn't. I was in the back of the car and we drove straight into the courtyard.'

'Well, if it has not changed, there will be a likeness of the Wolf of Hades in the centrepiece above the gate.' The old man raised his eyes to Ben. 'So, Signor Cartwright, the thing you found in Toni's hand binds his death to the Vitelli. In the old days the people would have believed that his soul had been claimed by the Wolf of Hades.'

'You do not fear this superstition yourself?' asked Ben.

The other man thought for a minute. 'Well, perhaps I do a little. The only thing that I do know is that there are more evil things in this world than there are in the next.'

'What does it mean if I have this in my possession?'

'Oh, do not fear for yourself. You have come by the mark by chance. If you were to throw it at another person and to hit them, they would fear that the mark was upon them and that the wolf would be coming to claim their soul.' He smiled at Ben. 'You may have a powerful weapon against some people.'

That comment made Ben wonder about the demand which the hood with the knife had made in the living room of the flat in Naples. He was almost sure the man had mentioned the word 'mock', or perhaps it was 'mark', the meaning of which had been unclear to him at the time. He said, 'Well, I now understand the background to the enmity between your two families. However I still do not understand why Toni was killed or why the Vitelli should wish to take away my business. I suppose my next step is to go to Mancino Vitelli for those explanations.'

The old man raised his hand with a finger pointing to the heavens. 'Please have great care if you are thinking of going to the Villa Rafallo. When Toni left me six days ago his intention was to meet Mancino Vitelli. We know what happened to him. The Wolf of Hades can be a very unforgiving man.'

Something in his words made Ben shiver. Looking out across the sea he realized that the evening was by now well advanced. To the west a deep magenta sun was sinking towards the horizon. It was laced across by a few thin tendrils of cloud. From the sun a carpet of flashing orange crossed the sea below them and nearly reached to the foot of the cliff where they sat. The sky was bathed in a variety of colours from rose to carmine. In the east the short Italian dusk was gathering over the land, preparing to spread its mantle of darkness over them.

Ben was tired. In this state, the story which he had heard from the pale, cultured voice of the old man seemed all too plausible. It was easy enough to believe that the evil Wolf of Hades would be abroad tonight under the cloak of darkness in its search for errant souls. He stood up, aware that he had been sitting for too long on the hard chair by the balustrade.

Francesca, in her thin cotton dress, was also feeling the cold. She leapt to her feet. 'Grandpapa,' she said, 'it is nearly dark. It is time for me to take you into the house.'

The old man slowly pulled himself upright. 'You will stay to dinner?' he asked. 'In fact you must stay the night, for the last of the *aliscafi* has gone and they do not run after sunset. I regret that I have only one spare bed. So, unless you are lovers, one of you will have to sleep on the floor.'

Francesca turned a smile on Ben that made his heart leap for a second. 'That is all right, Grandpapa. Signor Cartwright has had so many disturbed nights recently that I think it is I who should sleep on the floor. He has a busy day ahead of him tomorrow.'

But the old man seemed not to hear. His sightless eyes were gazing somewhere far away where an old memory had been reawakened.

'There is one more thing I should tell you while you are here. I am told that the volcano Solfatara is active again. The same old myths say that, when this happens, the Wolf of Hades is abroad once more and that he will not return to his lair without his bag of souls. You should think on that.' Then he gave a mirthless chuckle which made Ben's scalp prickle. 'It all depends on whether you believe the old stories.'

His words unsettled Ben. In fact, after they had enjoyed a meal prepared by Grandpapa's maid and a bottle of good Chianti, it took him a long time to get to sleep that night in his borrowed sleeping bag on the hard tiled floor.

Ben lay flat on his stomach on the bare hillside and stared down at the Villa Rafallo. Angular lumps of limestone dug into his chest and a tuft of dry brown grass tickled his ear. The sun still beat down mercilessly, but the sky had acquired a steely glint that heralded a storm brewing. It gave Ben a slightly uneasy feeling.

As far as he could see in either direction the magnificent Amalfi Coast stretched into the distance. Range after range of high limestone mountains tumbled almost vertically into the sea, great masses of bare grey rock with an occasional fringe of scrubby vegetation. Below him wound the Amalfi Drive – forty miles of tortuous roadway which picked its way carelessly, clinging to the sides of the cliffs, plunging into tunnels, striding across ravines on curving viaducts, twisting round headlands, climbing through narrow passes, falling to small seaside villages and enjoying some of the most splendid views of any road in Europe.

Ben tore his gaze away from the natural beauties all around him and set himself to study the terrain below. The Villa Rafallo occupied a splendid natural site. It sat on top of a high sloping promontory which was cut off from the mountain ranges behind it by the road. On three sides sheer limestone cliffs plunged 200 feet straight into the deep blue waters of the Mediterranean. On the fourth side the casual traveller along the road was kept at bay by a high stone wall topped by ornate and evil-looking ironwork. Approximately halfway along the wall was a pair of high, solid gates, surrounded by a carved masonry pediment, in the centre of which was a coat of arms.

Ben propped himself on one elbow and lifted the binoculars to his eyes. Sure enough, even at this distance he could make out that the carving looked like a grotesque dog. It was the Wolf of Hades, just as Francesca's grandfather had said.

Ben shifted his gaze to inspect the villa itself. It was a very large house. Although he judged that it was old, it seemed to have a bright, new roof of pink clay tiles. It was only a two-storey structure, built in a square around the traditional central atrium, but with an additional long wing on the eastern side which terminated right on the edge of the cliff. The wing was also two storeys high with a straight new roof in which were a number of small dormers.

Along the front of the house was a large paved courtyard where Ben could see at least two parked cars. Just inside the gateway on the right-hand side was a single-storey lodge or gatehouse. Beyond this building were formal gardens laid out with gravel paths enclosing beds of shrubs and flowers which extended around the west side of the main house and southwards towards the sea. In the middle of the southern side of the garden was a long flight of steps, broken by occasional terraces, which led down to a level grassed area occupying the centre of the promontory. Most interesting to Ben was the lowest terrace. This appeared to be almost circular and paved in tarmac. Because of the slope of the land he could not see the whole area. However he could just see part of what looked like a large white cross painted in the centre.

It looks remarkably like a helicopter landing pad, he thought to himself.

From behind the gatehouse Ben could see steps leading into a narrow ravine. They disappeared out of sight but he guessed they led down to the water's edge. It meant that the Villa Rafallo had potential escape routes by land, sea and air. Over the years the Vitelli had gone to considerable lengths to protect themselves in case they should come under attack.

Wow, what a place, thought Ben to himself. It's just like the modern equivalent of some medieval castle. Now he had to find an unguarded way into this stronghold.

He pulled a pencil and paper from his back pocket and started to make a rough sketch of the place, as far as his uncomfortable position and the uneven surface would allow. From time to time he raised the binoculars to check on certain details before he made a note of them on the plan. As he worked he began to realize that there was likely to be only one way in which he could get into the Villa Rafallo without being detected – to climb in. The only trouble with that idea was that he hadn't put on a pair of climbing boots since the day that Carlo died. Would he be able to restart now?

He lifted the glasses and surveyed the promontory for the last time. As he did so a movement caught his eye. A man stepped out of the gatehouse and walked across the paved courtyard towards the east wing. He was a long way away and, even with the binoculars, Ben was unable to make out the man's face. But from the style of the man's dress and the way in which he walked, he could have sworn that it was the hood with the knife who had twice pursued him.

Ben thought grimly to himself that sooner or later the two of them were bound to come face to face again. He only hoped the contest would be an equal one, because up until now he had felt at a distinct disadvantage each time they had met. Ben decided that he was feeling quite nervous about the next twenty-four hours.

Carefully he started to retrace his route to the car. He kept low until he was far enough over the brow of the hill to rise, first to a crouch and then to walking height. He picked his way over the rough, rocky hillside, skirting clumps of thorny undergrowth and frequent large boulders. After a while he reached the cleft by which he had ascended the half-mile from the road. He began to climb back down it with great care. In this rough, loose terrain it would be easy to turn an ankle, and that was the last thing he wanted to do at the moment.

When he was in sight of the road he paused to brush the worst of the dirt and dust from his clothes. He could see that Francesca was sitting on a part of the broken parapet across the other side of the road, swinging her legs idly as she looked down at the sea far below her. Donna was leaning against the side of the car which was parked in a rough gravel lay-by on the near side of the road. She appeared to be manicuring her nails. They were obviously avoiding speaking to each other. Ben was disappointed that the two of them didn't seem to get on. He supposed it was because they were such different types. He shrugged his shoulders and made his way painfully down the last, steep part of the ravine.

The women heard him coming. Francesca rose and sauntered back across the road as Ben returned to the car. She looked cool and self-contained in her light-green dress. It was Donna who looked overdressed and pink and uncomfortable in the breathless midday heat. She raised an enquiring eyebrow.

'Well,' said Ben, 'the place looks nearly as impregnable as Fort Knox, unless you've got a couple of attack helicopters up your sleeve. The Vitelli certainly know how to look after themselves.'

Donna leaned back again. 'What are you planning to do then? Hammer on the gate and demand your rights?'

'I will go in,' said Francesca. 'Signor Vitelli will see me. He thinks I am to be his daughter-in-law. He will talk to his son's future wife.'

'Are you joking?' asked Donna. 'Look what he did to your brother. A man like that doesn't bother about being polite to ladies.'

'But there is supposed to be friendship between our two families. I do not think he would openly do me any harm.'

'Who said anything about being open? You disappear through that gateway on your own, my girl, and who's to know whether you will ever be seen again.'

'Well,' said Francesca. 'If I do not come out again within two hours you can ring the police.'

'I don't think that would work.' Ben shook his head. 'I think the police would be very careful about charging somebody as important as Mancino Vitelli. They would accept anything he told them. And I don't think Donna and I would wield much influence.'

Donna snorted. 'All Signor Vitelli has to do is tell them that he doesn't know what we're talking about and he hasn't seen you for a week. Then they'll leave him alone and concentrate on sending us on our way.'

'I agree with Donna, Francesca. You probably won't even get as far as Vitelli himself. He knows that your appearance will mean trouble and he'll probably put one of his henchmen on to you. I'm not absolutely sure, but I think I saw that gangster with the knife I told you about. He was crossing the courtyard from what looks like a guardhouse by the gate to a part of the house which looks like a small factory or laboratory, or something like that. I don't like to think what might happen if that bloke got hold of you.'

'But I tell you that they will not think of me in that way.' Francesca was adamant. 'I have been to the Villa Rafallo before. The people there will know me.'

'Even if you did get in to see him,' said Donna, 'what could you do?

Vitelli isn't going to admit to you that he had your brother murdered and then say he's sorry. He'll deny it, won't he?'

'That's right, Francesca,' Ben agreed. 'We're going to have to squeeze Vitelli hard to get anything out of him. We need to surprise him and we need to find something that will let us put some pressure on him. You can't do all that on your own.'

'Is there no other way in except the front here?'

Ben grinned wryly. 'I think I could see a helicopter landing-pad. But we're not exactly the US marines, are we?'

'Don't look at me,' said Donna as Francesca turned to her. 'Joseph Carter's alimony doesn't stretch that far.'

'How about a boat?'

'It looks as if there might be a small cove where boats could come in to land,' said Ben. 'But the path comes right up beside the gatehouse and I can't believe that it won't be fenced off somewhere. Everything else is so secure.'

'Then that only leaves the front gate.' Francesca tossed her head rebelliously. 'If they will not let me in, I do not see how *you* are going to reach Mancino Vitelli. As you say, the place is so well protected that there is no other way except to persuade them to open the front gate to us.'

'Well, there is another way,' he said softly. 'But I don't know whether I can still do it.'

'What do you mean?'

Ben pulled a face. He found he couldn't look at them. He turned to face the sea. 'The only way in, other than the gate,' he said unhappily, 'is to climb up the cliffs on the east side of the house. On that side they don't have any way of seeing you until you get to the top.'

'Then that is what we must do,' said Francesca.

'But I haven't climbed for two years. I haven't been on a rock-face since – since the day that Carlo died. And the cliffs here are difficult. I can't do that climb on my own.'

There was a long silence. Then Francesca said, quietly but accusingly, 'You are afraid.' There was so much contempt in her voice that Ben found it almost unbearable.

'It isn't only that,' he said lamely. 'I don't have any equipment. This climb would have to be made in the dark and on difficult surfaces. It would be important to have the right equipment.'

'I know where there is climbing equipment,' said Francesca. 'It is at the bottom of the wardrobe in Toni's flat. I saw it only two days ago when we were there. Toni must have kept it there.'

'But it's not only the equipment. I would need practice – several days' practice – to rebuild my technique.' Even as he spoke he felt the shame welling up inside him, and when he looked at Francesca there was a look of utter scorn on her face.

'We cannot wait several days. It must be done now or not at all.' She flung her head back haughtily. 'Very well. I shall climb up by myself if you will not do it. I am not afraid. You can stand by the gate until I reach the top and I will open it for you to come in.'

'Come and look at this,' said Ben. He crossed the road to the sea side and the women followed him. He put a foot on the low stone wall which was all that prevented vehicles from going over the cliff and falling on to the rocks 200 feet below. He pointed over a lower headland which jutted out into the Mediterranean and across the inlet beyond to the sheer wall of rock below the Villa Rafallo.

'That's the cliff you've got to get up. It's not an easy climb. Have you ever done any climbing?'

'I have often talked to Toni. He knew how to climb. He has told me how to do it.'

'But Toni wasn't an expert climber, Francesca. He knew less about climbing than I did. *He* didn't have the technique for a climb like that. He had only done a few short climbs himself before – before the accident.'

She turned on him with her eyes blazing. 'Don't you say anything about Toni. He was brave – that is all that matters. He would not have been afraid to do this climb. Since he is dead I am now the only one left who can help the Cimbroni. Therefore I will do the climb.'

Ben hung his head. It was useless trying to make her see reason when she was in this mood. Besides, he knew she was right. They could not wait several days. 'No,' he said, so quietly that the others could hardly hear him. '*I* must do it.'

Francesca leaned forward. '*When* will you do it?'

'Tonight. There is no other time.'

Donna linked her arm through his. 'Now look, Ben, you don't have to climb up that bloody cliff just to keep this little madam happy. As you said earlier, you can't do it alone. Even I have enough knowledge of climbing to know that. One slip and it'd be feeding time for the gulls. I'm sure we can find some other way to get in to Fort Rafallo there.'

He smiled weakly at her support. 'They call it "bottling out" in England. I shouldn't have left it so long before I tried to climb again. I should really have gone straight out on a new rock-face the next day.'

'What exactly happened two years ago to make you feel so bad?' asked Donna.

'Yes, tell us.' Francesca looked almost eager. 'I want to know just how Carlo died. He was very important. Toni said he was the best of the Vitelli.'

Ben's thoughts were tugged unwillingly back to that day. He shuddered again as he began to talk about it.

'The three of us set out to climb a five-hundred-metre rock-face called the Brow of the Devil. Carlo had always wanted to do it. But he didn't have enough experience. And neither did I.'

He looked at them sadly. 'We started off too late in the day. We were roped together. Carlo was leading, Toni came second and I was the anchor man. It was the most difficult climb that I had ever done.' He shook his head. 'By evening we weren't halfway up and it was getting dark. It was then that Carlo took one risk too many. He fell and pulled Toni off with him. Luckily I was able to hang on.' He swallowed. 'Then I had to try to rescue the others. After a couple of hours I was able to get Toni into the chimney where I was when the accident happened. But I didn't have enough strength left to drag Carlo into the shelter.' He paused. 'When the rescue helicopter reached us the next morning he was dead.'

He looked at the two women. Donna seemed sympathetic, but Francesca's expression was no more than neutral.

'Of course, I blamed myself for Carlo's death although Toni told the court that it was the man's own fault because he took too many risks and they agreed with him.' He shrugged. 'Anyway, I have never climbed since.'

Ben sat silent on the wall on the edge of the cliff, looking down at the waves swirling over the rocks far below. He felt a deep sense of shame.

'I know I should have made more of an attempt to rescue Carlo,' he admitted, 'but I seemed to be so weak. My muscles had given up working. I hardly had enough strength left to hold myself up there.'

Donna spoke out, 'Well, I reckon you're a hero. I'd have just given up and only thought about saving my own skin.'

Francesca had said nothing and Donna prompted her, 'Don't you agree that he should have a medal for saving your brother's life?'

The girl was silent for a long time, then she blurted out, 'Carlo deserved to die. Toni did not.' She rested a hand on Ben's arm. 'My grandfather said he believed you are the tool of God.'

The other two looked at her in astonishment, but she didn't seem to think her words were strange.

'You have been sent to us in our day of need,' she said. 'I think you will destroy the Vitelli. My grandfather told me this. He said I must follow you.'

Donna burst out irreverently. 'Ben, you're obviously the new Messiah.'

'I don't know about that.' Ben tried to make a joke of it. 'I'm not sure I can even look after myself, much less sort out the Vitelli. We've still got to find a way to get up that cliff over there.'

Francesca glared fiercely into his face. 'We will do it. They will not be able to stop us now.'

'I tell you that will not be an easy climb,' said Ben. 'It'll have to be made at night. We may make a noise. If I had to put a bet on it, I would say the odds are two to one against us doing it without being caught.'

'I tell you we will do it. You will not be alone. I shall come with you to help you up.'

'That's out of the question.'

'Donna said you cannot do it alone. So you would not succeed. You must not do it alone. And also you will need to someone to show you the way when you get to the house. I am the only one who knows where to find Mancino Vitelli.'

'I've told you, Francesca, it'll be a very demanding climb. It will be dark and the rock is difficult. It's no outing for a beginner.'

'But I have to come,' she said. 'I am the last of the Cimbroni. Poor Alfredo is an empty shell. I cannot ask you to do something that is so difficult on your own. For the honour of the Cimbroni I must come.'

Ben shook his head. 'I tell you again that it is not a climb for a novice. A girl like you would not have the strength in her hands.'

'Do not talk to me in that way,' blazed Francesca. 'I may be a girl but I am equal to any man. I will show you that I am not afraid of anything.

123

And I am very fit and strong. I will probably leave you behind halfway up.'

Ben looked at the fury in her face. If sheer determination was enough, he could believe that she was more than capable of scrambling up 200 feet of sheer, friable limestone. However it would need more than that. He turned to Donna for support but she just shrugged.

'Oh, let the woman go,' she said. 'Then she'll find out what it's really like.'

'Even if she kills the pair of us?'

'You too,' said Francesca. 'Why should we not all climb?'

Donna shook her head vigorously. 'Not me, my friend. You won't get me anywhere near that rock-face. I'm scared of heights.'

'If I go, I go on my own. I don't want anyone else to slow me down or put me in danger,' said Ben.

'You *know* that is not safe,' said Francesca. 'We have already said that you cannot do it alone. I remember that Toni said many times that nobody should make a big climb on their own. It doesn't matter how good a climber you are – you must have someone to back you up and carry spare equipment. Besides' – she spread her hands wide – 'I ask you where you will go when you get to the top of the cliff if I am not there to guide you? You do not know the way into the building. You also do not even know what Mancino Vitelli looks like, or where he sleeps. You cannot even speak Italian. You will get nowhere without me. You will do all that climbing and then throw it away for nothing.'

She had a point there. Ben still felt it was wrong to expect a young girl to risk her life doing something that she had never done before. But when he looked to Donna for a way out, she was no help to him.

'I say let her go. She's got to learn to be a big girl some time.'

He shrugged. 'OK, you win. I'll take you with me.'

He saw Francesca's grim smile of success. Ben thought that probably she was only coming to make sure that he didn't have an opportunity to back out. It was likely that she didn't have any confidence in his ability or resolve to succeed. But he couldn't complain about that. He didn't feel much confidence in himself at the moment.

He thrust those thoughts firmly behind him. 'If we're going to climb tonight, we'd better get moving. We've got a busy day ahead of us – checking out the equipment and giving you some basic training, Francesca. I'm not climbing without the proper preparation.'

'You're the boss.' Donna stepped in before the girl could argue. 'Tell us what we've got to do next.'

'All right, then. First we go back to Naples to pick up the kit and check it out thoroughly. It hasn't been used for two years and it was packed away after an unsuccessful climb. It's bound to be in a mess. So it'll have to be cleaned up and possibly repaired. That'll take all three of us at least a couple of hours.'

He paused but there was no argument.

'We've got to plan our ascent properly. Speed is going to be important. A climb like this may take three to four hours in the dark. We can't start until all the light has gone and there's no risk of people in the villa spotting us. That means we won't begin climbing until about midnight. Dawn is soon after six at this time of year. We've got to be in the house long before that. Really I'd like to be in and out again by that time. So this afternoon we'll have a training session to try and instill some technique into you, Francesca – how to hold yourself, how to control the ropes – that sort of thing. We can do some low climbs on the cliffs where Toni used to train and I'll show you what to do.'

He was ready for Francesca to raise some objections, but she seemed to be keeping remarkably quiet. Perhaps she was so anxious to do the climb that she was prepared to do everything she was told, just to humour him.

'The other thing that I want to do is to take a boat out from somewhere near here so that we can give the cliffs below the Villa Rafallo a thorough survey. I need to have a good idea of the most suitable route up. For that I'll need a local boatman who isn't a friend of the Vitelli.'

'While you two are practising I'll see if I can come up with someone,' said Donna. 'I'm good at worming my way under the skin of the locals.'

'Thanks.' Then Ben suddenly thought, 'You're doing a hell of a lot, Donna. This isn't your fight. I'd understand if you didn't want to get involved.'

'Hey! I haven't had so much fun in years. I'm with you all the way – just so long as you don't ask me to do anything silly like climbing up cliffs. That's your department. And Francesca's, of course, if that's the way she wants to play it.'

Ben nodded. 'OK. Well, thinking about it, we ought to do the survey as soon as possible, before the shadows get too deep. The climbing practice can come later. If you can drop us back at Toni's flat, Donna, then Francesca and I will sort out the gear while you're off looking for a boat. Then you can come and pick us up as soon as you've got one, if that's all right with you.'

'OK.'

'Then let's get moving.'

He turned back to the car. His heart was thumping as he climbed into the back seat. I wonder whether I can go through with it, he thought miserably to himself as Donna did a U-turn and headed back to the city.

- 13 -

Another wave surged into the little cove, sloshing round the rocks and saturating him nearly to the waist. Ben cursed. He was going to get very cold without a wet suit and there was no chance that they could change before they started the climb. The rocks here at the sea's edge were incredibly slippery. In the darkness it was difficult to make out where the slime and seaweed ended and the dry rock began.

He could hear the scrabbling of Francesca's feet no more than five yards ahead of him but he couldn't see her in the pitch blackness. She was dressed overall in black and her dark hair was coiled on her head, making her nearly invisible from behind.

He realized that he should have been leading the way, since he was the experienced climber. However he had at last discovered that she had a weakness – a tendency to seasickness. She had been so desperate to get out of the lurching, swooping little boat that he had let her go first. Then she made a desperate leap to get ashore, risking a ducking and broken limbs to escape a queasy stomach. Ben shook hands with the boatman Donna had recruited and followed more carefully.

It was a night for taking care. The cold, blustery wind, which had got up from the south during the evening, and which had rolled a mantle of glowering clouds across the sky, was going to make the climb very uncomfortable. They would have to be more careful about finding their foot- and hand-holds. However the rough weather offered some compensation for the additional discomfort that it brought. There would be a lot more noise around the villa at the top of the cliffs. Up there the bushes and trees would be swaying and rustling, doors and shutters would rattle and creak, shadows would flit around. The enthusiasm of the guards would be lessened by the chill wind which carried the occasional squall of rain – and all that would be a help to them.

'Have you found the ledge yet?' he asked her in a hoarse whisper.

'I think it's just above me, but I can't find a way on to it.'

'Wait just where you are until I get to you. Remember what I told you – one slip now could land you with a broken leg.'

Ben shifted the rucksack containing their climbing gear higher on to his shoulders to balance himself better and started to move forward – feeling his way rather than seeing it. As he went he tried to memorize the route which he had studied so closely from the boat during the afternoon.

The boatman from Positano had brought them round here on what they hoped would appear to be a casual fishing trip. While the others had trailed rods and lines over the side, Ben had searched the headland thoroughly with his binoculars, looking for the best means of access to the cliff-top eyrie of Mancino Vitelli. Of course the easiest way up was the long zigzag staircase cut into the ravine on the west side. This led down to a tiny cove where they could easily have been landed in the lee of the boathouse. However the steps were protected at the top and bottom by high stone walls topped by barbed wire. The walls were pierced only by timber doors which appeared to be new and strong. He could also see that there were lights cut into the rock walls all the way down the steps. These would probably be switched on at night. He judged that there would be little chance of getting up that way unobserved.

The cliffs all around the promontory were never less than 180 feet high. They were formed of old and often crumbling limestone. They had been much weathered by winter storms and were patched with trailing clumps of vegetation. The problem on a surface like that was not the shortage of handholds, but the unstable nature of the rock. Ben knew from past experience that a surface like that would be fragile and friable. Whole boulders could break off quite easily when a person's weight was put upon them. You didn't have to be very clever to envisage what would happen if a disaster like that occurred in the middle of the climb. They just had to find a more protected route.

From his observations the only place which appeared to offer any real possibility of a safe ascent was a large fissure on the eastern side near the root of the promontory. Ben had asked the boatman to take them closer to that area and he had spent a lot of time studying it carefully. It was deep enough to provide protection and support on both sides during the climb. And there were several useful ledges. The only problem was that the fissure narrowed as it rose up the cliff and ran out completely when it was approximately thirty feet below where the eastern wall of the house seemed to almost overhang the cliff. When they reached the top of the crack it would be necessary to carry out an exposed traverse on an almost vertical rock-face to reach the middle terrace. At a height of 170 feet directly above the sea that was going to need nerves of steel, which Ben wasn't sure that he still possessed.

However, when he had discussed it with the others that afternoon, there had seemed to be no better alternative. Now the two of them had to test the theory. They would be in the dark, swept by the occasional shower, and trying to feel their way up with wet rock beneath their hands.

After a couple of minutes scrambling, Ben reached Francesca. She was still stuck below the first ledge. It was about six feet above her head and she had the beginner's worries about taking her feet off solid rock without any large hand-holds to take her weight.

'Wait there a minute while I get up,' he told her. 'Then I'll reach down to give you a hand.'

'Damn!' She was nearly crying with frustration. 'I have only been climbing for about five minutes and I'm stuck already.'

'You've not started yet. This is where the walking stops and the climbing begins.' Ben spoke flippantly to disguise the queasy sensation in his own stomach. Would he still be able to do it himself?

Thrusting that thought behind him he took off his back-pack and heaved it on to the ledge above his head. Then he felt about until he was able to find suitable hand-holds. It took him only a couple of minutes to get up. It was still surprisingly easy. But how would he feel when he had a hundred feet of clear space below his feet? Heights had never worried him in the past, but now he wasn't so sure.

He lay flat on his stomach and reached down to her. He showed her where the hand- and foot-holds were and reminded her how to keep her hips close to the rock while she leaned out. Then he took a grip on the collar of her anorak as she came up to give her confidence.

When he had her safely settled on the ledge he opened the rucksack and reminded her how to put on the harness and straps and fit the other items of equipment. He explained the use of each one to her again as she fitted them on.

'Actually you're mainly carrying this stuff as spares in case I run out. Since I shall be leading, most of it will be fixed before you get there.'

When they were kitted out, Ben folded up the back-pack and tucked it away in a crack in the rock. He had no idea when he might return to collect Toni's equipment again.

'Now – are you ready?'

Francesca nodded.

'Remember that we have to keep as quiet as possible. So, no calling out unless it's absolutely essential. Also remember to test each hand- or foot-hold with your full weight before you let go of your other holds. That way you'll never get caught out.'

He showed her again how to tie the ropes to her harness so that they wouldn't slip loose by mistake but could be quickly released in an emergency. 'When I want more rope I'll give you a jerk like this. If you want me to stop for some reason you give me a jerk. If it's OK to go on again, give two jerks. When I want you to start climbing behind me I'll give you two jerks. Three jerks from either of us means there is a problem. If I give you three jerks you must release yourself from the climbing rope as I've shown you, tie the safety rope to the nearest secure point and get down the cliff as quickly as you can.'

Her voice was low but insistent 'We are not to go back.'

He could imagine the set expression on her face and it made him grin. He pointed to the equipment dangling from her belt 'These funny-shaped things are called nuts or chocks. What I'll try to do is find a big enough crack and fit them in so that the sides pull against the rock and grip it tightly. I've shown you how to tie a non-slip knot on the end of the rope. Funnily enough we call them Italian loops. Otherwise it'll be free climbing for both of us, although I'll keep you on a tight rope to give you confidence.'

He didn't really doubt *her* self-confidence. It was his own nerve that he doubted. He didn't know why he reached out and squeezed her hand. 'Do you still want to come?'

He felt an answering pressure from her, but she said nothing. He couldn't really judge her feelings. Probably she wasn't too happy, knowing she was climbing with a man who was trying to regain his lost courage. But it was no good thinking of that. With a sudden movement he turned away.

He began to edge along the rough and rapidly narrowing ledge, scrambled over a couple of low boulders and moved into the fissure. Now he could feel the palms of his hands turning greasy with sweat and his heartbeat beginning to accelerate. He tried to tell himself that this always happened at the start of a climb, but he wasn't convinced. He used to be able to do climbs like this with his eyes closed. But his memory kept taking him back to the sight he had seen as he was lowered from the Brow of the Devil.

He could once again see in minutest detail the picture of Carlo's dangling, swinging body doubled up in the middle as though it had been snapped in half. That picture had returned to haunt him many times in the last two long years. And this would be the first time that his feet had been on vertical rock since that terrible night. He did not want young Francesca to be his next similar sight.

Somehow his confidence wasn't helped by the awkward little lump in the small of his back. Just before they had left Donna had taken him on one side and handed him a little canvas bag. When he opened it and peered inside he found it contained a small handgun.

She winked. 'Just in case you need it.'

'Where did you get this?' he asked suspiciously.

She shrugged her shoulders. 'Oh, you know us Americans – keen on personal security.'

'But isn't it illegal?'

'Not as illegal as throwing knives at people.' She looked straight up into his eyes in a disconcerting way. 'Look here, Ben, these guys aren't pussy-footing around. If you come face to face with one of them in the Villa Rafallo, you're likely to finish up dead.' She tapped the leather holster. 'This may even things up a bit.'

'But I don't want to kill anybody.'

'You aren't going to kill anyone with this little pop-gun unless you hit them straight in the head or the heart Remember to aim low for their belly. That won't kill them but it'll hurt them a lot.' She patted him on the arm.

'I don't know,' said Ben, doubtfully taking the thing in his hand. 'I've never shot anyone before.'

'Please take it for *me*,' she cajoled. 'Call it a little insurance policy.

It'd make me feel a lot happier.'

'It'll get in the way when I'm climbing. I don't want the bloody thing to go off and hit me in the foot or something.'

Donna chuckled. 'I've thought about that too. You should know it can't hurt anyone unless the safety catch is off.' She took the bag back and turned it over. 'Also I've sewed these two tabs on the back. If you take your belt off, it'll loop through them and tuck down inside your waist-band without being too uncomfortable. It's so small you can hardly see the bump it makes.'

They tried it and, to Ben's surprise, it worked all right.

'There, it hardly makes any lump at all. Can you reach back and get it?'

He tried as she asked, lifting his loose sweater and slipping his hand into the bag without any difficulty.

'I think that'll work OK,' she said. 'Nobody'll know a thing about it unless you need to use it.'

Ben still wasn't sure that it was a good idea. It seemed to make the whole matter far more serious. However he couldn't cause a fuss about it once he had it on. As Donna said, what had he to lose? But now it felt uncomfortable?

He wondered again how Donna had come by the gun. She couldn't have carried it through even the second-rate Naples airport security. He should have asked her more questions about it. Somehow it seemed to add to the fear and foreboding which he felt. He laughed grimly to himself. He could just imagine what Francesca was thinking as he hesitated there, rubbing the small of his back and thinking fearfully of his previous climb.

With an effort he tore his mind away from his memories of the past. He thrust his hand into the bag at his waist, generously rubbing chalk into his sweating palms and between the greasy fingers. What he must do was concentrate on technique – that was the thing. The rock here was damp but not slippery. As long as he kept his hands dry the grip would be easy.

He put his right hand into the fissure as far as he could push it. Then he clenched and balled it into a fist, squeezing it tight. He'd taped his hands but they still seemed very soft. How would his body stand up to a real climb?

Forget about that. Reach up two feet. Feel for the crack. Left hand in.

Same procedure. Bring up the right foot and ease it into the gap. Foot in, twist and arch to grip. Step up two feet and repeat with the left foot. Now he was off the ground. Release the right hand. Reach up two feet and start again. After a two-year interval he was climbing again. It was no problem! He could still do it!

He went quickly up the first twenty feet and then paused. The perspiration broke out on his forehead and the mists of fear closed in again behind his eyes.

Don't look down. Must keep climbing. Don't give fear a chance.

He started off again. By the time he was fifty feet up, the fissure had started to broaden out so that he was beginning to lose his grip. But here he found a crack big enough to put in a chock. He was twice as careful as he would have been in the past to make sure that it had the best possible grip and there was no chance of it slipping. He suppressed a grim little smile at the care he was taking. Then he moved up another two feet and put in another one just above his head. He told himself that was for Francesca and he would remove it later on. He put a krab into the upper one and was ready to move up. Then he gave two jerks to Francesca to get her started.

He leaned out to watch her progress. It took her a long time to get up to him. This was difficult climbing for her. Her hands weren't big enough. It was true that women were often better on open rock work, but they couldn't do the heavy hand work like this.

He kept the climbing rope tight to give her plenty of support and encouragement. But it must have taken her four times as long as an experienced climber to get up the fifty feet of rough cliff face. She finally made it, puffing and blowing, and rested on the ropes just below the nut.

'There you are,' he said. 'That's your first pitch, and you didn't do too badly at all.'

She managed a little smile but didn't have the breath to answer.

'You've got the usual beginner's problem of trying to hug the rock too closely because you haven't got confidence in your hands. Remember to hang your bottom out further and keep your knees in. I won't let you fall.' He looked at his watch. 'Well, it's after two thirty, so I'd better get a move on. We've less than four hours till dawn.'

He adjusted the ropes, deciding to leave the second chock in position for Francesca to rest on. Then he was off.

Now it was a question of hand-holds. Feel and pull your way. In the darkness he couldn't see to reconnoitre ahead. So he frequently had to retrace his steps. The first nagging worry about time began to seep into the back of his mind.

He came to a good fifteen-foot crack between the blocks. Here he could use the flat of his hand and arch his fingers for grip. His progress improved. At the top it ran out into a ledge. It was not enough to stand on but he could hook his elbow over to obtain some respite. He paused to relax his muscles in sequence and follow a pattern of breathing to build up the oxygen level in his blood again.

Damn it, he thought, I'm getting soft. I could easily have made this two years ago. He surveyed the rock ahead. It was sheer in front of him. He was about six feet away from the fissure which seemed to be narrowing again. So he decided that was the best route. He was too exposed at the moment to help Francesca up the next stage.

He moved along the ledge, carrying his weight on his hands and just using his feet for friction. This was tiring work. Of course the ledge ran out two feet before he reached the crevice and he had a difficult thirty seconds scrabbling around, trying to get a grip for his right foot. But then he was away again.

After a few feet he rested and put in his last two chocks. Francesca was carrying two which he could use at either end of the traverse. Then he pulled in the ropes and secured them.

He double jerked back to her and watched her start off. This was quite a short pitch, barely forty feet, but she had much more of a struggle. Despite his instructions to follow exactly where he had gone, she tried to cut a couple of corners in her haste and got into terrible trouble. Ben decided that he had to abandon silence and call down to her as quietly as he could.

'You'll have to retrace your steps to the little flake on your left and come up over the top of it instead of trying to get past below.'

There followed five minutes of sweating, scrambling effort from Francesca.

'Good. Now come straight up towards me for ten feet – er – three metres. That's right – along that little row of knobs.'

She was doing her best to follow his instructions now. She already knew that time was important.

'Nowt take that crack half a metre to your left. That's the one. Then at the top you'll follow the ledge. I can help you from there.'

At last she made it. He almost had to drag her over the last bit. He checked his watch. She had spent nearly an hour struggling up the forty feet and it had taken a lot out of her, both physically and psychologically. Ben thought grimly that she was probably regretting the blithe decision to climb which she had made in the sunshine of yesterday.

But he said cheerfully, 'Well, I think this next section is quite easy. I'll go right to the top of the crevice now. It's longer than the two previous pitches but it's straight. That means I'll be able to help you a bit more.'

He took Francesca's two chocks and looped them on to his belt. Then he set off. He went straight up the next pitch in not much more than ten minutes. He put in a single chock at the top. He wanted to keep one spare in case he needed it on the traverse.

He almost pulled Francesca up this next stage, taking a grip on both the lead and the safety ropes to get her up as quickly as possible. She did it in less than twenty minutes. When he checked his watch again he found it was just after ten past four. That was about forty minutes later than he had intended.

Ben settled Francesca as comfortably as he could, supported by the single nut. Then he gathered the rope together for the traverse.

'Right. This may take some time. You'll probably be here for an hour or more. There's a risk that you may get cold and stiff. But traversing is a slow old business on limestone like this. Do the exercises I showed you to keep your circulation going and to avoid getting too cold. You'll need everything about you when you start again.'

Francesca shuddered as she looked at the bare cliff-face. 'Have we really got to go across there?'

'You knew that all along.' Ben couldn't help grinning at the change in her tune now that she was close to the real challenge.

'It didn't look as big when we were in the boat.'

'Don't worry,' he said. 'When you cross there'll be a fixed rope for you to hang on to. I'll also have you on the safety rope if you lose your footing and let go. You'll probably skate across it in ten minutes or less. At the end you may have a problem going up the three metre wall on to the terrace, but I can pull you up there if you're getting tired by then.'

She nodded but said nothing. Did she guess that his cheerful tone disguised his own worries? Ben didn't pretend to himself that this next section wasn't going to be very difficult. The traverse was at least twice as long as he should have attempted without competent support. But it was too late to worry about that now.

He secured the end of the fixed rope to the nut and looped the rest to the front of his belt. Then he set off.

The surface was bad, as he had known it would be. It was less than five degrees off vertical and the rock was very crumbly and badly weathered. Now that he was out of the protection of the fissure the gusting wind was tugging at him as though to tear him from his precarious hold and throw him on to the rocks far below. His still damp trousers clung to his cold legs. Each hold had to be reached for, laboriously cleared of debris, and carefully tested before he could put his weight on it It was hard work and he was out of condition. But the wonderful thing was that he no longer felt any fear. He had overcome his weakness. He was determined to get the two of them to the top.

He cautioned himself to be careful not to hurry and make a foolish mistake. Even Francesca, with the help of the fixed rope to hold, was not going to find it easy. They had to go upwards at a slope of approximately twenty degrees from the horizontal. That meant that the fixed rope would be nearly vertical by the time she got to the far end. Coming at the end of the climb, this pitch would demand the last of their reserves of energy and muscular strength.

By the time Ben had reached the pocket just below the corner of the terrace every muscle in his body was quivering like a taught bowstring and the pain was starting to mist his eyes. Luckily there was a small sloping shelf here where he could take five minutes rest before he tackled the last ten feet up the wall.

He checked his watch. It was nearly 5.20. There was not much more than an hour left before dawn. Flogging his weary limbs into action, he set off again.

He'd been worried about the last bit of wall but it proved to be easier than he had expected. Luckily the masons who had built it had had decided to use ribbon pointing and it was in good condition. There were finger- and toe-holds of at least half an inch all over the wall and the slight angle made it child's play. After a couple of minutes he was cautiously peering over the parapet.

There was nothing in sight – just an area of concrete paving in fancy patterns with several flower beds laid out in a formal way. Three feet from this corner was the large creeper which he'd been able to observe from the boat He had decided that the end of the fixed rope could be safely tied to the main stem with hardly any risk of being seen.

He slid over the parapet, trailing the line behind him, and secured it firmly. That would leave him with the remaining chock to try to gain as much height to the line as possible. Then he went back over the wall again and down to the small ledge. As a reserve he decided to take the trailing end of the fixed line to provide an extra aid.

He tugged on the safety rope to signal to Francesca that she could start to cross. He had to do it twice before he saw her get up slowly from the huddle she'd been resting in. As soon as he watched her stretching he could tell that he had left her there for too long. She was cold and her limbs had gone stiff. He could see this by the tense way she was moving. But she started out, grimly hanging on to the rope and with her toes scrabbling for a foothold. The way she was moving made it look as though she had forgotten everything he had told her in their brief training session.

Ben was worried that something was going to happen to her. Keeping the safety rope as tight as he dared, he started to talk her across, not worrying any more about being overheard. It was essential that he tried to relax her and prepare her for the difficult pull at the end. She edged across the first thirty feet or so. Then, hanging by the full length of her arms, she began the increasing pull towards the shelf where Ben was waiting.

'Remember what I told you,' he urged, as quietly as he could. 'Keep your bottom out. Toes up. Remember to keep your elbows bent. Above all – try to relax.'

He kept taking in the safety rope, running it through the figure of eight which he'd fixed above his head, gently keeping. the pressure up – as much to give her confidence as actually to help with the pull. He even dared to begin to think she was going to make it. But suddenly, when she was only ten feet below him, her hand slipped.

As she looked up at him her face was white and desperate. 'Ben! Ben – I'm slipping! I just can't hang on any more.'

'Don't be silly. Of course you can. Now look, Francesca, there's no way you can fall. Just stop for a minute and try to rest. Try to find some footholds to take the load off your arms.'

She started to scrabble frantically with her feet.

'Do it carefully, for Christ's sake.'

But it was too late. The next second she had lost her grip and was starting to slide back down the rope, dragging the safety line with her. The grip failed in her stiff, tense arms and, with a frightened cry, she fell back into space.

- 14 -

Ben could only crouch and watch helplessly as Francesca swung away from the fixed rope in a long, arcing pendulum. Luckily, he'd got the safety rope locked round the figure of eight and was able to hold her quite easily as her weight brought the rope taut at the bottom of its swing.

'Don't worry,' he soothed as she swung slowly to a halt. 'You're quite safe. Just relax a second.'

'The harness is hurting me.' There was a note of panic in her voice. It has slid up around my chest. I can't breathe properly.'

'It's all right. I'll get you another rope. We'll soon solve that problem.'

Ben checked the distance carefully. She was about fifteen feet below him. From this narrow, sloping shelf he couldn't get sufficient purchase to lift her up. He would have to get up on to the terrace.

'Please hurry. I'm frightened my ribs might break.'

'It's just coming.'

He put a clove hitch on the safety rope and rested his foot on it to secure it. This left his hands free to get a rope to her. He grabbed at the trailing end of the fixed rope hanging down from the parapet. It was plenty long enough. He pulled it up and measured approximately the right length. Then he fashioned a large noose with a running bowline and dropped it down to her, holding it as close to the cliff as he could.

'Here you are, Francesca. Can you get your foot into the loop?' He forced himself to speak quietly and calmly.

She tried, gasping with panic and shortness of breath. The first time she kicked too violently and almost missed, knocking the rope away from her.

'Use your hand to hold it steady. Don't worry. You won't strangle.'

She had another go and this time she caught her foot in the knot With a bit of a wriggle she got her instep into the loop. Ben decided he'd made it a bit short, but that didn't matter too much. He allowed the rope to go taut under her weight.

'That's OK. Can you get your second foot in beside the first?'

She did as she was told.

'Now then, link an arm round this hanging rope and then get your thumbs under the harness round your chest. That's good. Can you pull the rope down?'

'Yes, I – I think so.'

The next moment her relieved face was looking up at him. 'Oh,' she exhaled, 'that's better.'

'Fine. Just stay there and rest for a few minutes. In order to pull you up I'll have to climb on to the terrace. Can you wait a few minutes?'

She nodded, her face white in the darkness. 'You won't be too long, will you? I don't think I'll be able to hang on much longer.'

She was tired and frightened and getting near to breaking point. Time was important. Ben wouldn't have time to do this the proper way with anchors on the cliff-face. He knew that Francesca wouldn't be able to help herself much when the hard work started. But he had to try a straight pull.

As quickly as he could he went back up the wall and over the parapet. He checked it out. Luckily, the masons had built strongly.

'Are you ready?' he called down. 'I'm going to start pulling you up. Mind you, it might take some time, because I'm not as strong as I was earlier this evening. Try to keep the safety rope taut if you can. Take the loop about your wrists as I showed you.'

He gripped the rope behind the parapet and tried to pull. But the friction was too great. He leaned over again and called down to her. 'Have you got the safety rope taut?'

'I – I don't know.'

She took a couple of turns about the wrists. The fall appeared to have knocked the stuffing out of her. She seemed to have lost the ability to help herself.

'Right, when I tell you to pull, try to take as much of your weight on the safety rope as possible to help me with the lifting.' Ben took a grip on the rope below the parapet.

'Are you ready?' He braced himself. 'Pull!'

He wasn't sure whether she had heard at first. But the tension in the lead rope seemed to relax slightly and Ben gave it a sudden desperate heave. He was able to pull her up about three feet before his strength gave out. Holding the line taut he edged backwards to the creeper and secured the slack end above the fixed rope.

On each subsequent pull he became a little weaker and it took nearly ten heaves to get her head up to the level of the shelf. Ben could feel his strength beginning to give out.

'Hang on there,' he told her. 'I'm coming down for you now.'

She didn't seem to be able to reply any more. Ben secured the rope again and went back over the parapet and down to the shelf. He clipped himself on to the safety rope. Then he reached down with both hands, grabbed her unceremoniously by the jacket and dragged her on to the ledge. She collapsed in a shivering heap. He could tell that she was nearly at the end of her reserves now. But he still couldn't leave her in this position.

'Come on,' he ordered her roughly. 'We've got to get up this last bit. Stand up and catch hold of the rope.'

He half lifted her into a standing position and tied the fixed rope around her back and under her armpits in a loose bowline. Then he got his shoulder behind her little rounded buttocks and heaved her up until her hands were over the edge of the parapet. He belayed the loose end of the rope to support her feet.

'Stay there and I'll go up and pull you over.'

He used the final burst of his own strength to free climb up the masonry for the third time. Sitting astride the parapet, he grabbed her by the belt of her jeans and the back of her anorak and dumped her unceremoniously on to the terrace. She collapsed on the paving, clinging gratefully to the solid stones while he released her from the ropes. Then he pulled her to her feet and helped her to the shelter of the creeper.

He put his arms around her and began to massage her back, shoulders and buttocks, trying to rub warmth and life back into her tense and knotted muscles. After a while she began to sob silently into his shoulder. He spoke to her like a child, trying to find the soft caressing words to make her feel safe again.

'There now. You're all right. Don't worry. You won't have to do it again. You did fine. I'm proud of you.' He murmured other things which she wouldn't understand. He told himself they were just endearments to relax her.

At last she began to unwind. Her breathing slowed and her crying ceased. She looked up at him with a tear-stained face. 'I'm sorry, Ben,' she sobbed. 'I'm so, so sorry.'

'There's nothing to be sorry about. You've just done a climb that most inexperienced people wouldn't even be able to contemplate. You've really done ever so well.'

'No, I'm sorry about what I said to you – what I said this morning. I just didn't realize what you must have gone through after that climb when . . . when Carlo died.'

'Oh that.' Ben grinned. 'You shouldn't worry about that. It was just what I needed. I probably wouldn't have had the guts to do the climb without you needling me.' He patted her shoulder. 'You've succeeded in getting me climbing again after nearly two years.'

She looked deep into his eyes. 'But I had no right to talk to you like that. Donna was right. I was so stupid. I didn't know what I was talking about.'

'Shush,' he said gently. 'Forget it. Don't talk about it any more.'

'I know now that you ought to put me across your knee and spank me. You must hate me for the way I've behaved to you.'

'Hate you?' Ben looked down at her in surprise. 'How could I ever hate you?'

Francesca's lovely, tear-besmirched face was very near to him. 'Do you promise?'

Her voice had a little lilt at the end and it was that which made him kiss her – that and the half-open lips, the very soft lips. He knew that he shouldn't really do that to a girl of good Italian family. But to his surprise he found that she didn't object. In fact the hands which clasped around his neck seemed to have recovered a surprising amount of strength. Her face was deliciously wet and salty. The skin of her cheeks and nose were cold. But her lips were burning hot and trembling slightly. And they were – oh, so soft!

Ben undid his anorak and pulled her slim and shivering body inside it. She slid her hands round his back and clung to him as he wrapped her in its warmth. She buried her face into his sweater and muttered little endearments in Italian. He stroked her dark soft hair with his lips and smelled its damp, fresh scent which seemed like wild roses.

He had a strange feeling in his chest It was different from the way he had felt about girls before. He felt as though he wanted to protect and care for this one. She had so many problems now – problems not of her making. She seemed small and vulnerable. Her self-possession and occasional bursts of temper were a mask for the soft and gentle girl underneath. He had allowed her to accompany him into hardship and danger; now he must do his best to see that she got out of it safely.

Under this stimulus his mind started to function properly again. It was time for them to get moving. Dawn was fast approaching. He looked at his watch, expecting it to be well after six o'clock. But, incredibly, it was still only a quarter to. Less than ten minutes had passed since Francesca had slipped off the rope.

'Come on,' he said gently. 'This is the last lap for you. You must show me where to find this Mancino Vitelli and then you must lie low somewhere.'

She looked up at him and Ben saw that the stubborn glint had come back into her eye. 'I am not leaving you now. It is best if we stay together. They will find the two of us – how do you say? – a tougher nut to crack.'

'OK.' Ben grinned. 'We'll sort that out later.' Reluctantly, he let her go. 'Which way is it now?'

She took his hand and they set off along the foot of the wall below the upper terrace. 'There are steps in the centre,' she whispered. 'We need to be careful at the top.'

At the foot of the steps he stopped and peered up. It was just a short flight of about twenty steps with a landing halfway up. It presented no problems at this stage. He went up quickly in his soft shoes and paused below the top. Only his head projected above the terrace to survey the lie of the land.

Here there were mainly gravel paths so they would have to go carefully. But there were quite a few shrubs around for cover, swaying in the blustery wind. He couldn't see any lights on in the house. He searched all the windows as best he could and they all appeared to be tightly shuttered.

Ben turned back to Francesca. 'There's nothing open at the back of the house. I think we'll have to go round to the front. We'll take this diagonal path to the left. The bushes will give us extra cover.'

He laid his hand on her shoulder as she made to move. 'We'll have to walk slowly and carefully to avoid making a noise on the gravel. Remember to put each foot down gently and transfer your weight on to it little by little before you lift the other foot.'

She nodded, her eyes wide with excitement It was incredible. She was already enjoying herself again and seemed to have forgotten the traumatic experience of a few minutes ago. Ben found her vitality was catching. He squeezed her hand and felt the ready response. But that was not for now. He tore his mind away from Francesca and concentrated on the business in hand.

They went along the path at a crouch, moving in a strange, slow-motion walk to cut down the noise. They reached the corner of the house and Ben looked round. Then he realized they would have no luck there. Floodlights illuminated the front and part of the side, lighting up the whole of the driveway clearer than day. There was no cover.

From his viewpoint Ben could look straight into the lodge beside the gates. It had the appearance of a military guardhouse with large windows giving unobstructed views over the front and side of the villa. Furthermore, the door of the gatehouse was standing open and the lights were on inside the building even at this time of the night. Clearly someone remained on guard here all the time while the Vitelli were in residence.

Ben hastily stepped back out of the brightness and turned to Francesca. He hadn't realized that they would keep such a permanent watch. From the expressive shrug of her shoulders it seemed that she was as surprised as he.

'Well, there's no chance of us going that way,' he said. 'We would certainly be seen before we got into the house.'

'What about making a run for it? There's no one watching at the moment.'

He shook his head. 'That wouldn't work: you can't run silently on this gravel'

Ben checked his watch. It was eleven minutes to six. He looked to the east and fancied he could detect the first lightening of the sky that warned of the approach of dawn. They couldn't risk hanging about much longer.

'Come on. We'd better try the other way.'

He led Francesca along the back of the house, trying the shutters as he went to see whether by chance the occupants had forgotten to fasten one. Now they were walking on stone paving so they could afford to move faster. But he had to be careful to avoid making a noise as he tried each window. Francesca went ahead of him casually, waving cheerfully when he hissed a warning not to make any noise.

There were nine windows along the back of the house. Then there was a set-back of some twenty feet or so before the start of the new wing. They had no luck at all with any of the ground-floor windows. But the east wing had balconies at first floor level. Ben carefully selected one which appeared to him to offer the best possibility. Here he fancied he could make out a shutter standing slightly ajar. Perhaps they would have a chance of getting in that way.

He inspected the wall below the balcony. The newer masonry was in good condition and offered fewer handholds. However he was ready for a small problem like that. He unwound the short rope he was carrying from round his waist and tied a soft heavy knot in the end to make it swing. Then he carefully measured the length of rope he needed. Standing back a little he tossed it over the balustrade parapet. As it swung over the rail he released more rope and the weighted end plunged back towards the ground. He stopped it at head height.

Stepping forward, he caught the two ends together, then pulled enough rope through to let the free end reach the ground. He tied the rope ends together and put his weight into the loop. He suspected that the parapet might not be strong enough to take his weight. The last thing they needed was to bring it all crashing down. However, he decided that, with his support, it would carry Francesca's weight.

'Are you willing to climb up first?'

She nodded enthusiastically.

'I'll support you until you're out of reach, so it will only be a few feet of free climbing. Here you are.'

She came over and caught hold of the ropes.

'Remember to hold your knees out, your feet tight together and keep your arms bent – just like rock climbing. Are you ready?'

'Yes.' Her whisper was full of excitement.

'When you get up there, I'll undo the rope. Then you must pull it up, move it along to the end near the wall and lower it down to me again.' He pointed. 'Then I'll come up and join you. Understand?'

She nodded.

'OK, then. Here we go.'

He trapped the end of the rope to the paving with his foot and steadied her as she started to climb. He told her to pause when she got to the limit of his reach while he made sure that her legs were properly positioned. After that it took her only a few seconds of scrambling to make the last few feet Then she was hanging on to the rail and pulling herself over the parapet with a great deal of noise. However, there seemed to be no reaction at present from within the house.

She removed the rope as he'd instructed to the more secure fixing against the wall. Ben was able to swarm up it in just a few seconds and get on to the balcony.

He immediately started checking on the shutters. The left-hand one wasn't locked but it was extremely stiff. As delicately as possible he prised it open far enough to get his body through. He slid inside to see whether he could make any impression on the window.

It was there that he came upon a strange phenomenon. Between the shutters and the window a framework of vertical steel bars was firmly fixed. It was as though the room had been turned into a prison.

Ben felt around the steel frame. His fingers encountered three hexagonal bolt-heads with new, sharp edges which were securing the frame to the masonry. No doubt the other side was the same. He would need the right tools and would make a lot of noise getting through this window. Disappointed at yet another obstacle, he slid out from behind the shutter and gently pushed it closed again. He shook his head at. Francesca and she smiled sympathetically.

He stepped to the edge of the balcony and looked along at the other shutters. As far as he could tell they were all tightly closed. Ben glanced again to the east. The heavy, rolling clouds were keeping the dawn at bay but he fancied he could detect the first shadings of grey seeping into the blackness of the night. If they stayed here much longer they would soon be clearly visible to anyone who might be patrolling in the garden below. He looked up to heaven for inspiration. Just a few feet above his head were the deep, overhanging eaves of the roof. That gave him an idea.

The only possibility now was to get in through one of the small dormers he remembered seeing. The roof itself was fairly shallow-pitched and should be quite easy to climb. The eaves would have been too deep to reach anywhere else around the building. But these projecting balconies made it possible.

Ben inspected the balcony rail carefully. The ornate ironwork had started to rust in the sea air but it still appeared to be quite sound. He tested it by putting as much of his weight as he could on it without risking over-balancing. It took the load without protest. He climbed on to it near the junction with the wall and stood up. It still seemed to be strong enough. He moved out from the wall to the front of the balcony. Now the edge of the roof was just above his head and he was relieved to see that the gutter was solid cast iron, not the cheap, modern plastic stuff, and seemed to be strong and sound. He let his weight hang on it and it didn't deflect under the load. Then he jumped down lightly on to the balls of his feet, pulled up the rope and coiled it on the balcony behind the shutter where no one would see it.

'I'll get on the balcony rail first. Then you get up beside me. I'll show you what I want you to do.'

He helped her up and supported her with an arm round her back. She was shivering and he wasn't sure whether it was excitement or cold. For himself, he could feel the chill of the wind on his hands and cheeks but the rest of his body was glowing warm.

'All right,' he whispered. 'Can you reach up and catch hold of the gutter? Now, when I say, spring up as far as you can. I'll give you a push to get you on to the tiles. Keep as low as possible and crawl towards the nearest dormer.'

Her white face looked up into his. 'Oh, God. I don't like this.'

'Don't worry. I'll be just below you and I won't let you fall. It's nothing after what you've done this evening. Are you ready?'

She nodded.

'Right, then.'

He reached down to find something to catch hold of so as to give her the greatest lift. The only obvious place was to put his hand in her crutch. It was hardly correct behaviour towards a young woman. He hesitated, but now was not the time to bother about such niceties. He explained to her.

'Sorry about this,' he muttered.

Francesca hardly flinched as put his hand between her thighs. There was the ghost of a smile on her face, but she said nothing.

'Are you ready?' They crouched down and he took a firm grip. 'Now!'

She sprang up and he hoisted her as she went. She was surprisingly light. His heave had her right up on the roof with just her legs dangling over. He pushed one foot as the rest of her disappeared from view with what seemed to be a large amount of rattling and creaking. He hoped the noises made by the wind would disguise it.

Now Ben had to get up himself. This was more of a problem. It was a jump of over six feet and he had to get the whole of his body as far as the waist over the gutter or he would lose his balance and fall back again. If he did fall he wasn't sure he would find the balcony rail as he went down. He might well land inside the balcony and make a noise. Even worse, he might miss the rail altogether and be left dangling from the gutter.

Well, there was no point in hesitating. He had to get on with it. He bent at the knees and went down to the full reach of his arms, flexing his body to prepare his muscles. Then, with a sudden furious burst of energy he threw himself upwards and outwards and over the gutter.

He landed flat on his face on the tiles with a tremendous crash. His hands were too close together. They were trapped underneath his body and he hadn't got enough of his weight over the edge of the gutter. For a second he wobbled about his point of balance and he knew he was going to fall back. He tried to prepare himself to let his weight go down slowly enough to prevent losing his grip and falling to the ground.

The next moment a small hand had grasped him firmly in the crutch and was pulling him on to the roof.

Francesca hissed in his ear, 'Sorry, but I couldn't find anywhere else to catch hold of.'

Ben was too breathless and startled to reply at first. Then he said, 'Until a few days ago I thought you were a well-brought-up young woman.'

'Until a couple of days ago, I was.' She grinned roguishly.

There wasn't time to pursue that conversation further. The new tiles were quite rough and gave a good grip, but Ben didn't want to be out on the roof any longer than was necessary. The nearest dormer was almost directly above them and about ten feet away. He crawled up to it and offered a hand to Francesca as she followed. The dormer was very small and had a fixed glass pane about two feet square. The only way to get in was to break it.

He decided there was no point in messing around. Nobody seemed to have heard the noise of them climbing on to the roof, so he might as well make a little more noise. Arching his back, he pulled off his warm anorak. The wind immediately seemed to cut into him like a knife, giving new urgency to his actions.

He rolled the jacket into a ball and placed it against the centre of the glass. Then he put his shoulder to it and pressed hard and firmly until there was a sharp report. When he took the jacket away there was a large star of cracks spreading to all the sides of the pane.

He selected one of the biggest pieces and, wrapping his jacket round his fist, he applied more pressure to this part. It took a surprising amount of effort to make the glass give. Suddenly it snapped near the frame and fell into the room, followed by several smaller pieces. There was a resounding tinkle. Surely someone must have heard that.

Well, there was nothing to be done but to continue. Using his jacket like a mitten he started to wriggle away the pieces of glass around the hole. Piece by piece he wriggled it out and rested it against his crooked leg. It took him another ten minutes to remove the rest of the glass from the frame and during that time there had been no sound. With a bit of luck no one had yet heard them.

He brushed the bottom of the frame clear of broken fragments. Then he carefully wrapped the pieces of glass in his jacket which he handed to Francesca for safe keeping. 'You can hand it to me when I'm inside.'

As he looked at her he realized he could see her face more clearly then he had before. He glanced to the east. It was definitely starting to get light now. The sky was full of angry, lowering clouds. Clearly the fine weather had deserted them.

Must hurry, he thought.

There was no longer any chance of them getting out unobserved. But they might still have a chance of finding Signor Vitelli before the rest of the house woke up. The fleeting idea of taking him hostage to get them out again crossed Ben's mind.

Forget that for now. The first thing was to get in. He peered through the window to see what was inside. However, his body blocked out what light there was and he couldn't manage to make out any features inside. He couldn't even see if there was a floor. But there was nothing for it but to go in as quietly as he could.

Catching hold of the front of the dormer, he pulled himself into a standing position. Then he slid his legs through the window and felt about carefully in the blackness with his feet. He didn't come into contact with anything anywhere.

Little by little he eased himself through the opening but still his searching feet could find nothing. How far down was the floor? Was there a floor? He daren't just jump down because he didn't know what he might land on.

It wasn't until he was resting on his shoulder blades and in considerable discomfort that his pointed toes reached the floor. It seemed to bear his weight. Cautiously he lowered himself until he was standing firmly with his head at window sill level.

For a moment he waited for his eyes to adjust to the even dimmer light in the loft. As far as he could see the place was almost bare of the clutter which normally seems to gather in roof spaces.

Ben turned back to the window and took his jacket and its burden of glass from Francesca. He placed it carefully on the floor behind him then went back to help her. Her feet were already on the sill. He helped her to sit down, then he caught her by the waist as she sprang through, landing lightly on her toes in front of him. Her face was smiling up at him. It dawned on Ben that she was actually enjoying this adventure.

'What a nice secret place.' Her lips were only inches from his.

'We've got to get a move on,' he said, reluctantly tearing his gaze from her.

She pretended to be put out. 'Oh,' she asked innocently. 'Are you in such a hurry?'

She stepped back and, with a noise like thunder, she disappeared through the ceiling into the room below, leaving a hole more than a foot and a half in diameter.

- 15 -

Ben looked aghast at the hole which had opened in the floor beneath him. The light was on in the room below and obviously their breaking in through the dormer skylight had woken the occupant. Now it was likely that the whole house had been aroused and a reception committee would be ready for them. After all that effort they had failed.

And what state was Francesca in? She might have broken something or knocked herself out. She would certainly be in no condition to escape from Vitelli's minders. She was likely to be kept under very close control from now on. And Ben's own chances were no better.

By the light coming from below he was now able to see that only the centre part of the loft floor had been boarded. The planking ended just beyond the window. But no barrier had been provided. Francesca, with her lesser height, had been able to step back without hitting her head. She had stepped off the edge and had fallen between two joists. She had obviously been so startled that she hadn't even been able to catch hold of the timber either side and had crashed through to the floor below. What had she done to herself?

Ben dropped to his knees and peered through the jagged opening. What a relief! By great good fortune Francesca had fallen flat on her back on to a double bed below the hole and had escaped serious injury. He was delighted to see her startled and breathless face gazing up at him, surrounded by chunks of plaster and rubble.

Recovering from her shock she rolled over and sat up on the edge of the bed. Suddenly she froze stock still. The colour drained from her face and her mouth opened wide. She seemed to be trying to say something but no words came out. What was she looking at? Or had she suffered some form of paralysis as a result of her fall?

'Francesca! Francesca – what's the matter?' He knelt at the edge of the ragged hole, unable to get down for the moment to help her.

Then he saw a little old man move into the circle of his vision.

'Francesca!' The old fellow's voice was hardly more than a hoarse whisper. He opened his arms wide.

'Papa?' she gasped. She leapt from the bed and rushed into his arms. She hugged him to her and smothered his face with kisses. 'Oh – *Papa mea, Papa mea,*' she cooed as she rocked his frail body back and forth.

Her father looked up to heaven and mumbled in Italian. Ben felt a lump rise in his throat when he saw the tears in the old man's eyes. He felt a keen sense of frustration as he watched their loving reunion without being able to join them, or understand what they were saying to each other.

At last he could bear it no longer. He called out, 'Francesca, what is it?'

She looked up to him with a tear-streaked but radiant smile. 'Oh, Ben. My papa is still alive. He is not dead. He never died. He is still with us.' The colour had returned to her cheeks. The sudden shock had been replaced by joy. Ben thought how extraordinarily beautiful she looked.

She turned back to her father. 'Papa, do you remember Ben? He is Toni's friend. And he is my friend – my very good friend.'

'*Si! Si*, Francesca.'

Ben thought that Signor Cimbrone seemed to have recovered from his first breakdown of emotion and now had himself under control.

'Of course your father knows me, Francesca,' he said. 'I last met him after the accident on the mountain when Carlo was killed.'

Then suddenly the awful truth burst upon Francesca and she whirled round to face her father. She spoke to him in a flood of Italian to which he replied with a shake of his head.

'What are you saying?' asked Ben.

She looked up at him. 'We buried someone a week ago who we thought was my papa. How did that happen?'

'I don't know. I think it's another question for Mancino Vitelli to answer.' Ben stopped further discussion. 'I'm sorry, Francesca, but there is no time for this. If you do not get out of that room your papa will be in greater danger. And so will you, for that matter. You are both in mortal danger. The Vitelli will be here any minute and they will not want anyone to know that they have been falsely imprisoning your father.'

She looked up at Ben with a horrified expression as she absorbed the meaning of his words. Then she went and tried the door. It was obviously locked. She looked round the room quickly and then back up at him.

'How can I get out? I cannot reach the ceiling. Papa is not strong enough to help me.'

Ben, too, had realized there was no practical way that she could get back into the loft. It was up to him to get her out. 'I'll try and get to the outside of the door. Let's hope the key is in the lock so that I can let you out. Hide under the bed until I get there in case anybody comes. Perhaps they won't try to look for you.'

As he stood up, Ben knew that was a fairly slim chance with the great hole in the ceiling above her father's bed. It was up to him to try to save them. He turned away from the hole and went to collect his jacket. He carefully unwrapped the glass and put it to one side. Then he shook the jacket thoroughly to get rid of any fragments before he put it on. Walking as quietly as he could, he set about finding a way out of the roof space.

Just about halfway along the floor he came to a trapdoor. Of course it had no handle but there was a length of rope fixed to the back which appeared to have been used as a stay to keep it open when people were in the loft. He caught hold of it and lifted gently.

The trapdoor was heavy and the hinges were stiff and it required a lot of effort. Ben raised it only few inches before cautiously looking out to see what was below. It was just as well that he did, for the first thing he saw was the back view of a person's head walking along the lighted corridor. The man stopped in front of a door about twenty feet away and inserted a key into the lock. Ben realized, with a sinking feeling, that he was entering the room where Papa Cimbrone was imprisoned. Francesca was in great danger of being discovered.

The man opened the door and went in. Looking upside down from his elevated position, Ben had only the sight of a pair of feet – bare except for sandals – a long, dark dressing-gown and a head covered in slick black hair. But he felt there was something about the man that he recognized.

He didn't need to be very clever to work out what would happen next. The man would see the hole in the ceiling and the mess all over the bed and the floor. It wouldn't take him long to find Francesca. Within a few minutes the whole house would be alerted and there would be other men climbing into the loft to investigate. Ben had to do something – and fast.

In a few seconds he had the hatch open and his legs were dangling through. His mind was obsessed with two things. Firstly, he must keep quiet; secondly, he must leave the hatch closed so that they shouldn't think he had come down into the house before they searched the loft. As he wriggled through the aperture he let the half-closed trapdoor rest against his body. He eased his way through the narrowing gap until he was hanging by his arms above the corridor carpet with the door trapping his fingers against the framing of the hatch. It was the last bit which was the most difficult. In the end there was no way he could avoid a nasty graze to his knuckles as he let go and jumped down, landing softly on his toes.

Sucking his damaged fingers he looked round for somewhere to hide but there was nowhere obvious. The corridor was straight with only a couple of large niches containing stands with vases of dried flowers. They weren't large enough to conceal him. At the end there was a window looking east across the sea towards a grey and troubled dawn.

Loud noises were coming from the open door to Signor Cimbrone's prison room. Ben's heart jumped as he heard Francesca answering angrily. She obviously hadn't been able to hide. But there was nothing he could do for her at present. The best thing would be to get out of sight until he had a better chance of effecting a rescue.

At that moment Francesca let out a squeal of pain. It was that cry which made him change his mind. Ben felt the anger build up inside him as he thought of someone hurting her. There was also a feeling of humiliation stirring in him. It seemed that ever since he had landed in Italy he had been running or hiding from the Vitelli and their henchmen. It was time that he turned and fought back and now was the time to start hitting them while he still had the element of surprise on his side.

With a sudden furious resolve that startled him, Ben made for the open door. He paused for a second, just out of sight outside, to try to work out where the fellow was. He wanted to catch him off balance. There was a heated argument going on in Italian. Occasionally, he could hear Papa's tired old voice interjecting. But nobody took any notice of him. The main argument was between Francesca and the man whom he suddenly recognized from the sneering nasal twang. She was arguing with her nearly betrothed: Dino Vitelli.

There was a sound of a scuffle and somebody grunted. Ben balled his smarting fists and prepared to wade in. Then he heard the noise approaching the door. He waited for a little longer. The next second Francesca was pushed through the doorway. Ben swung his arm back ready.

Francesca saw him and her jaw dropped open. Ben winked at her but he was concentrating on the two hands which gripped her left arm. Aiming a few inches below that level he swung the hardest punch he had ever delivered in his life.

Coming through the door behind Francesca, Dino walked straight into it. Ben felt his fist sink up to the wrist in the man's soft stomach. Dino's hands let go his captive's arms and grasped his paunch as he doubled up in pain. The next second he received a violent upper cut full in the middle of his face followed by another one to the jaw as he straightened up. He collapsed on the floor as though he'd been poleaxed.

Ben stood gasping with the pain to his damaged knuckles and the shock of the anger and hatred which had surged through his body. He'd never felt like that before in his life. He felt Francesca's hand flutter lightly on his arm as though not sure whether she should touch him. When he raised his eyes he found himself looking straight into the startled face of Signor Cimbrone. It brought him back to his senses.

'We must get you away from here before the whole house is awake,' he said. 'Can you soon be ready to escape?'

He bent down to check Dino. The man seemed to be out cold. Ben hadn't realized the destructive power of his own fists.

He looked up at the girl. 'Can you help your father, Francesca?'

There was a gleam of amusement in her eyes as she turned back to the old man. Ben felt embarrassed. She probably thought he had over-reacted. She would be thinking what a fool he was to have lost his temper. In the long run it wasn't going to help him to get his business back.

He dragged the limp body into the room away from the door. He wondered briefly whether he should bind and gag him, but there didn't seem to be much point. No doubt Dino would make plenty of noise when he recovered, even if he couldn't shout. It wouldn't take him long to wake the house.

Ben turned back to the others. Signor Cimbrone was already fully dressed except for a coat. That was apparently downstairs. He fancied that he detected a slightly crafty gleam in Papa's eye.

'OK,' said Ben. 'Let's get moving as quickly as we can before someone else turns up.'

He ushered the others out of the room, at the last minute remembering to lock the door on Dino and pocket the key. The fellow was groaning and writhing a little already. It wouldn't be long before he recovered full consciousness. Ben wanted them to be out of the house before then. His mind was grappling with the problem of getting from the front door to the gate past the guards.

Following the old man, who seemed to know where he was going, they set off along the corridor towards the main house. At the end they turned right and almost immediately came to the staircase. Papa peeped over the balustrade and set off nimbly downstairs. At the foot he glanced around almost sheepishly, then led them to a door into a cupboard under the stairs.

He opened the door and disappeared into the coat cupboard. Ben stood back and waited for him to find his coat and come out again. But the old man turned and beckoned them to follow him into the cupboard and closed the door behind them. Then he switched on the light. With a cheerful comment he burrowed into the coats at the back of the cupboard and pulled them aside to reveal another door which he opened.

He clicked another switch inside the door. A further light sprang on, revealing a flight of stone steps leading down under the staircase. Papa set off down the steps, muttering something as he went.

'Papa says to switch off the cupboard light,' said Francesca.

Ben did so and followed the other two down the winding steps into the bowels of the earth, pulling the door closed behind him as he went. At the foot of the steps they came into a narrow stone-lined corridor. Papa turned unhesitatingly to the right along the tunnel. Within ten feet this opened out and became a wide, modern corridor of white painted concrete blocks. Ben guessed that they had entered the basement beneath the new wing.

Papa opened the first door on the right and walked in, switching on the light as he did so. Ben discovered they were in a long, low room which was set up like a laboratory. At the far end were dozens of boxes the labels of which proclaimed they contained Italian wines. He recognized some of them as brands which the Cimbrone family shipped regularly to him in London. The first stirrings of suspicion began to work away at the back of his mind. Perhaps he was getting nearer to discovering why the Vitelli were so interested in taking over his business.

Some of the crates were open on the central laboratory bench. A stack of full bottles stood on the bench with their foil seals removed. A little further along was a modern corking and sealing machine. To the left of that stood a case of bottles which had been newly resealed.

'They're doctoring the wine,' Ben burst out. 'No wonder Italian wines get a bad name if that sort of thing still goes on. Toni would never have allowed that sort of wine to get through to us in London. He must have found out about it.' Was that the reason why the Vitelli had killed him?

Papa took no notice of him. He walked across to the bench, picked up one of the newly sealed bottles and tucked it in his coat pocket. Despite his interest in the scene, Ben was beginning to fret about the amount of time they were wasting on the trivial pursuit of messing about with a bottle of rough wine. Any competent taster would immediately pick it out anyway. He was anxious to get away before they were discovered.

Signor Cimbrone beckoned and they followed him back to the door. He switched off the light and led them back into the corridor. He took two paces and froze. Ben was following close behind him and he bumped into the old man's back. Then he saw what had made him pause.

There, not five yards away, was the hood he had seen in the guardhouse. He was balancing the knife that Ben remembered so well on his thumb and forefinger. Behind him stood the other two gangsters. He felt the hair on his neck slowly stand on end as he gazed in fascination at the hovering knife.

- 15 -

For a second Ben toyed with the idea of slamming the door and trying to barricade himself into the cellar, but on reflection he decided that would not be appropriate at the moment. He couldn't abandon Francesca and her father to these criminals. So he stepped into the corridor and pulled the door closed behind him. The man with the knife said something to them.

'What was that?' asked Ben.

'He said to turn round and put your hands on the wall.'

'Not on your life. I don't want a knife in my ribs.'

'Please do as he says,' she pleaded, 'or it will be bad for all of us. He will not knife you now unless Mancino Vitelli tells him to.'

Reluctantly Ben turned round. The two gangsters came forward and frisked them. Ben presumed that they were looking for weapons. He couldn't help admiring the complete disdain with which Francesca ignored the grubby, lingering paws. She was once again completely self-controlled – the proud, superior lady.

The search wasn't very well conducted. The man searching Ben removed Donna's mobile phone from his jacket pocket, but missed the little pistol tucked into the back of his belt. They didn't even bother to search Papa. They just took away the bottle of wine projecting from his coat pocket

The hood barked out another order.

'We have to go upstairs,' said Francesca, with a slight note of relief in her voice.

One of the gangsters preceded them up the steps and through the coat cupboard. On the ground floor they were instructed to turn right after a few yards in to the corridor leading into the new wing. They stopped outside the third door on the right The thug came forward to unlock the door and gestured for them to go inside.

They found themselves in a large, palatial office with full height hardwood panelling around the walls. There were three windows along one side which looked over a grey, early morning garden. Bookshelves were let into the walls at either end of the room. To their left was a conference table circled by ten chairs. Filling the right-hand end of the room was a large ornate desk with an inlaid leather top and an expensive executive chair behind it.

'What's going to happen now?' asked Ben.

'I don't know,' she said. 'I think they have gone to fetch the *capofamiglia* – Signor Vitelli.'

They were left to stand in the middle of the floor, guarded by the man with the knife and one of the gangsters. Weary from his exertions, Ben pulled out a chair from the table. It provoked a violent outburst of Italian from the hood.

Francesca translated. 'He says you are to remain standing up.'

'Surely he's not going to make an old man continue to stand up.'

'Yes, you are right.' With a brief comment in Italian, she picked up the chair and took it to her father.

The man stepped forward with a torrent of abuse. He slapped her sharply across the face and took the chair back to its original position. Francesca gasped, but kept herself under control.

'What a charmer.' Ben started forward. He felt an almost overwhelming desire to catch hold of the little bastard by the throat and shake him till his teeth rattled. But the Italian was ready with his knife in case he was attacked.

'Please don't, Ben. It was really nothing.' She seemed worried in case he started a fight with their captors.

So he clenched his fists and forced his anger to subside. In the long silence that followed he thought furiously about ways of taking his revenge.

After about ten minutes a hidden door suddenly opened in the panelling behind the magnificent desk. A small man of about of about fifty entered. He was a strange apparition. He had short, brown, furry hair of an unusual hue for this part of the world. If it was a wig, or if it had been dyed, then so too had his eyebrows and his small brown moustache. His eyes were also of a neutral brown colour. Even his skin had a dirty tint, as though he'd been soaking in a bath of rust-coloured water. However, he was smartly dressed in a pale-cream suit with a matching shirt and a brown tie. His neatness gave the impression that he had spent some time getting ready. Ben checked his watch and was amazed to find that it was still only ten past six.

Francesca spoke quickly in Italian to the man whom Ben guessed to be Mancino Vitelli. Her voice had a submissive note. Ben assumed she was asking whether her father could be permitted to sit down. Vitelli asked several questions of the man he called Guido. The man replied expansively with several extravagant gestures. Vitelli made a flapping movement of his hand and the next minute the two gangsters moved in.

'What's happening?' asked Ben.

'We're being taken back to Papa's prison room.'

Ben started to move but the next second he found himself looking at the blade of Guido's knife. Vitelli reached inside the right-hand drawer of his desk and his hand came out holding a large, black automatic.

'Please sit down, Signor Cartwright,' he lisped, in passable English. Francesca had said that he could not speak English. However it seemed the *capofamiglia* was a man of hidden talents.

Ben subsided into a seat as Francesca and Papa were led from the room. He wondered whether they would be able to get back into the room since Dino's key still nestled in his pocket. When they did get in, Ben's problems would start to multiply.

Vitelli looked across at him. 'Signor Cartwright, how did you get here?'

There was no doubt that a quick search would uncover his route, but Ben didn't see why he should help them at this moment.

'I climbed in.'

'I don't believe you.' Vitelli's eyebrows rose. 'Nobody has ever climbed into the Villa Rafallo.'

'I'm a good climber.'

The Italian's face darkened. His eyes turned into little intense black dots. His mouth was sneer. 'You are the man who left my son Carlo to die on the Brow of the Devil.'

Ben was startled. Had the man been nursing a grievance against him for the last two years? He tried to explain. 'I did all I could to try to

160

reach him but I couldn't move his rope. Then I raised the alarm. When the rescuers arrived they said he had been dead since he fell and hit the rock-face.'

'Mr Cartwright, I read the report. Carlo was left hanging from a rope for sixteen hours before the rescuers got to him. Nobody can survive like that for sixteen hours.' Suddenly the little man was seething with rage. 'You were there all the time. You tell me you are a good climber. Why did you not rescue him in sixteen hours?'

'I tried.'

His moustache bristled pugnaciously. 'You managed to save your friend Antonio. Did you truly try to do the same for Carlo?'

'Toni was close to the chimney where I was anchored. He was alive. I did my best to try to reach Carlo, but my strength was giving out'

'The report also said that you lost your nerve and had to be lifted off the mountain. In Italy we just say that men are afraid.' He pointed a finger at Ben. 'It was your fear that killed my son.'

It hadn't occurred to him before that this man might hold him responsible for Carlo's death. Toni had assured him that everyone agreed that it was the fellow's own foolishness which had caused the accident.

'Signor Cartwright.' The *capofamiglia*'s head was jutting forward and his eyes were fastened on Ben as he pushed home his message. 'To me you are the man who killed my son because you did not try to save him when he was still alive.'

'That is not true,' Ben burst out 'You read the report. It said that he probably died much earlier. He might have been killed by the shock of the fall. He fell a hundred feet – more than thirty metres – before the rope stopped him. That would have been enough to kill him.'

'But he still had his safety helmet on. Why did you not try to reach him?'

'I did try. I tried for at least half an hour. But he was dangling sixty feet down the rope. It was nearly dark. It had taken two hours to get Toni up into the chimney.' But now Ben felt a terrible shame again, for it seemed that somehow he ought to have tried harder.

'So you saved a Cimbrone but did not try to save a Vitelli. That is not liked by my family. In Italy we believe that you owe us a debt of honour.'

'What do you mean? How does one pay a debt of honour?'

'Only by giving your life for his.'

Ben was stunned into silence. He couldn't explain to this man who was thirsting for vengeance what it was like on the mountain. Vitelli would never understand what it felt like to be at the end of his resistance – to be exhausted and cold and – he might as well admit it – frightened of death. But Ben couldn't blame him. Nobody else understood either. The accident had been foolish and unnecessary. It was his misfortune to have survived it without injury. The Vitelli seemed to be unable to forgive him for that.

The *capofamiglia* switched the line of his attack. 'You have come into the Villa Rafallo without an invitation. Why did you come?'

Ben dragged his mind away from that dreadful day on the mountain and back to the present. 'I came because I am told that you are the man who is trying to take my business away from me.' Now he found that he could look him in the face again. 'I want to know why.'

Signor Vitelli paused for a moment, as if weighing his answer in his mind. 'I would say that the business is not yours.'

'Part of it is mine – a large part. My father started the shop and I took it over. Then together Toni and I built it up to the position that it is now in.'

The man looked thoughtful. After a while he said, 'Well, it may be that we can be of some use to each other. You also have something that is *mine*.'

'What is that?'

'You mean you do not know?'

At that moment the door suddenly burst open and Alfredo stormed in. He was walking irregularly as though he was the worse for drink. He went up to Vitelli's desk and launched into a torrent of excited Italian. Ben was able to pick out the words 'Papa' and 'Francesca' and he guessed that at last the man had begun to realize a little of what the Vitelli were doing to his family.

Mancino Vitelli appeared to be largely uninterested in Alfredo's excited denunciation. The gun in his hand was pointing vaguely in the direction of the younger man's stomach but it was completely unheeded by his son-in-law.

The long tirade was only silenced by the creak of the door opening again. Ben turned to see Dino entering the room, followed by the two bodyguards. Guido crossed the room in two strides, caught Alfredo by the arm and thrust him into a chair beside Ben. But all eyes were on Dino.

Ben realized as he looked at him that he had hurt the fellow more than he intended. Dino was doubled up with the pain to his stomach. He was supported on both sides by the toughs. He looked as white as a sheet except for the area of flesh around his mouth which was badly bruised and swollen. When he spoke it was with a peevish but muffled squeak.

He complained long and bitterly to his father about the attack. Ben could see the sense of outrage growing on Vitelli's face as he listened. He also noticed the way that Guido was fingering the blade of his knife. Ben had a feeling that the next few minutes were going to be acutely uncomfortable for him. Surreptitiously, he began to edge forward in his seat. He made as if to scratch his back as he felt for the little gun which Donna had loaned to him.

Vitelli turned to face him. 'Did you do this?' He indicated his son with a sweep of his hand.

Ben nodded.

'I want to watch him pay for it,' complained Dino in painful English.

The *capofamiglia* pointed at Ben. 'You are bad news for the Vitelli,' he hissed. 'I do not want you around any longer than is necessary. In a minute I will give you to Guido to play with. But first I want something from you. If you give it to me quickly then I shall tell Guido to be quick with you. If not, I will let him take as long as he wants. I warn you that he can take a very long time to strip the skin off a man with that little knife of his.'

Ben gulped down a spurt of fear. 'What are you talking about?' he asked. 'You haven't told me yet what it is that I'm supposed to have of yours.'

'Ah, but I think you know.'

'I have got no idea what you want. What makes you think that I've got something?'

Vitelli half-closed his eyes as he looked down his nose at him. The image reminded Ben of some of the paintings he had seen of Napoleon, but in paler colours. 'I know you have it. You showed it to old Emilio. That is how you got into the Villa Cimbrone.'

He reached down and opened his desk drawer. He put down the gun and lifted out a small object. 'It is one of these. This is the mark of the Vitelli. This means death to anybody who holds it without the right.' He held up a twin to the one which nestled in Ben's pocket.

Ben had just succeeded in removing his gun from the holster in his belt and releasing the safety catch. He let it lie on the chair seat and sat back on it It was hard and painful but very comforting. It gave him renewed courage.

'I found a thing like that on the body of Toni Cimbrone,' he said accusingly. 'His throat had been cut. I think it was you who ordered that.'

'He had found out too much.' Vitelli did not attempt to deny it. He must be feeling completely secure. 'He had also stolen a very important thing of mine. I think that now you have it.'

'Not any more,' lied Ben. I must have left it around somewhere. I thought it was just a piece of pretty metal.'

Vitelli spoke very slowly. 'I regret that I do not believe you. I think that you know more than you admit about this token. Why else would you show it to Emilio to get you safe passage?'

'It just came out when I put my hand in my pocket.'

'Why don't you put your hand in your pocket now and let me have it?' said Vitelli. 'It may save you from the same treatment as your partner.'

Ben did as he was told. He reached around and brought his hand out empty. 'It's not there I must have left it at the hotel or dropped it somewhere.'

'Perhaps Guido can help you find it' Vitelli nodded at the hood, who advanced towards him.

The thought of the sharp little knife galvanized Ben into activity. He jumped to his feet 'All right. I don't want the damn thing.'

He pulled it out of his pocket and tossed it at Vitelli. Reacting to the tension of the moment he tossed it harder and higher than he had intended. The *capofamiglia* put up his hand to shield himself but he was not quick enough. The badge struck him sharply on the cheekbone and rebounded against the panelling before falling at Dino's feet.

With a weird fascination Ben watched a droplet of blood trickle down Vitelli's face. The man's hand went to the cut. He took it away and stared down at his blood-smirched hand. Like an automaton he sat back heavily in his chair, still staring at it.

'The Wolf of Hades,' he gasped hoarsely and his brown face turned as white as a sheet. His eyes rose to look at Ben and the fury came pouring back into them. He pointed an accusing finger.

'Kill him,' he shouted.

Out of the corner of his eye Ben saw Guido moving to attack him. The knife arm was swinging wide for the thrust. Ben half-turned to meet the onslaught. His hands were ready to grab the arm when he was attacked. But at that second a shot rang out and everything froze.

The only movement was from Mancino Vitelli who toppled slowly back in his chair. There was a neat black hole in the middle of his forehead and his face bore the startled look of a man staring at his own death.

Ben spun round. Alfredo had half-risen from his chair. He had Donna's pistol in his hand and a small spiral of smoke rose from the barrel. Then, as Ben watched, Guido suddenly changed the line of his attack and buried his knife up to the hilt in Alfredo's stomach.

That change of direction was all Ben needed. His weight was already moving forward to meet the expected blow from Guido. Now he grabbed the man's knife-arm and carried him backwards into the face of the other two gangsters. The three of them crashed backwards over several chairs and disappeared under the table. There was the sound of several things breaking. Ben fervently hoped that it included a few of the gangsters' arms and legs.

He knew that he had to move quickly now if they were to get away, or he would be overwhelmed. Dino was turning to face him as he let go of Guido's arm. He saw Ben charging at him and dived frantically for the sanctuary provided by the desk. He caught the side of his head on the top as he fell. With a clear path, Ben scooped up the Vitelli emblem from the floor and made for the door.

He grasped the ornate handle, swung the door open and crashed in to Sylvia. He grabbed her before she fell. She let out a little cry but did nothing to obstruct his passage. Ben looked back to where Alfredo was lying doubled up on the floor.

'Look after your husband,' he said. 'He needs you.'

She rushed forward and bent over his body. Ben couldn't tell how badly hurt the man was, but he knew there was nothing he could personally do to help him. To stop now would endanger Francesca and Papa.

The first thug was emerging from under the table. Ben waited no longer. He slammed the door shut behind him and made off down the corridor.

- 17 -

Ben sprinted down the corridor and up the stairs three at a time. As he made for the prison he pulled the key out of his pocket, sincerely hoping that Papa and Francesca were still there.

Luckily they were. The door swung open to reveal their startled faces gazing at him.

'Hurry,' he gasped. 'We've got to get out.'

He helped Papa to his feet and led the way back into the corridor. As they started back towards the stairs one of the gangsters came loping round the corner. He stopped and let out a yell. Ben made as if to fire a gun at the bloke, although Donna's weapon was still downstairs beside Alfredo. He was rewarded by seeing the villain dive for cover. Without further hesitation Ben grabbed the handle of the door opposite. He blessed their luck as it opened.

'In here.' He pushed them through into the darkened room and followed, slamming the door behind them. Francesca switched on the light to reveal an unoccupied bedroom with a massive bed beside the door.

'Quick. Get the bed across.' The ancient piece of furniture seemed to weigh a ton. Ben felt his muscles crack as he tried to drag it the few feet to the door. Francesca threw her weight in beside him and it moved a little at first and then with a rush as the feet came free. He heaved it as tight against the door as he could. That should take some moving from outside.

Beside him there came a rattle at the door handle and it opened a fraction. There was a heavy thump as the man applied his shoulder. With a protesting squeak the bed moved perhaps half an inch. Francesca and Papa hurried to push against it as though to keep the man out.

Now they could hear voices outside the door. It was only a matter of a minute or two before they broke in. Ben crossed to the window and tried to open it but it appeared to be locked. He applied both thumbs to the catch and suddenly it gave and he heaved the creaking casement open. A cold gust of damp air swept into the room.

He pushed back the protesting shutters and looked down into the forecourt. As yet there was no one below. Away to the left the gatehouse appeared to be empty, the door standing open. Presumably, whoever might have been on guard had rushed into the house to deal with the emergency. How long had they got before the men came out again? Ben guessed they had no more than a minute or two to get out of the place before they were pursued.

The high wall round the villa garden was about thirty feet away. Beyond that, in the miserable grey dawn, the countryside didn't look in the least like southern Italy. Heavy clouds were streaming in from the grey, wild sea and buffeting into the mountains. The blustery wind tugged at the thorn bushes clinging to the limestone hillsides. The gravel in the forecourt looked damp and greasy.

'Francesca,' called Ben. 'If you go first and hang on to my hands you'll only have a drop of about six feet – er, two metres – to the gravel. Remember to bend your knees as you land.'

There was another crash against the door.

'Come on. Hurry up.'

She looked startled, but leapt into action as soon as she realized what he intended. He helped her over the window sill and held her as she jumped to the ground. She toppled on to her back as she landed but immediately got up, obviously without injury.

As soon as she was ready he picked up the little old man. He hardly weighed any more than Francesca. Holding him by his wrists, Ben lowered him as far as he could towards her waiting arms.

'All right? Try to catch him under his armpits as I let him go. Here he comes.'

More thumps came from the door behind him and the timber creaked as one of the joints gave. He let go Papa's wrists and Francesca caught him magnificently. Although they both fell over on to the gravel, they began to get to their feet and it appeared that neither was hurt.

There was another crash behind him and the bed moved another half-inch. A few more like that and someone would be able to squeeze in. Without further hesitation Ben hurdled the window sill. He hung on to the frame for a second to slow his descent and then toppled forward as he hit the ground with bent knees.

'Try the gates,' he suggested to Francesca, as he got to his feet. They only had a couple of minutes before their pursuers realized they had got out of the room. 'I'll cover the front door to slow them down.'

He made for the porch. His route took him past a big Mercedes parked on the forecourt. He eyed it speculatively. That was the sort of thing they needed for an escape. On a whim he tried the door. It was open. They hadn't bothered to lock it because it was inside the compound.

Ben hesitated for a moment as his mind took in the possibilities. He climbed in to the driver's seat and checked the controls. If only. . . .

Then he saw the keys were still in the ignition. What a stroke of luck!

'The gates are locked.' Francesca turned towards the gatehouse with Papa trailing behind her.

'Don't bother with that.' He checked the control to the automatic gearbox.

He saw her pause uncertainly by the gatepost.

'Keep clear.' He slammed the door and turned the key in the ignition.

It was a beautiful car. The engine started first time. The electronic choke set it running at a fast tick-over. Ben set the gear lever to reverse, released the handbrake and pressed his foot down experimentally on the accelerator. With a deep grumble of the engine the car swooped backwards towards the porch as he swung the wheel to line up on the gates. In the rearview mirror he saw Guido come through the front door and he deliberately crashed the tail end of the car into one of the porch pillars, sending the man into a frantic dive to avoid being crushed by the heavy vehicle or any falling masonry.

Before the crunch of the impact had died away, Ben moved the lever to 'Drive' and stamped the throttle pedal to the floor. The engine roared and the big car lurched and shuddered as the tyres bit into the loose gravel. A shower of stinging stones was thrown into the faces of the other pursuers as they came through the front door. The next second the car began to move forward, but not quickly enough as he aimed it at the gates. Ben had a fleeting glimpse of Francesca and Papa crouching by the left-hand gatepost as he ducked down behind the steering wheel.

The Mercedes hit the gates at a slight angle at about fifteen miles an hour. There was a fearsome crash. Ben's nose came into violent contact with the padded steering wheel and a mist of tears blotted out his vision for a second. The laminated windscreen crazed across but stayed in the frame.

The gates must have been solidly built. For, despite being comprehensively bent out of shape by three tons of luxury limousine, they still held together strongly enough to deflect the right front wing of the car into the gatepost and to stall the engine. The car slewed sideways and stopped, nearly blocking the entrance. For a further second there was a deathly silence.

Ben shook his head. There came a rattling at one of the rear doors. It brought him back to his senses and he looked round. Francesca and Papa were just outside. The gangsters were starting to run the thirty yards or so towards them. He leaned across and opened the door for them. They tumbled in and Ben snapped the lock down before the pursuers got to them. The crooks started to hammer furiously at the side of the car.

Ben looked round for inspiration. He could see that the gates had remained locked at the top but had been forced outwards about three feet at the bottom. He found he could open the driver's door about a foot. He forced it further, cracking the glass and bending the thin top frame.

'Follow me.' He slipped out at the bottom on to the wet gravel.

He saw there was room to get under the gate. He turned back to help Papa who was being pushed out of the car by Francesca. Somehow they managed to drag the old man out. But shouts from the other side of the car made them realize that the gangsters were after them. A minute later a hammering broke out on the other side of the car as the men attacked it.

'Quick. Through the gap at the bottom.'

The three of them went down on their knees. Ben forced his way through the narrow gap. Papa was dragged through unceremoniously with Francesca pushing from behind. Then Ben pulled her through and the three of them staggered out into the roadway. The tinkling of glass as the car windows were smashed in told them they were only half a minute ahead.

'We'd better run for it. Let's hope we can hitch a lift.'

Papa shook his head, gasping for breath already as he tried to speak.

Francesca spoke for him. 'He says you must leave us. He cannot run.'

'I'm not leaving you,' said Ben. 'We're sticking together. If necessary I'll have to carry him.'

'Wait!' Francesca looked up. 'I can hear something.'

The next second a little white Alfa came hurtling round the bend and skidded to a halt. The front passenger door swung open and Donna leaned out.

'Here comes the cavalry,' she called cheerfully. 'Well – get in! Don't just stand there. We've got to get a move on.'

Ben obediently helped Papa into the back while Francesca ran round to the other side to get into the front passenger seat. As Ben climbed in he saw the first man struggle out of the door of the damaged Mercedes and start to scramble over the fallen masonry. It was only at that moment that he realized that the arch carrying the stone carved shield with the carving of the Wolf of Hades had collapsed into the roadway and the emblem had shattered.

'OK, let's go,' shouted Donna gaily, as she let out the clutch. With a squeal of protesting rubber the Alfa shot off down the road, the half-closed door nearly clouting the furiously gesticulating gangster.

'You seem to have made a mess of his hundred thousand-dollar motor,' said Donna as she glanced through the gate. She turned to wink at Francesca. 'Huh! Men drivers!'

'It was the first time I'd ever driven a big Mercedes.'

Francesca laughed. 'Probably the last.'

Ben thought he detected an air of unjustified gaiety in the car. 'I don't think we're in the clear yet. They'll soon be able to back the Mercedes out of the gateway.'

'You're right,' said Donna. 'It isn't going to hold them up for long.'

Francesca pulled a face. 'And there's a Ferrari in the garage. I've seen it.'

'In that case we'd better get a move on. Hang on, folks.' Donna put her foot down harder and the little car leapt forward.

Ben reminded them, 'The guide books say that the Amalfi Drive is one of the most spectacular roads in Europe. Be careful. It has more than eleven hundred hairpin bends in forty miles of road.' He thought that should be enough to keep even Donna quiet.

He watched in awe as she hurled the little car around the curves with apparent aplomb. She never seemed to hesitate, clearly unworried by the fact that the surface had been made greasy by the damp wind. Often they were in a four-wheel drift only a few inches from the low concrete wall which was all that prevented them from plunging over the sheer cliff edge with a drop of 200 feet to the sea. The sight made Ben gulp and he noticed Francesca had suddenly gone silent.

Fortunately there was no traffic around so early in the morning as they rushed into short black tunnels through the rocky headlands where the road was scarcely wide enough to allow two cars to squeeze past each other. They soared over viaducts, through deep cuttings and round bend after corner after hairpin bend with never more than a hundred yards of straight road between them.

Francesca clung tenaciously to the front dashboard. Papa had shrunk down into the corner of the back seat where he sat with an ashen grey face and closed eyes. Ben tried to stop himself being flung about the car as it slewed and slithered and gyrated round the succession of corners. Whenever possible he tried to look behind for signs of pursuit. Only Donna seemed cheerfully unconcerned as she kept up a bantering conversation with him.

'Lucky there aren't any cars out today. These Eyeties are fair-weather drivers. Begging *your* pardon, of course.' She nodded to Francesca as she casually corrected a tail drift coming out of a bend with a bit of opposite lock.

They dived into their fifth tunnel. This one had a bend in it so they couldn't see to the far end. Donna switched on the lights. 'Are you keeping a look-out behind?'

'I can't see a lot just at the moment,' Ben reminded her.

'That Ferrari will make mincemeat of this road once it gets moving. We've got to find somewhere to get off as soon as possible.'

They screamed round the bend and into the daylight again. She tossed a map over her shoulder. 'See if you can find anywhere suitable.'

Ben struggled to open it as he clung to the arm-rest. He found the appropriate part of the map. 'I don't think there are many side roads along this way.'

'I know somewhere,' said Francesca unexpectedly.

'What's that? Come on – tell us, girl.'

'Oh, there is a small villa called La Procida which belongs to some people I know – the Pomorelli. It is down a little narrow lane. We could hide there while the Ferrari goes past. Then we could return to Amalfi.'

'Is it out of sight of the road?'

'Yes, but it is very difficult to find unless you know just where the turning is. It is just round a corner.'

'All the better,' said Ben. 'What do you think, Donna?'

'I'd say it's worth a try. How far is it?'

'I'm not sure. I think perhaps five kilometres. But I will know better when we get near.'

They rounded a bend and crossed a ravine. The road wound alongside a precipitous cliff as they approached another headland. From here they had a good view back along the way they had come. It was then that Ben caught his first glimpse of the low, red Ferrari. It was about a mile behind them and even at this distance he could tell that it was travelling fast.

'I've just seen the opposition,' he announced. 'I don't know whether we'll be able to go another five kilometres before they catch us, the speed they're going.'

'That isn't all.' Donna indicated out to sea and all their eyes followed her pointing finger. Coming towards them at an oblique angle and half-shrouded in the low cloud was a helicopter.

It came straight for them until it was about fifty yards away. Then it banked and followed parallel to the road, but a little behind them.

'What are they doing?' asked Donna. 'Have they got any weapons?'

Ben had quite a good view of the occupants as the helicopter pitched forward to come closer. He was almost sure he could see the damaged features of Dino on the man sitting beside the pilot. In the back was one of the big gangsters. There was a slight figure seated next to him. Ben guessed this was probably Sylvia.

'They don't seem to be intending to fire at us at present,' he reported. 'They seem happy just to sit and watch us until the Ferrari catches up. They're probably reporting our progress to the car on a mobile.'

Francesca pointed back. 'That will not be long now.' The red car had almost halved the distance between them.

'Hang on!' cried Donna. 'I'll go into overdrive.'

With a violent squeal of tyres she flung the car into the next bend and they had to brace themselves to prevent being thrown across the vehicle.

'I nearly lost my stomach that time,' said Francesca.

'I always wanted a couple of laps with a racing driver,' said Ben.

Donna laughed as she accelerated out of the hairpin, seeming to move forwards and sideways at the same time. The next second there was a violent buffeting and a roaring sound.

'My God! What was that?'

The helicopter swung low overhead, banked and headed away across the bay.

'Wow!' Donna exhaled. 'I thought the engine had blown up or something.'

Ben scratched his chin. 'I wonder where they're going? Is there somewhere they can land ahead to cut us off?'

'There is a viewpoint at Il Practice,' said Francesca. 'The helicopter could land on the car park if there are no sightseers.'

'There won't be any today. How far is it?'

'I don't know. Perhaps three kilometres – perhaps less.'

'Does it come before your friends' house?'

'No. That is just around the other side of this bay. There – you can see the roof above that little inlet.'

When Ben looked where she was pointing, he could make out a couple of buildings projecting from the side of a narrow ravine which appeared to lead down to the sea. It didn't look very hopeful. It was probably a dead end from which there would be no escape. But anything which might confuse the Vitelli would be a relief.

'I think we might just about make it,' said Donna, checking in the rear-view mirror. 'Warn me when we're coming to the turning. And we might all have to be ready to move quickly when we get there.'

They roared down a short straight and through a small clutch of houses clinging to the steep hillside above a little sandy cove. There was no sign of life. They were probably all empty holiday homes. Then the car started to climb the hill on the other side, winding round nearly vertical cliffs which overhung the road in places. There was a sheer drop below them. Ben looked back just in time to see the Ferrari come round the corner across the other side of the bay and begin the descent to the village. The next second it was blotted from sight as they squealed round a bend and into a steep guilty. When they came out the other side the red car was out of sight.

'I think the villa is just around the next bend,' called Francesca. 'Go carefully. It is here! Just here! Look!'

'Whoops,' yelled Donna as she braked hard. She flung the car over the small hump which Francesca was pointing at and they rushed down a dirt track which appeared to be pointing straight at the sea.

'Careful! Be careful!' yelled Francesca, but she was too late.

At the last minute Donna realized that the track only ran a scant fifty yards before it ended in a small level parking area. Beyond that there was just a low parapet wall to stop them from going straight over the precipice.

Donna put the Alfa into a violent sideways skid down the track to try to stop in time. Luckily the car didn't turn over, but the crazy slide only came to an end when they crashed heavily into the parapet. The car tipped precariously on to one side and hung there for a long five seconds. Then it smashed down on to its wheels again with a tinkle of broken glass and a crunch of torn metal. It came to rest with the bonnet sticking up at an awkward angle. Everyone seemed to let out a silent sigh of relief.

Ben was the first to recover sufficiently to leap out. He saw immediately that the front left wheel had been smashed off completety and an ominous cloud of steam was issuing from under the bonnet. They had lost their means of escape.

Donna joined him in surveying the wreckage. She sighed. 'Oh dear. I don't know what the rental company will say.'

'Somehow I don't think your little car's going to do many more miles.'

They turned back to where Francesca was bending over the old man. As they watched he sat up in his corner apparently all right, but Ben guessed it would be some time before he chose to take another trip along the Amalfi Drive by car.

The thought was chased from his mind by the snarl of an exhaust above their heads as the Ferrari swung round the corner and chased off to its rendezvous with the helicopter. They had temporarily succeeded in throwing their pursuers off the trail. But Ben didn't doubt the Vitelli would soon be back.

'Well,' he said, 'we can't escape by car now. What do you suggest?'

'We stay and face them.' Donna's fighting comment made them all look at her.

'We can go down to the house,' suggested Francesca.

'I don't think your friends will be very pleased if we turn up out of the blue with a pack of the Vitelli at our heels.'

'Oh, I do not think they will be here now. Usually they only come for the holidays and at weekends in the summer to get away from the heat and the bad air of Naples. But I know where they keep the keys. Maybe we could hide in the villa.'

Ben shook his head. 'They would soon find us. We can't hide the car and that'll give us away. I think we may be better going back to the village. There might be somebody there who can give us a lift to Amalfi in their car.'

'The village is fifteen minutes' walk,' said Francesca. 'I know. I have walked it. I was here on holiday two years ago.'

'I didn't see anybody in the village.' Donna tossed her head. 'I vote we stay and defend ourselves. I've got a gun.'

'Another one? Are you running a private army?'

She laughed as she went back to the car, opened the glove compartment and took out an automatic pistol.

'That won't keep them off for long,' said Ben. 'But it might give the police time to get here. We'd better ring them straight away.'

'There's no signal on my mobile.' Donna looked at him. 'What about yours?'

Ben looked shamefaced. 'I had it taken away at the Villa Rafallo.'

'Is there a phone in the house?'

Francesca shook her head. 'There is no telephone. It is just a holiday home.'

'Well,' said Donna, 'it looks like this weapon is the only friend we've got.' She gestured towards the villa. 'Come on. Let's see what we can find down there.'

They helped Papa Cimbrone out of the car and down the steep winding steps between the bushes of myrtle and oleander. It was quite a long way but he coped gamely with the help of a hand under each elbow from Ben and Francesca. Donna went ahead, carrying the gun in her handbag and shivering in her inadequate clothes. The wild wind tugged and buffeted at the hillside, sometimes carrying a spattering of rain in its bosom.

They reached the shelter of the front porch to the villa. Ben saw that the place was little more than a small bungalow occupying a concrete terrace cut out of the precipitous slope. With only the slightest hesitation, Francesca reached up to a ledge on one side of the door and removed a small bunch of keys. She looked at them carefully.

'I think this one is the boat and the little one is the padlock to the boathouse. That means this will be the one to the front door.' She started trying to fit it into the lock.

'Wait a minute – what sort of boat have they got?'

Francesca's eyes glowed. 'Oh, it is a lovely boat. It is a speed boat.'

'Is it big enough to get us to Naples?'

'It is quite big.' Francesca shrugged. 'But I do not know if it will go to Naples.'

'I reckon that's a better idea than trying to defend ourselves in this villa,' said Ben. 'Let's go and look at it.'

Donna and Ben set off again down the path, leaving Francesca behind to help her father. The steps became even steeper as they started to drop into the small gully. The roof of the boathouse came into view. It covered a deep, narrow inlet cut into the rock. The steps went down the side of the building and on to a small concrete landing stage. The door at the front was an up-and-over grating which was padlocked to a shackle let into the concrete. Ben undid the padlock without too much difficulty. It had obviously been used fairly recently.

He led the way inside. The boat was tethered to the catwalk with its nose pointing out to sea. He went down to check it out. It was a sporty motor cruiser with a half-cabin and a spray-shield to shelter the helmsman in the cockpit. He was pleased to note it had in-board engines. The controls were to the left of the cabin door. They looked simple enough – a starter button, twin throttle levers and a small steering wheel. He only hoped there was enough fuel in the tank to get them to Naples. He couldn't find a fuel gauge on the control panel.

While he was doing this Donna had climbed some steps from the catwalk to a storage platform at the back of the boathouse. 'Hey,' she called, 'there's a little window up here – only about a foot square. There's a great view of the steps. I believe I could hold them off for a month from this position.'

177

'I'm more interested in getting away.'

Ben unlocked the cabin door and peered in. There were two long seats with a table between them. Otherwise there was little of interest. He returned to the cockpit and climbed on to the helmsman's seat. He tried the key in the ignition. The electric starter turned the motor over immediately. After a couple of seconds the first engine fired, followed almost immediately by the second. He moved the throttle levers forward experimentally and experienced a surge of power as the boat tugged against its mooring ropes. A wash of water splashed over the rocks at the back of the boathouse. He closed the throttles and the engines settled down to purr contentedly.

'This seems a quite potent vessel.'

He looked ahead to the closed doors of the boathouse. They stopped about a foot above the water. They needed to be opened. Ben got out on to the catwalk and went forward to the front of the building. The doors were secured in position by two steel angles which slotted into brackets on each side. These lifted out quite easily. Then the doors concertinaed to the side of the catwalk. They had become a little stiff with rust in the salty atmosphere but a hefty pull slid them across. Ben returned to the boat.

Francesca and her father had arrived by now and Ben helped her get the old man into the cockpit and then into the cabin.

She followed him back into the cockpit. 'You are taking the boat?'

'It's the only way I can see of escaping. You'll have to apologize to your friends when you see them next. Let's hope we can return it to them undamaged.'

Francesca opened her mouth to reply but at that moment there came a shout from Donna and a furious beckoning. In a few seconds Ben was at her side on the storage platform.

'See this, Ben. Looks like they haven't taken long to tumble our little game.' Coming down the steps were Guido and the two gangsters.

Ben looked at her. 'I don't think we'll have a problem getting away in the boat if we keep our heads down. But we'd better get a move on. If you undo the bow rope I'll deal with the stern.'

She looked straight at him. 'I don't like boats any more than I do aircraft. I'll stay here to protect your rear.'

'Don't be silly, Donna. You know what these characters are like. They won't give you a free lift home just because you're a woman.'

'Sorry.' She turned back to the window. 'I don't want to leave my little car. I've got sort of attached to it.'

'Donna,' Ben remonstrated, 'those men out there are killers.'

She lifted the automatic and took aim. 'Don't worry about me. I can look after myself. Those guys out there will lose interest in me as soon as you take off.' She reached in to her hip pocket and took out a card. 'When you get to Naples, go to this address and ask for Jacob Smith. Tell him who you are and everything that's happened. He'll know what to do.'

Ben glanced at the card. The address meant nothing to him. 'What's all this about, Donna?'

'No time to tell you now. I'll explain later. Just get moving while you can.'

She smashed the glass in the window with the muzzle of the automatic. The Italians froze, looking for the source of the sound. Ben could see they were coming down the steps, less than thirty feet away. Donna took careful aim. There was a flat report followed by a howl of pain. As if acting in unison, the three men dived off the steps out of sight.

'Flesh wound,' said Donna casually. 'But that'll slow them down a bit. Now, Ben, you get going while you still can.'

'Just as you say, ma'am.' Ben squeezed her shoulder. 'Take care and don't expose yourself.'

She looked up at him and her eyes were soft. 'You too, you silly fool.'

Somebody called in Italian from outside and Ben was galvanized into action. He ran to the bow of the boat and undid the rope, coiling it roughly before he tossed it on to the foredeck. Then he went to the stern and released that one. He looped the tail through the ring on the quayside and handed both ends to Francesca who was waiting in the cockpit.

'Hang on to this and let go of the loose end when I open up the engines. Then coil it up on the seat. OK?'

'All right. Shout when you are ready.' There was excitement in her eyes as she took the rope.

Both these women seem to be treating this like a game, he thought to himself. He jumped aboard, went to the wheel and eased the throttles forward. The engine snarled and the boat tugged at the rope.

'Let go!' he shouted, and pushed the levers further forward. His over-eagerness was nearly their undoing. Released from its tether, the cruiser roared off down the creek straight towards the rocks on the far side. He flung the wheel over to prevent them hitting the entrance jamb and scraped the other side against the end of the concrete walkway. He corrected it properly this time and they were free, heading down the little inlet. Ben would have liked to wave back to Donna but he didn't dare take his hands off the wheel or his attention from the rocks on the left-hand side.

He heard a plop from behind and a soft echo from somewhere near him. That meant they were shooting.

'Get below!' he yelled at Francesca, and pushed the throttles hard forward.

With a roar of exhaust the stern sank and the boat leapt forward. Ben prayed there weren't any half-submerged rocks in the mouth of the inlet. A few seconds later they shouldered into the first wave in the open sea and the boat seemed to take off in a cloud of spray. Ben hung on to the wheel with grim determination.

However, he knew they couldn't carry on like this for long. As soon as they were out of range of stray bullets, he slowed down and the boat stopped bouncing across the surface of the waves and settled down to plough through the choppy sea. Not that it was any more comfortable. Ben set a course parallel to the shore and about half a mile out to sea. They were heading in a generally north-west direction with the waves rolling in across their path. As a result the boat worked its way through the water with a kind of cork-screw motion. Ben knew it must be most uncomfortable below, but he couldn't spare the time to go to help. All he could do was hope to get into more sheltered waters as soon as possible.

- 18 -

Half an hour later they rounded the Punta Campanella and began the run north across the Bay of Naples. The only time Ben had ceased to concentrate on the steering of the boat was when the helicopter had made a couple of low passes over them. But there had been no attempt to attack them or delay them in any way. After a few minutes it had flown off in the direction of the city.

Now that the wind and sea were behind them, the motion of the boat became less violent and he could begin to ease the throttles forward again to make better speed. Naples was still more than twenty miles away and anything could happen in the time it took them to get there.

Francesca poked a rather grey face out of the cabin door. 'There are the things here to make a cup of coffee,' she announced. 'But you will have to take it black.'

Ben suddenly realized he was both thirsty and hungry. 'I don't mind what it is.'

'Also you must slow down, or the kettle will not stay on the heater.'

Obediently Ben reduced the speed again. The need to have some food was greater than the urge to get back to Naples and a somewhat uncertain kind of safety. He checked his watch. It was now nearing eight o'clock. Time seemed to be passing very slowly. Away to his left he could see the twin mysterious peaks of Capri disappearing into the low cloud. It was less than twenty-four hours since he and Francesca had taken leave of her wise old grandfather there. A lot seemed to have happened in that time.

He wondered how Donna was getting on. He regretted now that he had left her. He ought to have insisted more strongly that she should come with them. But somehow her competence and her self-assurance made him feel like a small boy. He grinned to himself. He hadn't noticed that he aroused any maternal instincts in her.

Whatever she was doing, she certainly seemed to be keeping the pursuit away from them. Ben again turned to search the sea and sky behind. There was absolutely no movement in sight. Most Italians had more sense than to be out on the sea on a miserable day like today. Even the regular steamers from Sorrento to Capri seemed to have been called off, unless of course it was still too early for them.

Ben turned to study the shore which was about a mile away. It was wild and unpopulated here. He checked the chart which Francesca had found for him before she took to her bunk. From this he could see that there was a small town ahead calle Massa Lubrense. He couldn't yet see it in the misty, spray-filled atmosphere. He wondered whether this place might be where the Vitelli would try to intercept them. He couldn't believe that their enemies would allow them to motor across the bay straight into Naples.

He also checked for off-shore rocks and found there was a small islet somewhere to their right. He couldn't see this either. But he decided to alter course a little more west of north to make sure he kept well clear of the area.

Francesca's head appeared in the doorway. She had a smile of triumph on her face. 'I have opened a tin of pasta in sauce,' she announced. 'Are you feeling hungry?'

'You bet I am. Where did you find that?'

'There are some stores in the cupboard under the cooker. Here – put it somewhere safe and I will get your coffee. Then I will steer the boat while you have breakfast.'

A minute later she emerged with the steaming cup of black coffee. She had wrapped herself in a woollen blanket which she must have found in one of the lockers below. It made her look very small. Ben found himself feeling strong and protective again. However there was nothing weak in the way she took control of the cruiser while he sat on the spray-spattered seat and wolfed the pasta. It was one of the most delicious meals he had eaten in a long while.

From time to time Francesca cast a sideways glance at him as he ate. He tried to think of something witty or intelligent to entertain her with. No doubt she was used to the company of eligible young Italians. She would expect to be kept amused by her companions. He had never considered himself to be quiet or introverted before. But somehow she seemed to tie up his tongue. He feared he must cut a very poor figure in her eyes.

Even now all he could think of saying was, 'What about you? Have you had something to eat?'

She shook her head. 'No. I do not much like that pasta. I have had a cup of coffee.'

'What about your father?'

'I am worried about him. He will not eat because he feels seasick.'

'Well, in something over an hour – two hours at the most – we will be in Naples. Then he will be able to rest and eat.'

'You haven't told me yet about how you got away from the *capofamiglia*,' said Francesca.

'I'm sorry. I should have told you before.' Ben recounted the events in Vitelli's office. It was the first time he had found the time to go over the shooting of Mancino Vitelli and Guido's knifing of Alfredo since they had got out of the Villa Rafallo. The car chase and the escape from La Procida had driven the thoughts from his mind.

'I suppose you'll think I should have stayed and tried to help Alfredo, but I didn't see what good it would have done and it would have resulted in the imprisonment of all of us. I told Sylvia to take care of him. I hope she is still prepared to look after her husband.'

Francesca let out a sort of hiss. She seemed to be concentrating very hard on controlling the boat. Ben felt depressed again.

'I always seem to find myself in a position where I have to make decisions which have serious consequences for the people affected. Afterwards I wonder whether I made the right decision.'

Francesca shook her head. 'I think you did right. How could you have done any different?'

'What would your father say about me abandoning his eldest son?'

'Papa would understand. He told me that Alfredo had gone over to the Vitelli. I think he is completely changed. He was never a strong man of action like Toni or you. But now he seems to have no interest at all in the Cimbrone family. I think that Sylvia has changed him. I am ashamed of him.'

'I think you're being a bit harsh on him. Perhaps he has only just woken up to what is going on. Maybe you will be able to forgive him in the light of what happened this morning. I don't know what would have happened if he hadn't shot Vitelli. Guido's attack was intended for me. I think he only knifed Alfredo as a kind of reflex action.'

Francesca was silent but Ben continued, 'I don't know how badly hurt he was. I hope they got him to hospital. If they did, I think he might be all right.'

'It is no good for you to feel sorry for him,' said Francesca firmly. 'You have to accept what happens. If he is well, then that is good; if he is not – it is not your fault.'

Ben looked down at his lap. Francesca had revealed another more fatalistic side of her personality which he wasn't quite sure that he understood. However, he supposed she was right. He noticed his forgotten, half-eaten meal. With less enthusiasm than he had started, he swallowed the rest of the coffee and pasta.

'The food was good, Francesca. Thank you.' He set the tin plate down and stood up, waiting to take over from her at the wheel.

She looked up at him meekly. 'I don't want to go into the cabin. Please may I continue to drive for a little time? I am enjoying it.'

'All right. You can speed up a little if you like. It won't make things much rougher for your father down below and it will get us there faster.'

He showed her how to increase the throttle revs gradually until the boat was planning smoothly across the surface but without jumping wildly from the wave-crests. Then he leaned against the bulkhead and searched the sea astern again for any sign of pursuit. He spent some time checking all round, occasionally allowing his eyes to linger on Francesca's slim, windswept form. She must be feeling cold. He stepped over and pulled the blanket round her neck. She smiled gratefully but was still shivering.

'You should be in the shelter of the cabin,' he said, his voice sounding weak and husky to his own ears. He didn't want her to go yet.

She shook her head. 'I hate it down there. It makes me feel sick. I would rather be cold up here.'

'I'll get you another rug.'

'There isn't one. There were only two and I have wrapped Papa in one. It helps him to sleep.' She smiled at him. 'Really, you should have one. It is you who has been up here in the cold all the way from La Procida.'

'I'm not cold. The lining of this jacket is warm. And I've had something to eat to recharge my batteries.' Ben suddenly felt daring. 'It's the wind coming in from behind which is chilling you. Here – this will keep you warm.'

He moved behind her, opened the front of his jacket and wrapped it round her, clasping his hands round her waist to hold it in position.

'You appreciate that I'm only sharing my body-warmth with you out of a sense of generosity,' he murmured in her ear.

She said nothing. Was she working out how to rebuff his forwardness? Yet he had the feeling that she was moving slightly against him. Her hair was tickling his face and he could smell the tang of salt on her cheek. She shivered again and the next second she had twisted in his arms and was kissing him with an urgency and an excitement that took his breath away. The boat described a crazy S-bend as Francesca let go of the wheel.

'Here, I'd better take over,' said Ben. 'We don't want to disturb your father.'

He took his hands from around her waist and got the cruiser back on course. Francesca swivelled to face him and slid her hands up his back and round his neck. They were like chips of ice.

'You English! You are so slow. If I had been here with an Italian he would not have been talking about what was good for my brother. He would have had other things on his mind.'

'A young Italian girl of good family is not supposed to know about things like that,' said Ben. 'She should never allow herself to be alone at sea with any young men.' All the time he was acutely aware of her small, hard breasts pressing against his thin T-shirt. He tried to keep his mind on the sea ahead.

'Do not worry,' she soothed. 'I have never been to sea on my own with a young Italian man. My parents would never have allowed it. Besides, I have been keeping myself for a young Englishman.'

'Even if he is so slow?'

'We have a saying in Italy which translates something like this: if the journey is long and slow it makes the arrival even more important.'

'I'm not sure whether to take that as a compliment or not,' said Ben, bending to kiss her again.

After a while it was Francesca who stopped him. 'Perhaps you are not so slow,' she joked. 'You should not put your hand in that place when my father is on board. Also it is not good for your steering of the boat.'

Ben was silent for a while. 'Will you come with me on your own when I take the boat back to your friends at La Procida?'

'I shall not let you go without me.' She laughed gaily at the idea.

Ben studied the sea ahead and thought, with tendrils of her hair flicking across his face. His view of the future had suddenly changed. Now there was an urgent reason for going on with the fight against the Vitelli. And the penalty for failure had become much greater. As soon as he could he must get Francesca and her father to a safe place. Then he could face his pursuers unencumbered.

'What are you thinking?' She was watching his face. 'You are looking very serious.'

He smiled a little shamefacedly. 'I was thinking about the future.'

'Tell me about the future – our future.' She half-turned from him and hooked her shoulder under his armpit.

For the next half an hour they talked of the things that dreams are made of, discussing plans that both of them knew were unlikely to happen. The boat steadily made its way across the wide bay, usually so soft and beautiful, but today a cold, wet and unpleasant place. However Ben didn't even notice the discomforts. He wouldn't have changed his circumstances for the most luxurious surroundings imaginable.

The buildings of Naples were already beginning to grow large on the horizon when the helicopter found them again. It came up low from astern and was overhead before either of them saw it. It roared past with an ear-shattering noise and climbed ahead of them, looping round and crossing behind them again.

'You'd better get below and get the old man into a safe position,' said Ben. 'They may start shooting.'

Francesca opened the door, slid back the hatch and took a step down into the cabin. However, she went no further. From that position she looked up and studied the helicopter closely. 'I cannot see a gun. I do not think they will want to shoot us. I believe that we have something which they want very much. That is why they chase us so hard.'

'Well, I don't see what is so important – unless it's your father. They won't want anyone to know they've been keeping him prisoner while pretending he's dead.'

'That may be the reason,' she agreed, but however it seemed she was right about the shooting, for after a couple of minutes the helicopter made off in the direction of Naples.

'We'll have to watch out when we get to the harbour,' said Ben. 'I think they'll try to organize some sort of reception committee.'

'We will go straight to the harbour police. My father is still quite an important man in Naples, especially since they will think he has come back from the dead. The police will protect us.'

'OK. You can direct me.'

Ben settled down again, concentrating on keeping the boat on a straight course and now more alert for other craft. In the next twenty minutes they only came close to one Capri steamer, ploughing past them on its way to the island. The vessel was pitching heavily as it shouldered into the rough sea and the decks were clear of any curious watchers.

Away to their right the top of Vesuvius was hidden in thick cloud which boiled around its lower slopes like a slow-moving stormy sea. The land began to close in around them. He began to wonder what would happen in the next half-hour.

It was Francesca who first noticed the other boat. She drew Ben's attention to it, pointing almost dead ahead. Her eyesight was excellent. Screwing up his eyes, his searching gaze could just make a small blur coming in their direction from the port of Naples. At this distance it was impossible to make out what it was or even its size. It seemed to be moving fast for it was growing at a rapid rate as it headed almost straight for them. Ben began to feel uneasy as he saw the dark-blue hull rise for the first time above the turbulent grey sea and then drop out of sight again.

Even though there was no certainty that the other boat was interested in them, Ben wasn't going to take any chances. He decided it would be prudent to give them a wide berth. So he swung the wheel to take them in a more northerly direction towards Cape Posillipo.

He had to repeat this manoeuvre three times in the next five minutes as the other craft moved closer to their path. In the end they were pointing away at an angle of almost ninety degrees from the route they should have been taking and they were beginning to get close to the land. Each time they changed course the other boat followed until it was closing on their starboard quarter. There was now no doubt that it held their pursuers. Ben studied the vessel as carefully as he could while still steering his own boat. It was a fast cruiser with a sleek superstructure and looked quite a lot larger than their own boat. No doubt the Vitelli would have access to something big and fast.

He swung the wheel over again and headed directly away from them, opening up the throttles to full power as he did so. The noise and vibration increased greatly. The boat began to leap in great, staggering jumps from one wave-crest to the next. But he knew that somehow they had to get far enough away from their pursuers when they landed to give themselves time to find someone to help them. Looking ahead, he could see a strange hump-backed headland. Beyond that was a large bay almost completely surrounded by land.

'What is that place ahead?' he asked Francesca.

She came up to his side clinging on to the rail on top of the bulkhead as the boat bucked around. She focused on the coast ahead. 'I think it is the Gulf of Pozzuoli.'

'Is there anywhere to land there – any harbours?'

'There is a harbour at Pozzuoli but I do not know what it is like. It is many years since I last went there. The town is partly closed because of the action of the volcano Solfatara of which Grandpapa told you.'

Ben looked behind quickly. As far as he could see the other boat wasn't getting much closer while they were at full throttle. But it was now dead astern and was preventing them from turning away from the coast ahead.

'I think,' said Francesca prophetically, 'that we should keep away from Pozzuoli.'

'We haven't got much choice. We'd have to turn right round to get out now and they would catch us straight away.'

She pulled a face. 'It is not a good place to choose.'

Ben was inclined to agree but it was really too late now to do anything else. It seemed likely that the Viteli had set out to drive them into this narrow trap. Even at this minute they were passing the strange headland which looked almost like an island with a castle on top and the land was closing in right round them. 'I'm sorry Francesca,' he said. 'It seems that Pozzuoli has chosen us.'

- 19 -

Ben throttled back as they rounded the stone mole and headed into Pozzuoli harbour. A strange sight met his eyes. It appeared that the volcanic activity of the last few years had caused the land to rise and this meant that the majority of the harbour was now nothing but dried and cracked mud-flats. There wasn't a single boat in the whole place. He had to decide soon where to run the boat aground on the rapidly shallowing shore.

He chose a point near the harbour wall, cut the engines and ran the cruiser firmly on to the hard mud. In the tideless Mediterranean it would probably stay there until they came back for it – if they ever had the chance.

'We'd better get ashore quickly,' he suggested. 'We haven't got much of a lead.'

He jumped over the side on to the hard-baked harbour bed. Then he reached up to help Papa and Francesca as they hurried over the side. He lifted the old man across the slightly slippery surface to a flight of stone steps a few yards away which ascended to the top of the pier. Then he and Francesca took an arm each and propelled him up the staircase as speedily as he could make it.

Pozzuoli seemed to be a ghost city. There was no human life anywhere. Along the stone harbourside there were already signs of the huge earth movements which were slowly taking place, tearing the very ground apart under their feet. Just a few yards from the top of the steps the whole pier had cracked right through. They had to jump across a gap at least two feet wide and up a step about nine inches high. As they hurried up the quay they passed a small stone kiosk. One of its walls had collapsed outwards and the roof now sagged in the middle. The windows had fractured and glass littered the ground all around.

But it was when they reached the end of the pier and started to climb the hillside into the old city that they began to realize the full extent of the devastation. Many of the most magnificent old buildings had cracks in their walls. It was not uncommon for fissures to run the whole height of the building from road level to the roof. Ben thought that some of the cracks would have been big enough for him to insert his clenched fist into them. Stone copings and cornices had fallen from the tops of walls; rotten frames hung loosely from their openings; doorways and windows had been boarded up; parapets had collapsed; holes had appeared in roofs; signs warned people to keep clear of the dangers. In fact some of the buildings had been completely demolished by the movement of the earth and now lay in hillocks of rubble. Weeds were starting to appear. The whole place had the appearance of a bomb-site.

They had to pick their way carefully. In places, massive wooden shorings had been erected to prevent edifices from collapsing, often half blocking the roads. Scaffolding and timber support work had been constructed around buildings. But what was even more disturbing was that some of the supporting structures were themselves collapsing. Often they littered the pavements and blocked narrow side-streets, sometimes partly covered by the rubble of the buildings they had been intended to support. It was as though Pozzuoli had been abandoned by the human race and had been left to crumble back into oblivion. A civilization which had prospered for 3,000 years was in the process of being swallowed up again by nature.

They kept to the centre of the road, but even there they felt vulnerable. Over the whole city hung a tense and tingling silence, as if the place was holding its breath and waiting for something catastrophic to happen. One could almost hear the creaks and stresses which the slowly moving earth was putting on the buildings. Even at that moment there came a rumble and a scattering of shallow echoes as another pile of masonry collapsed and for a full minute afterwards they could hear stones and slates and glass clattering and tinkling on to the ruptured and tormented streets all around them. It continued for so long that they wondered whether the whole city was starting to collapse. But it gradually died away and the ominous silence returned.

Where would it strike next?

'It's so lonely.' Francesca sounded frightened.

She was right. The strange thing was that no cacophony of squawking birds rose from the funeral pyre of the latest building; no scurry of rats escaped from the danger. The city had even been abandoned by the scavengers and rodents. They were the only living creatures left here.

'Come on,' urged Ben. 'The Vitelli will have landed by now. Once they do, it won't take long for them to catch up with us.'

They hurried as best they could over the rough surface. In the circumstances Papa was doing magnificently, but he was being half-dragged and half-carried by Ben and Francesca, tripping over stones and rubble as they went. Obviously it was many months since any vehicle had attempted to pass along the broken and cluttered streets. What purpose would they have had? The population seemed to have moved out completely and taken their belongings with them. There was no longer a living thing within sight.

They came into what must have once been one of the main streets, but which was now a scene of utter devastation. Shop fronts and ground-floor windows and doors had all been boarded up, but the upper parts of the buildings were often partly destroyed. In some cases the hoardings themselves had collapsed. Lamp-posts had fallen or leaned at strange angles. Electricity cables festooned the roadway and were draped across piles of rubble. Now they presented no danger for the power had obviously been turned off in the abandoned city.

At the end of the street was a grand piazza which had once been graced by a splendid central fountain, now sadly deteriorated. This would have been the main meeting place for the populace for centuries and must have been a fine sight before earth tremors had caused the central statue to collapse into the cracked bed of the dried-up pool.

'We must stop for Papa to rest,' pleaded Francesca.

When Ben looked at him the old man was gasping for air and his face had turned grey. It was clear he could go no further at present.

'All right. We'll have to spare a couple of minutes.'

They helped him to the crumbling wall which had once surrounded the pool. He sat there with his hands on his knees, trying to suck in enough oxygen to keep his feeble frame moving. Francesca sat beside him and loosened his shirt collar.

Ben surveyed the devastation. 'When you look round you realize how weak our buildings are when they're up against the forces of nature,' he observed.

'Isn't it horrible?' She looked up. 'This has happened so many times in southern Italy. You would think they would learn to build in safe places.'

'It seems strange to find nothing moving anywhere.'

'I remember reading that the whole of the centre of the town is shut off,' said Francesca. 'Nobody is allowed to enter. All the entry points are barricaded and guarded. The old city and all the area by the sea is out of bounds except to the police.'

'In that case I'm surprised that someone wasn't there to intercept us when we landed.'

She shrugged. 'Ah, this is Italy. Nobody will do anything about it until there is a problem.'

'Do the police patrol the city?'

'Why should they? There is nothing here to be stolen and nobody to keep under control. There may be some police in the area, but they will be outside the barricades, sitting in their hut and drinking wine.'

Ben glanced back down the street. They couldn't risk remaining here much longer. 'Do you don't know where the nearest barricade is?'

'I haven't the least idea.'

'Well, let's hope we're going in the right direction.' He checked his watch. 'Come on. The two minutes are up. Can your father move again?'

'I'm sure he will do his best.'

As if he understood, the old man stood up as soon as they did. Ben decided to take the road to the left. It still led up the hill but, with the change in direction, they would be less easily seen by their pursuers. After a couple of hundred yards they came to a crossroads and paused. Papa was already gasping like a fish out of water.

'I hope it won't be too long before we reach one of the barricades and we can find some help,' said Ben. 'I will carry your father until then.'

He bent down and lifted the light old frame on to his back. Papa had no breath to argue. Ben selected a road going up at an angle to the right and set off at as fast a pace as he could manage with the old man wobbling about on his shoulders.

The sky ahead seemed dark and heavy. Now they were higher up they could hear the sound of the blustery, teasing wind high above them as it rolled the forbidding clouds off the sea. It was the only sound that came to them, making a strange, unworldly noise.

'I think we're going to have some rain soon,' he suggested.

Francesca only nodded.

Within a hundred yards Ben found he was panting from the effort of plodding along with the extra weight on his back. But he forced his body to push on. They had to get to safety before the Vitelli found them. With his eyes misting from the effort, he set himself the target of reaching the next junction before he rested. It was about 150 yards away and he was gasping by the time he got there and lowered Papa to the ground.

They seemed to have reached what used to be a main road – broader than anything they had seen before and with larger, more modern buildings. Here also the devastation seemed less serious although all the openings were boarded up and there were still signs of structural movement. Ben looked to right and left, hoping to see a barrier across the road and guard post near it, but there was nothing in sight. Surely if they followed this road to the right they would find someone soon.

The old man said something to Francesca and she translated. 'Papa says you are to let him walk now to give you a rest.'

Ben didn't argue. It was blessed relief to be able to stand upright instead of being doubled up under the old man's weight. In addition the slope was less steep and Papa could probably walk further here without getting tired.

They carried on at a steady pace. They passed a side road and Ben looked down. At the far end of the street was a man whom Ben instantly recognized as Dino Vitelli even though he was 300 yards away.

'Quick! Get out of sight,' he hissed at the others.

But they were too late. At that moment Dino looked up the street and his high-pitched shout told them that they had been spotted. They set off again at a shambling run, he and Francesca helping Papa on each arm. After thirty yards or so the road opened out into a large dusty piazza. They turned left along the hidden side of the square. Ahead of them was a large building which looked as though it had once been a hotel. Now the sign was missing, the stucco was cracked and had fallen off in places, and the paint was peeling. In the middle of the building was a large archway with an unmanned barricade in front of it.

'Ah! At last!' said Ben. 'We've only just reached the police in time.'

'No! No!' Francesca held him back. 'That is not a police barricade. I think that is the entrance to the Solfatara.'

'What do you mean?'

'It is the way in to the volcano. We should not go in there.'

He looked through the arch into the gardens beyond – a landscape of great palms and exotic shrubs, bright greens and vivid coloured flowers. It looked more like a colourful jungle.

'It doesn't look much like a volcano.'

'Oh,' she said, 'the Solfatara is not like Vesuvio. It is not a great mountain. The crater is at the same level as the ground. On this side there is not even a – how do you say? – a rim to the crater. That is why the plants are so green. It is the warmth and the steam from the volcano. But I have heard that it is very dangerous to go into Solfatara at the moment. It is trying to erupt. Nobody is allowed near the place.'

As they hesitated in front of the hotel there came a shout from the road to their left. Turning to look, Ben saw one of the Vitelli gangsters coming towards them. The man was no more than 200 yards away. When he looked the other way he saw Guido run into the square. His knife was already in his right hand.

'We've got no choice,' said Ben. 'I'd rather risk the volcano than those characters.'

'The volcano is very hot,' warned Francesca. 'Everyone within a kilometre has moved away. The crater has cracks and fumaroles and hot mud pools.'

'Well, I'm not waiting to be knifed.' Ben lifted Papa over the barrier and hurdled it himself. Possessed of a new urgency, he hoisted the old man over his shoulder in a fireman's lift and ran with him through the archway, leaving Francesca to follow.

The garden behind the hotel was very overgrown. To the right was a single-storey building with a peeling sign above the door which said 'Entrata ˘ 5'. But the turnstiles were open. There had been nobody to collect the entrance money for several years.

At the end of the building they took one of several overgrown paths into the dense jungle. Francesca explained that most of the west side of the volcano was filled with luxuriant vegetation. The only difference now was that it seemed to be turning brown, drooping and dying. The smell of death was all about them.

Ben carried Papa about thirty yards into this undergrowth before he set him down again on his feet. But they didn't pause. He led the way through the thick tangle of forest away from their pursuers. He kept glancing over his shoulder but they were already well out of sight of the buildings. Hopefully the Vitelli wouldn't know which path to follow through the dense vegetation.

Listening for sounds of pursuit, Ben didn't at first notice a new sound which formed a soft background roar. When he did detect it he had difficulty in working out what it was. Then suddenly the jungle thinned and they came out on to the floor of the crater and the noise was explained.

All around them was a vision from hell. Most of the crater was a savage sight of grey-coloured earth without any vegetation. It was like the surface of the moon. Dense clouds of yellow gas and steam issued from a series of massive blowholes. The clouds drifted across the flat surface and climbed the steep cliffs on the north side to the top where they were whipped away by the wind off the sea. It was these fumeroles, which seemed to be spurting up wherever the eye rested, that gave rise to the constant roaring noise.

Across the crater, the humped grey earth was criss-crossed with meandering cracks varying in width from a half an inch to more than a foot wide. From these there also issued a variety of gases, often in thin wisps, occasionally in irregular bursts, sometimes in continuous powerful jets. It was like walking across the top of a gigantic cracked pie-crust just after it had been taken out of the oven.

The sides of the cracks were edged with yellow sulphur crystals and other strangely coloured minerals. In places the cracks gathered into areas of weakness where the large blowholes occurred. These fumaroles had built up small cones of lapilli and lava fragments which glowed bright as they danced in the escaping gases and looked like mini-volcanoes. In other areas they sank into pools of bubbling mud from which occasional bursts of activity would splatter boiling deposits around their rim.

'I came here a few years ago. I thought it was horrific then, but now it has got very much worse.' Francesca pointed to a building on the eastern side of the crater. 'That was the observatory where they were checking the volcanic activity. But they closed it a year ago because it was becoming too dangerous for the scientists to work there.'

Ben could see that the small building had tipped over towards one side and the protective boards were hanging out of the windows.

She pointed to the centre of the area. 'This used to be flat right across the bottom of the crater. Now you see it has become domed.'

'My God. That means the centre must have risen twenty feet or more. It's like a great big balloon.'

'It is so high in the middle that you can't see the other side where the hot springs are. That was part of a health spa before it became too dangerous.'

The smell of rotten eggs was overpowering. It made them all gasp and induced a feeling of sickness in the pit of the stomach. Papa had a bout of coughing which brought him to a halt. Ben took out his handkerchief and Francesca tied it round the old man's face and told him to breathe through it. As she did so Ben watched the belt of lush vegetation behind them for any sign of their pursuers. He didn't think the terrors of the volcano would have put the Vitelli off and he knew they didn't dare to stay here, trapped between the chaos in front of them and the vengeful pursuers behind.

'We'd better try this way.' He led them off to the right where the volcanic activity seemed less intense.

They skirted the dense, dying vegetation, making for a point where the rim of the crater climbed out of the jungle and began to rise towards the highest point on the south side, perhaps 200 feet above the floor. Ben felt he wanted them to gain some height, maybe to escape from the volcano but also to reach a point where they could defend themselves if the Vitelli followed them.

Gradually the vegetation thinned and disappeared. They dragged Papa up slopes of crumbling soft, grey gravel. Steam was rising through it and they could feel the heat striking through the soles of their shoes. From time to time Ben looked back to survey the edge of the jungle, checking for Guido and his friends.

The visibility was poor. Often they seemed to be cut off by the clouds of steam that were being blown across the crater by the billowing wind. However, looking back, Ben was able to see enough to work out that about two-thirds of the crater was surrounded by walls of multi-coloured rock which rose from a few feet high to over 300 feet in the highest places. To the west these dipped down to disappear behind the vegetation through which they had entered. Peeping above the northern rim could be seen blocks of flats which must have once had splendid views but which were now presumably empty and abandoned like so many other buildings in the city.

Francesca squealed and paused to hastily pull off her shoe. A piece of lapilli had burned a hole clean through her sock and raised a blister on the skin beneath. Ben steadied her as she put it on again.

'We must try to gain more height,' he said. 'It should be cooler further up the slopes where we aren't so close to the volcanic activity.'

They struggled up a steep slope and emerged, puffing and panting, on to a rough sloping area. To one side were some large, irregular rocks. They were warm but not too hot to touch and Ben decreed that they should rest here again to allow Papa to recover his breath.

As he turned once again to survey the landscape below them he heard a shout. Nearly half a mile away, across the other side of the crater, their pursuers had come into view. There were four of them spread out over a stretch of about fifty yards. As Ben watched a fifth came out of the jungle. They must have taken the wrong direction in their chase and this had enabled Ben, Francesca and Papa to gain a valuable lead. But that wasn't going to be much help now.

It was obvious from the shouting that they had been seen. The group set off in a broad line, cutting straight across the centre of the crater, and only deviating around the active fumaroles and mud-pools.

'It looks as though they aren't as worried as you were about the dangers of the Solfatara,' observed Ben.

Francesca said nothing, but he noticed she was tightly gripping the small crucifix which hung round her neck.

He looked around. About fifty yards away the crater walls began to climb in rough, irregular terraces towards the rim. He had very little hope that they could climb the whole of the 200 feet with Papa. All they could do was get as high as possible and try to defend themselves. With another burst of furious energy, Ben picked up the old man and set off with him up the steep slope. Francesca pushed them from behind.

A further fifty feet up they reached another small platform and Ben stopped, gasping for oxygen in the foul air. He could see that they wouldn't be able to go any further. The walls in front of them were nearly sheer and the surface was very crumbly. Ben hadn't had the opportunity to check ahead for the best route. Now they had at last come to a dead end. This was where they must stand and defend themselves with whatever they had to hand. He deposited Papa and turned to look for suitable missiles to throw down on their enemies as they climbed towards them.

'Look at them,' shouted Francesca.

Their pursuers had now bunched together in a short column as they threaded their way through a gap in the centre of the crater between a big mud geyser and a roaring fumarole. From this vantage point they seemed to be surrounded on all sides by ever-increasing volcanic activity. Even as Ben watched, a great column of steam burst out of the ground a few feet in front of them and they retreated hastily. Another and another jet spurted up until it seemed as though they were standing on a raft in the middle of a boiling sea.

There came a deep rumble and the whole volcano gave a violent shiver. Rocks were detached from the cliffs above them and came leaping and bounding down the slopes followed by showers of smaller stones which rattled all about them. Ben ducked involuntarily. If this were to continue they would need to find a protected corner. At that moment it seemed they were being attacked from above and threatened from below.

Out in the centre of the crater he could see the ground was shaking violently and steam came shimmying out of holes all around. Two of the men fell down but were quickly on their feet again. They clustered fearfully in a group in the middle of their island which seemed to be rising magically out of the storm all around them.

Ben watched with a terrible fascination as the great table of rock lifted slowly and began to tilt over on one side. Around its rim showed bright orange lava which spurted and leapt out in great cascades, scattering over the surrounding ground where it glowed dull red before slowly cooling to grey-black. Even greater bursts of lava followed, climbing high in the air in slow motion before falling unwillingly back towards the crater bed in irregular trails with dozens of minor explosions.

One edge of the table slid under the red-hot magma which seemed to bulge out to swallow the victims who were still clinging together in the centre. With ponderous slowness the raft began to tip ever more steeply towards the vertical. Suddenly it broke across the centre but Ben couldn't hear the screams emanating from the open mouths as four of the five slid into the writhing mass of red. The black blotches remained there for a few seconds before they were swallowed up from sight. Only one person remained clinging to the sinking island. Although he couldn't make out her features, Ben somehow knew that it was Sylvia. He realized that he couldn't just leave her there without trying to do something to help her.

Although he knew in his heart that there was no hope of saving her, he began to scramble back down the slope towards the crater floor. He ignored Francesca's shouts, dimly heard through the turmoil. But the next moment there came another, more violent earth tremor which threw him off his feet. Massive cracks, greater than ever before, split the floor of the crater. And, as he watched, a tongue of lava reached out and knocked the last of the Vitelli off her precarious perch just like a gigantic lizard swallowing an errant fly. Ben thought that he could actually hear her shriek of terror before it was extinguished in the boiling lava.

He lay rooted to the spot for a long minute by the shock of it. All the hairs of his body tingled with horror. In a few short seconds the last member of the Vitelli family had been consumed by the volcano. At that minute he could believe every word of the legend of the Wolf of Hades.

As he lay there, watching the writhing magma throwing out ever more spectacular fireworks, he became aware of Francesca tugging at his arm. 'Quick! Quick!' she screamed above the noise. 'We, too, will be overwhelmed. We must try to get Papa out of the crater before it gets any worse.'

Ben came back to his senses. The ground was almost constantly shuddering and vibrating under his body as explosion after explosion tossed red-hot rocks and lava out of the centre of the volcano. Even as he watched a more violent earthquake shook free a massive area of the northern rim of the crater and the landslide came rolling across the floor towards them. Some of the larger boulders rolled into the bubbling lava and burst apart as the moisture in them expanded, creating a further display of pyrotechnics.

Ben climbed to his feet. He shook his head to clear it and tried to make himself think logically. 'No. We must go back the way we came. We'll never climb up to the rim. In any case the tremors are likely to bring down big chunks of the cliffs.'

'I won't go back across the crater.'

'We'll keep close to the edge and hope we don't get caught in any landslides.'

They scrambled back to where Papa was cowering on his lonely shelf and helped him to his feet. Francesca explained to him what they were going to do and he agreed with a weary wave of the hand. Carefully they started down again, picking their way over the unstable surface. Then another violent earth tremor shook the ground around them and they had to cling to each other to keep their footing. With a tearing rumble another great crack opened up in the ground just ahead of them. It must have been at least four feet across and an eerie glow was emitted from deep inside it. Ben hesitated to jump across it. He didn't want them to find themselves in the same sort of position as the Vitelli.

The way that the activity was building up in the Solfatara it seemed more than likely that they would be prevented from getting out through the jungle area by the massive earth movements which were now taking place almost every minute. But if they stayed where they were, they could easily be overwhelmed by a landslide or injured by falling rocks. There was almost no choice. It seemed as though the Wolf of Hades was still on the prowl.

'Come on,' Ben urged. 'We must cross this crack ahead before it gets any wider.'

Papa said something and Francesca translated. 'He says he cannot jump across the chasm. He is afraid he will fall in.'

'No, he won't. I'll stand the other side and you can hand him to me. Come on! We mustn't delay any longer. The gap may get wider.'

At first it seemed as though Francesca was about to argue with him, but she said nothing and made to follow him. However Papa sat down and refused to move another inch.

'He says he would rather die here than in the bottom of a crevasse,' she said. 'He says you are to go on without him.'

Ben looked down at the old man helplessly. 'What are we to do then?'

'I will not leave him. Why don't you go by yourself? You will be able to move faster without us. When you get out you can bring the police back to rescue us.'

He weighed the idea in his mind. 'That might take hours. This thing seems to be getting worse all the time.' He pointed at the ever more violent activity going on in the centre of the crater where a cone was already starting to build up. Lava and red hot rocks were starting to creep across the ground towards them. At the nearest point they were probably only seventy or eighty yards away.

Ben pulled a face. 'I don't think you will last that long.'

'We will climb back up to the platform where we were before. We will be safe there for much longer.'

'You might easily get caught by a landslide.' He pointed at it. 'Look, Francesca, it's only a four-foot gap – not much over a metre. He could easily make that.'

'But there will be others.' Francesca seemed to have made up her mind. 'I understand how he feels. He has had enough of running.'

Ben could see there was no point in further argument. 'All right. I will help you back.'

Together they helped Papa to his feet and started back up the slope again. But they hadn't gone more than twenty yards before there were more violent tremors and another massive rumbling. When Ben looked back the crack had widened to ten feet or so and lava was starting to bulge out of the ground.

'It's too late now in any case.'

'I'm sorry.' Francesca's face had gone white. 'But somehow I couldn't force him.'

Ben shrugged. 'I think it's better if we stick together anyway. Perhaps the volcano will quieten down in an hour or so now that it's had its victims.'

They set off again, scrambling silently back up to their little shelf where they could sit and watch the most spectacular show on earth from a ringside seat.

- 20 -

It was about half an hour later that Ben fancied he heard the roar of engines. He couldn't be sure at first above the pandemonium produced by the developing volcano. It was now hiding most of its sights behind a great pall of black smoke which the wind off the sea was carrying away to the north. He looked to where Papa was asleep with his head on Francesca's shoulder. She was dozing as well but her head jerked up as he looked across at her. Perhaps she, too, had heard it.

Ben got up and tried to tell from which direction the sound was coming. A few seconds later the helicopter came into sight over the eastern rim of the crater. It was a small glass bubble of a machine with a couple of occupants. It was moving in a broad circle around the perimeter as though they were photographing or observing the volcanic action.

Francesca woke her father and jumped to her feet. She started waving and gesticulating long before the helicopter got close enough for the crew to see them. Ben thought it more than likely that they would be too busy watching the spectacle to notice them.

The craft seemed to follow the line of the rim, keeping at a respectful distance from the main activity. For a while it disappeared from sight behind the rising cloud of smoke and dust. When it appeared again it was heading straight for them. As it started to come closer Ben took off his jacket and waved it in wide, expansive movements. The action seemed to work. Almost at once the helicopter dropped towards them. He and Francesca waved and shouted furiously. The pilot came down inside the crater and dropped towards their little shelf. The two occupants waved and gesticulated at them. Then they suddenly passed right over their heads, zoomed up over the rim behind them, and disappeared. Francesca was mortally disappointed.

'Don't worry,' said Ben. 'At least they know we're here. That helicopter was too small to help us. I expect they've gone to report what they've seen and soon we should have someone else coming.'

He hoped he was right. He knew that if they stayed in the crater much longer they were likely to be overwhelmed by volcanic activity or landslips or hit by falling rocks. The next twenty minutes passed desperately slowly. Then suddenly a big military helicopter appeared over the rim just above their heads and dropped down towards their little platform. On the side of its hull Ben could see the insignia of the United States Navy and a large door was open with two men sitting, their legs dangling into space. A gale of downdraught battered around their expectant faces. A few seconds later one of the men was being winched down to the flatter terrain below them.

'Come on,' Ben shouted. 'They won't want to stay here for long.'

They helped Papa down the rough slope to meet the waiting American who was standing there with a big grin across his face.

'We thought you might want a lift,' he drawled.

Ben shook him warmly by the hand. 'Boy, are we pleased to see you. How did you come to be here?'

'Tell you that when we get up top. Come on, let's have the old feller first.'

The man fastened Papa into the harness and explained through Francesca how he should hold himself with his head back and his legs loose. Then he gave a thumbs-up sign and the old man was whisked up into the sky. They certainly seemed to be in a hurry. Francesca went next and Ben followed a couple of minutes later, leaving the crewman to come up last.

He found himself hauled in through the door by a burly American with a crew cut and dumped unceremoniously on his back on the floor. There was sharp snick as the harness was released from the middle of his stomach and the winch whirred again as it was dropped down to the waiting crewman. At almost the same time the helicopter seemed to buck in a gust of hot air and Ben was precipitated across the cabin into Francesca's waiting arms.

'Wow! That one was a bit close,' shouted the winchman.

Ben picked himself up and turned to face the clear blue eyes of another American who must have been well over six feet six inches tall.

The man grinned. 'You sure seem to have got yourselves into a hot situation there. Now get shackled on to this safety rail.'

He turned back to help the other man as he scrambled inboard. The door was pulled shut, a couple of words were spoken over the intercom, and the helicopter started a powerful climb. On one side the walls of the crater seemed to be only a few feet away from the whirling rotor blades. Ben looked out of the other side window at the eruption of the volcano. Now there seemed to be massive jets of steam and smoke spurting everywhere. The bulging centre of the crater seemed to be collapsing slowly into the magma beneath. Great boulders, some half the size of a house were being tossed out of the core. Glowing gobbets of lava were scattering all about in recurring bomb-bursts. Bright red magma streamed up out of the ground and poured across the floor of the crater which had remained semi-dormant for centuries. Ben saw it lap up against the building which housed the observatory. It pushed in the side wall and the flat roof collapsed into the lava. Flames flared as the combustible elements vaporized. On the other side the trees around the edge of the forested area burst into flames in the intense heat even before the hot magma reached them. They had just got out in time. Nothing would survive for long in that superheated cauldron. Solfatara was starting to blow its top.

'Jesus Christ,' blasphemed the winchman.

Nobody else spoke. They were all silenced by the terrifying scale of the eruption. The next second the helicopter slipped over the rim of the crater and the scene was abruptly wiped from their horrified gaze. All they could see now was the trailing black plume of smoke which climbed erratically into the lowering skies as they fled from the awful sight.

The craft pitched forward and began to forge out across the bay in a southerly direction. Soon they were over the sea and looking down on the grey, white-combed waves.

'Where are we going?' asked Ben.

'Don't ask me, chum. I don't get to give the orders around here.'

'Where have you come from?'

'Us? We're carrier-based. We were just coming in for an official visit to Naples. Look over there. That's the *Franklin D. Roosevelt* anchored down there just outside the harbour. We only got in half an hour ago. No sooner do we get here than the word comes to send up the whirly-bird. That's all I know.' He shrugged apologetically.

'I'd still like to know where we're going.'

A female voice said, 'Perhaps you'd better ask me that.'

Ben spun round. 'Donna! How did you get here? It's incredible, the habit you always seem to have of turning up in the right place at the right time.'

'I don't know how I ought to take that.' She looked as cool and well-manicured as though she had only left her hotel room five minutes before.

'Donna, it was only three hours ago that we left you to fight off a bunch of crooks with nothing but a little handgun. Your only means of escape was a wrecked car. How the hell did you manage to end up here so quickly?'

She came over, took his arm and seated him beside Francesca. Then she sat on the other side of him. 'It's better if we talk here than on the flight deck. It's even noisier up there.'

'Go on then,' urged Francesca. 'Tell us what happened.'

Donna patted her hair into place. 'Really, it was just as I said it would be. As soon as our friends saw that you'd made a break for it they lost interest in me and couldn't wait to get to hell out of the place. I held them up for about ten minutes – managed to wing one of them. Then they were away as if they'd got a hornet up their backsides.'

'So how did you get back? Just hail a passing cab?'

She looked at him a bit sharply to try to judge whether he was pulling her leg.

'No. We're a bit more sophisticated than that. I forgot to tell you that I had a two-way radio in the car. Top secret stuff, I'm afraid. I got picked up nearly two hours ago.'

'We?' asked Francesca. 'What does *we* mean? Who are these people who have been playing around in helicopters while we were nearly being burned alive in the Solfatara?'

'It's just a way of talking,' said Donna shortly. Ben had noticed before that the two women seemed to rub each other up the wrong way.

'But how did you come to be sitting in this helicopter?' he asked.

'You've got to admit it's a bit of a strange coincidence, Donna. The woman who sits beside me on the plane to Naples is conveniently on hand to rescue me from thieves when I get into trouble. That could more or less be explained by your claim that you were following me. But then you just happen to be passing when Francesca and I are escaping from the Villa Cimbrone.'

'And what about arranging the hotel room?' Francesca chipped in.

'After that you give up part of your holiday to help us break into the Villa Rafallo; you give me a gun to protect myself when we're inside the villa; you come roaring round the corner to pick us up when we escape. Finally you turn up in the helicopter that rescues us from Solfatara. There's got to be some reason for it all.'

Donna's smile had faded. 'This is getting to sound like a bit of third degree.'

'Well, you can't expect us to accept that it's all pure coincidence. That's stretching our credulity too far.'

She was silent for a while, biting her lip as she looked down at the floor. At last she said, 'Well, I guess it does need a bit of explanation. But, I'm sorry, I can't give it to you at this minute. There'll be someone meeting us who may be willing to explain it to you. I'm afraid you'll have to wait till then.'

After that she looked out through the window and would tell them no more. Ben followed her gaze. He saw that they were approaching land again. In those last few minutes they had crossed the Bay of Naples and soon they were climbing through a valley in the Sorrento peninsula. On either side Ben could see the rugged limestone crags reaching high above them. Some of the highest were topped with spectacularly-sited shrines and crosses.

However Ben's thoughts were on other things. He didn't know why but he felt a certain sense of betrayal. He began to wonder whether Donna and the shady people behind her had been using him all the time. He felt as though she had been lurking in the background, pulling the strings that had him running all over southern Italy. Now she was going to turn him over to some boss of hers to extract what further help he might still be able to give. But why did he feel bitter about it? Perhaps he'd grown fonder of her than he realized. Now it just seemed that the whole thing had been nothing more than a job to her.

They were soon back over the sea again and swinging round to follow the coast to the east. In another five minutes they began to lose height. Peering out of the side window, Ben guessed their destination: it was the Villa Rafallo again. As they came in to land on the lower terrace, Ben could see the red-helmeted Italian police swarming everywhere. The long arm of the law had arrived at last.

They touched down gently on the circular landing platform, the engines were cut, and the helicopter settled forward on to its undercarriage with a sigh. The door was opened and the four of them were helped out. With profuse thanks and shaking of hands, they left the crew who had rescued them.

Halfway up the steps they were met by a tall, grey-haired man. Donna said a few quiet words to him and turned back to introduce them. Ben supposed this must be the *someone* she had mentioned during the flight. They were being passed on up the line.

For a few seconds further conversation was prevented as the helicopter's engine was started up and it rose into the air again with a roaring whoosh of air from its busy rotors. Waves were exchanged and it pirouetted and headed out to sea. As the noise died away Donna spoke again.

'Ben, this is my boss, Jacob Smith. Jacob – Ben Cartwright.'

'Hi!' They shook hands and the man turned back to Donna. 'The house is clean. There's nothing here of any interest.'

'What about the laboratory in the cellar?' asked Ben.

Smith looked at him sharply. 'We haven't found that. You'd better take us there.'

Ben obediently led the way into the house. As they crossed the terrace Smith beckoned to an Italian police officer who joined them. Ben took them to the coat cupboard, pulled the coats to one side and showed them the narrow stairs which led down to the basement. The laboratory was just as they had left it that morning.

'What are you looking for?' he asked.

The laconic reply was, 'We'll know when we find it.'

Nothing seemed to have been moved since they were here last. The crates of bottles were still stacked by the bench and the corking machine stood ready.

'Funny place to have a wine-bottling plant,' said Donna.

'I think they're adulterating the wine. You know – mixing the good wine with inferior stuff and selling it off as original quality. I don't know how long it's been going on. We import some of this label to England. We'll have to stop straight away or we'll get a bad name as well.' Ben felt the anger welling up inside him again as he thought of the damage the Vitelli had done to the business that he and Toni had so carefully built up over the years.

Smith looked over the top of his spectacles at him. 'So you think that's what had been happening? That's very interesting.'

'What do you mean?' The truth was beginning to dawn on Ben.

'I don't mean anything special.'

Ben faced up to him. 'Yes, you do. I think it's about time that you did a bit of explaining to me and the Cimbrones.'

'Explaining? Like what?'

'Like what are two Americans doing running the show on the Italian mainland.'

'We're not running the show,' said Donna. 'We're here with the agreement of the Italian Government.'

'Just as we have with your own government,' added Smith.

'And what's the reason for all this happy co-operation?'

Smith considered him carefully for several seconds. 'Well, Mr Cartwright, what I'm about to tell you is classified, but I guess it's better that you know the facts rather than start poking around with half the story. Donna Carter and I are from the Federal Narcotics Bureau but we're seconded to Interpol.' He paused. 'We're looking for narcotics trafficking routes. We've suspected the Vitelli family of being involved in this trade for some years. It was when they got involved with the Cimbrone family that we saw a chance of getting close to them.'

'Do you mean through my partner Toni?'

He nodded.

'So that's the reason he was killed.'

'You are responsible for his death,' accused Francesca.

Smith faced her. 'Your brother volunteered to help us, Miss Cimbrone. He did that because he hated the way that his in-laws had taken over the Cimbrone family business and were using it for criminal purposes. Of course, we had no idea that he was putting himself in such danger or we would have suggested he should back out.' He shook his head. 'But I don't think he would have backed out, even if we had given him the chance. I think you should be very proud of your brother, Miss Cimbrone, for being a very brave man and for stopping the Cimbrone name from being dishonoured.'

'It's incredible that the Vitelli should have killed Toni and tried to kill me just for drugs,' objected Ben.

'It wouldn't be the first time drug traffickers had killed someone who stood in the way of them making big profits.'

Donna chimed in, 'I don't think drugs are the reason why they have been chasing Ben.'

'What do you mean?'

'As you instructed, Jacob, I've been keeping close to Ben since he left London.' She winked at him. 'The Vitelli have been after you ever since you landed in Italy, haven't they?'

'Was it you who put them on to me?'

'It certainly was *not*.' She grinned. 'They've been watching you very closely, Ben, and I've been watching them just as closely. That's why I kept appearing in your life when you least expected it.'

Francesca pulled a face. 'That explains it.'

'I'm sorry, Ben. But I've got to say you had no idea what you were doing, or where you were going. The Vitelli could have easily left you to stumble around and get lost without causing them any trouble. Yet they pursued you from the moment you got off the plane at Naples Airport. Why did they attack you in the middle of Naples? Why did they follow you to Pompeii? Come to that, why did they chase you all the way into the crater of Solfatara? They seem to have been trying very hard just to catch you and tell you they wanted to take over your company – which is what you already knew, in any case.'

There was a silence while they all digested this point. At last Smith said, 'Well, Donna, have you got any ideas?'

She shook her head. 'Ben didn't know anything about the drugs until just now. I'm sure of that. I've never come across *anybody* more innocent than he is.'

'Perhaps you've got some information they wanted.' Smith looked at him. 'You may be in possession of something of theirs without knowing it. You may even have the courier route from Afghanistan. We'd really like to know that – if anybody's written it down.'

'I don't have the least idea what you're talking about. Toni never said anything to me about drugs, or trafficking, or courier-routes. I thought we were just importing wine.'

'Have you got anything on you that might carry a message? Perhaps it's something your partner gave you to look after for him.'

Ben shook his head. 'No. I've got nothing with me which I had from Toni. We didn't bother with birthdays or anything like that.' Then suddenly it dawned on him. 'Wait a minute. Mancino Vitelli did say that I had something that he wanted.' He dived in his pocket. 'Here it is – this metal thing. It's called the Wolf of Hades.'

He handed it over and Smith examined it carefully.

'I've already looked at it several times,' said Ben. 'I can't find anything special about it. It looks just like a heavy piece of metal with a picture on it to me. There are some rough scratches on the back like Roman numerals but they don't seem to make any sense.'

Francesca came forward. 'It is the badge of the Vitelli. It is their family motto since – oh, since many hundreds of years.'

'I described it to Francesca's blind grandfather. He told me that the legend says that whoever is struck by it will become a victim of the wolf from the underworld.' He joked without humour. 'I suppose you could say that's what happened to the Vitelli when they were chasing us.'

Smith and Donna laughed at the joke, but Francesca was furious.

'You should not laugh.' Her eyes were sparkling. 'In this part of Italy we are very close to the underworld. The Lake of Avernus is only twenty kilometres from here and we are told that is the entrance to Hell. We know better than to joke about things like that.'

'Sorry,' said Donna contritely.

Smith was concentrating on the emblem. 'It looks straightforward enough,' he agreed. 'But I'd like our people to have a look at it if you don't mind. They may come up with something.'

Ben nodded.

The American pocketed the badge. 'Now let's turn our thoughts to finding the drugs.'

'You want to find the drugs?' Francesca asked.

'We certainly do, ma'am.'

She addressed a question to her father who replied at some length. She spoke again and he pointed to the bench.

'There are your drugs,' said Francesca. 'They are put into the bottles of wine. Papa says he has been told it is a thirty per cent solution.'

'What – these bottles standing on the bench?'

'That is right. They are the ones with the Wolf of Hades badge on the seal. They are the drugs which are being exported by the Vitelli to the rest of Europe and to North America.'

- 21 -

It was nearly two days later that Francesca drove him to the airport to catch his flight back to Gatwick. Until then Ben hadn't realized that she knew how to drive. It was obvious to him that she wasn't very experienced and didn't feel comfortable in heavy traffic. This may have been the cause of the brittle silence which reigned in the car as she drove and which contributed to the almost tangible tense atmosphere.

It had been a difficult two days, dominated by the news of the continuing eruption of Solfatara which had consumed the last of the Vitelli. Fortunately the main activity had been contained within the existing crater and any wholesale loss of life had been avoided. Experts were confidently predicting that the volcano would gradually calm down over the next few months. It seemed that the wolf had returned to its lair, having satisfied its hunger for the while.

The happiest moment had been the reunion of Papa and Mama Cimbrone. No great outpouring of pleasure and gratefulness had occurred. In fact, for Italians, their meeting had been strangely free of gesticulations and shouting. But Francesca and Ben had watched their reactions with lumps in their throats. Mama had suddenly seemed to come alive again and once more take up the reins of power in the family. She fussed around her husband, seeing to his every wish. And Papa had been to see his lawyers about setting up the Cimbrone business ready for his son to take over.

Now they were concentrating their efforts on getting Alfredo back to health to take over the running of the family businesses from his father's old hands. At present he was in a secure clinic where it was hoped he could be weaned off the drugs introduced into his body by the Vitelli. The police had indicated that he was unlikely to be charged with Mancino Vitelli's murder under the circumstances.

Ben had been to further interviews at the office which Jacob Smith had been loaned by the Italian police while he tried to tie up the ends of the operation and gain the maximum results in terms of arrests and information. However, it seemed that the whole trail had gone cold. The police had picked up two more middle-men but apparently those knew nothing beyond their contacts with the Vitelli.

'It's usually like this,' said Smith morosely. 'All we can do is nibble away at the little ones in the hope that we'll catch a big boy some time or other. At least the Vitelli are out of the business.'

After their second meeting Smith decided there was nothing more that Ben could tell him so there was no reason to hold up his return to London. The business might be needing his attention. This was the moment of decision. Ben wrestled with it for a few hours before he made up his mind. He admitted that for some strange reason he didn't really want to go back yet. His enthusiasm for work seemed to have been temporarily blunted. But every logical argument said that he should now leave Naples.

Papa had not been very well since his return to the damaged Villa Cimbrone. The family had understandably been involved in the pleasures of reunion and the worries about Alfredo's condition. Ben felt an intruder in these family matters. He thought he should leave the family on their own as soon as he reasonably could. So, on the second night, he announced that he had booked a flight to London for the next day.

Francesca said very little when she heard he was leaving. Ben waited in vain for some expression of regret, some suggestion that he should stay for a few more days. Instead she volunteered to run him to the airport. After that the subject appeared to be closed, as far as she was concerned. Ben was depressed by the finality of it all.

The last evening Francesca declined dinner and went to her room with a headache. Ben was disappointed because he had hoped to have a private word with her. This would have been their last opportunity. She never seemed to be available on her own to talk and discuss the possibility of something happening in the future. By now he was convinced that she was avoiding him.

Of course it was easy to understand why she would. No doubt she felt embarrassed about some of the things she had inadvertently said

213

and done over the last few days. Probably it was just the stress of the experiences she had been through. They must both accept the fact that her family wouldn't be at all pleased if she were to disclose to them that she had fallen for an impecunious English Protestant.

So Ben had spent his last night dining alone with Mama. It had been a painful affair. Neither spoke much of the other's language. Although she responded politely to his feeble attempts at Italian, he could sense that her attention was not on him. It was a relief at the end of the meal when old Emilio approached her and, after a few words, beckoned for Ben to follow him.

The old servant led him upstairs and took him to Papa's room. The lights were low and the old man lay with his wrinkled hand on the counterpane, breathing slowly and noisily. It seemed to Ben that his health was now worse than it had been when they were escaping from the Vitelli. Ben was worried about him.

Papa raised his hand and signalled to Ben to approach the bed. The old man spoke quietly in Italian, presumably thinking that Ben's knowledge of the language was greater than it really was. Ben could understand almost nothing of what he said. Papa mentioned Francesca on two or three occasions and nodded appreciatively. Perhaps she had given him a good report. The old boy also talked about London and smiled and patted his hand. Ben wasn't sure what he meant but he hoped he was receiving Papa's agreement to his remaining in control of the London company. He told himself that he really must find the opportunity to ask Francesca whether she knew what was going to happen. But for now he just smiled and was profuse in his thanks and best wishes to the old man. Papa patted his hand again and gave him a cheery little wave of dismissal.

Ben backed away from the bed reluctantly. The old man's eyes were closed even before he had left the room. Ben hoped fervently that this was only temporary worsening of his condition and that he would soon be back in better health. Quite apart from Signor Cimbrone's importance to his future, he had also grown rather fond of the old fellow.

He didn't feel he could pressurize the old man about formalizing an agreement at this stage. He decided he would definitely discuss it next morning with Francesca no matter what obstacles she tried to put in his path. He couldn't leave without sorting out the original reason for his travelling to Italy.

That night he slept fitfully. Everything seemed to have died on him, leaving a flat taste in his mouth. In a way he had succeeded in what he had set out to do. But so much more had developed in the few days while he had been here. When he returned to London the next day he would be leaving everything behind unresolved. The prospect of life back in England seemed insufferably dull.

The next morning started badly. Ben wasn't quite sure what the reason was. When Emilio brought his breakfast there was a note on the tray. It was from Donna. It said: *I hear you're quitting Naples tomorrow. Please call in to see me. I have something for you.*

At first Ben was cheered by this interest from someone whom he now thought of as an old friend. When he met Francesca in the hall he showed her the note and asked if they could leave early so that she could drop him at Donna's hotel on the way to the airport. She agreed curtly. He glanced at her, aware that the request seemed to have upset her.

'I'll only be there a few minutes. It shouldn't delay us long.'

But his assurance didn't seem to mollify her. All she said was, 'Then we must be going very soon. Have you packed your things?'

'We've got more than three hours before the plane leaves.'

'You have to go to the bank and the traffic is very bad in Naples at this time of day.' Francesca was straight-faced. 'I will bring the car to the front door in five minutes.'

'I must say goodbye to your father and mother and thank them for having me.'

She shook her head. 'Papa is still asleep and Mama is sitting with him. I will give your thanks to them later. Please be ready as soon as possible.'

She swept off down the corridor, very much the fine lady with no time for Ben.

The drive to the Hotel Excelsior was completed in almost total silence. Ben's few attempts at conversation drew no response. She was completely absorbed in her driving, which Ben found a little erratic to say the least. She narrowly avoided a collision when pulling out from a side road. That was after he asked her how she felt and whether she had any problems. After that Ben decided to keep quiet.

They drove into the hotel forecourt and squealed to a halt. Ben got out with alacrity. 'I shan't keep you waiting long,' he promised, as he slammed the door.

He asked at the desk for Donna Carter. There was a brief telephone call by the reception clerk and Ben was told to go up to her room. The door was opened to his knock and Donna stood there, wrapped in nothing but a large bath towel.

She laughed at his expression. 'You always seem to catch me in the shower.' She shepherded him into the room and closed the door behind him.

Ben laughed too. It was a relief to be back with someone cheerful and relaxed after the rather tense last couple of days. He walked a little way into the room. He felt big and clumsy. Donna was really quite small when she had no shoes on, despite her ample curves. He was surprised that he hadn't noticed it before. Or perhaps it was the comparison with the tall, slender Francesca.

'I got your note at breakfast.' He was aware that he sounded stiff and formal.

She also seemed a little uncertain of what to say. 'Come and sit by the window,' she suggested.

They sat in basket chairs on soft cushions facing each other. Donna crossed her legs and Ben couldn't help noticing the pink, rounded thigh which protruded from under the snowy white towel. The window on to the balcony was open and the curtains waved in the soft morning breeze. The fine weather seemed to have returned after three dismal days. She shivered a little and Ben was on his feet in an instant.

'Can I get your dressing-gown?'

'No. It's all right.'

'Don't be silly. You've only just come out of the shower. You'll catch a chill.'

'OK then. My robe's in the bathroom.'

Ben went to collect the light, diaphanous garment and draped it about her shoulders. 'This thin thing isn't much use anyway.'

'That's fine, honey.' She stroked his hand.

Her blonde curls smelled damp and fresh. Her swelling body under the towel seemed infinitely desirable. With a conscious effort Ben pulled his hand away and returned to his chair. She smiled at him, apparently unaware of the effect that her undressed condition was having on him.

'I wanted to thank you, Ben, for the few days we had together and for the help you gave me. I'm sorry if I wasn't always as straight with you as I would like to have been. But I hope you understand that there were things which I wasn't allowed to tell you.'

He smiled and relaxed a bit. 'That's all right. It's been rather like living in a thriller for the last few days. Even now I can hardly believe everything that's happened.' He shook his head. 'I just don't know how much of it was true.'

'Most of it was true, Ben. The job was the only thing that I invented. That's our normal cover.'

'What about Joseph A. Carter – the creep?'

'Oh – he's real all right. Everyone can make mistakes. And the alimony is true as well. Drug-enforcement agents don't earn enough to pay for a pad like this, even on expenses.'

Ben grinned. 'I can believe *that*, anyway.'

'Truly. I'm still allowed a private life and everything I told you about that is gospel.'

He nodded. He didn't know what to say next. He looked out to the splendid view beyond the balcony.

'How's Francesca and the old boy?' Donna asked brightly.

'Well, Papa's not very well. We're a bit worried about him, but Francesca says he's been in poor health for a long time. She seems to think he'll be all right in a few days.'

'And Francesca?'

'She's waiting for me down in the car. I told her I'd only be a few minutes because she seems to be worried about getting me to the airport in time to catch the eleven-thirty flight.'

'So, you're off in a couple of hours. That reminds me – I've got something of yours.' Donna rose and went into the bathroom.

When she came back she had shed the towel and had nothing on but the thin negligee which totally failed to obscure the splendid view he had of her voluptuous body.

She was carrying a razor and a bowl of shaving-soap which she gave to him.

Ben looked at it. 'That's not mine.'

'It certainly isn't *mine*,' said Donna.

Then he remembered. 'That's what I found in Toni's flat the other day. I don't know what to do with it.'

'Well, I don't want it. People will start to talk if they find things like that in my room.'

Ben roared with laughter. 'Donna, you're fantastic. I can't believe you mind in the least if some man is found in your room – with or without his shaving-kit.' He smiled. 'I'm sorry to be leaving before I get the chance to make good my offer to hold your hand on another flight.'

She cocked an eyebrow. 'And what about the little lady down there?'

'What about her?'

'You can't kid me, Benjamin Cartwright. You're crazy about her.'

He grimaced. 'Unfortunately, she doesn't feel the same about me.'

'Rubbish. Of course she does. I've seen the way she looks at you.'

'Donna, you heard the way she was pitching into me about the climb. She despises me.'

'She does not! Every woman pitches into her man when he doesn't seem to be doing what she wants. But you showed her who was right.'

Ben shook his head. 'We're just not made for each other. Our backgrounds are so different. Her family is almost aristocracy in Italy.'

'Oh,' said Donna, 'Francesca won't let that make any difference. I tell you she's crazy about you. I can't believe she's going to let you go that easily – unless she's got all mixed up about me.'

'What do you mean?'

'She may think you're sweet on me, just because you spent a bit of time in my bed. You'd better put her right on that score.'

Ben looked at her, puzzled.

Donna came close to him. 'I tell you what, my dear, I'd have been willing to throw away my alimony for you.' She shook her head. 'But I know it wouldn't be any good. I think I could persuade you to run off with me all right, but you'd always be thinking of what you might have been doing with that skinny Italian girl.'

'Donna,' said Ben tenderly.

'Now, you get going before I change my mind.' She pecked his cheek and propelled him towards the door. 'Remember,' she called after him as he went down the corridor, 'you've only got a couple of hours left. Don't mess it up.'

The door closed behind him with a soft click.

It was only when he reached the car that Ben realized he was still carrying the razor and the shaving soap. He slipped the razor into his pocket as he opened the door.

Francesca turned the starter. 'I am pleased you were not too long in there,' she said. 'I was afraid we were going to miss the plane.'

Ben got into the seat. He reached across and switched off the ignition. 'There's no hurry, Francesca. I want us to have a little talk.'

'But we still have to go to the bank.'

'We've got two and a quarter hours.'

'The traffic is very difficult at this time of day.'

'There's loads of time yet. I want to talk to you.'

'What about?' Suddenly she seemed quiet and submissive.

'I want us to clear up a few things before I leave. You may not know that, when you were in your room with a headache last night, I was asked to go and see your father. I didn't understand most of what he was saying. But he talked about you. I don't know what you had told him, but it sounded as though you had given me a good report. I want to thank you for that.'

Francesca tossed her head. 'He shouldn't have said anything.'

'He also talked quite a lot about London. If I understood him right, it seems he was giving me his blessing to continue the business as Toni and I have been running it for the last few years. And I think that must be partly thanks to you.'

'It is nothing to do with him,' she said. 'He should have kept out of it.'

'I don't see how you can say that,' said Ben. 'But that's not what I wanted to talk to you about anyway. That just clears the air before I carry on to the next thing.'

'What do you mean?'

'Just now Donna said something to me. If she's right – it's fantastic. In any case I can't leave Italy without clearing it up with you.'

'What did she say?' Francesca's voice seemed very small.

Ben looked down at his hands and swallowed. 'She said several things. First she said that it was obvious that I was crazy about you.'

'I see.'

Ben glanced quickly at her. Was she smiling? He looked back at his hands.

'She also said that you – well, she thought that you felt the same about me. Now,' he hurried on, 'I know the things you said a couple of days ago were said at a time of stress when you needed a shoulder to cry on – when you needed to relax. I'm not taking those things seriously. But Donna also said that you were probably keeping away from me because of her – because you thought she was important to me – which she isn't. Well, that is, I like her of course, but it's nothing more than that. Anyway, I've been trying to talk to you for two days now and you seem to have been avoiding me and I didn't know why. So I wanted to clear it up with you and ask why – well, you know. . . .' He tailed off miserably.

There was a long silence before Francesca spoke.

'Ben. Look at me.'

He looked. She was smiling. He had wondered whether she would be smiling.

'Ben, for God's sake, will you please kiss me?'

Like an automaton he reached out towards her. Then suddenly she was in his arms and kissing him passionately. Salty tears were wetting her cheeks. She was murmuring little endearments in Italian. Suddenly, magically he knew she really did love him. He hugged her beautiful body to him. His hands were entwined in her soft, long hair and his lungs were filled with her exquisite scent. She nibbled his ear. He buried his face into the side of her neck and she shivered delightedly. Her fingers worked their way up the knobs of his spine and set his body tingling all over. He felt her small, hard breasts and slid his hand down her body. The hem of her skirt was already nearly up to her waist.

'Not here,' she whispered. 'I feel as though half of Naples is watching what we are doing.'

Ben thought that the people of Naples had seen so many provocative sights that they would not disapprove. But he took his hand away.

She drew back a little. 'I have something that I must tell you,' she whispered in his ear.

He buried his face in the valley between her breasts, nuzzling into the soft silk of her blouse. 'I'm listening.'

She slid her fingers through his hair, clasping his head to her chest as though she was nursing a baby. 'You did not understand what Papa was telling you last night. What he was actually doing was poking his nose into my private affairs because he knew that I despaired of you ever telling me that you loved me.'

He lifted his head to gaze into her dark, troubled eyes.

'It's true, Ben. I think he was actually saying that you had his blessing and that you could take me to London with you when you go back to run the wine importing business. He hoped that if he said that to you it would persuade you to ask me.'

'Do you mean he would give his blessing to our getting married?'

'Of course he would.' She hugged him to her. 'He likes you very much. He appreciates how much you have done for the Cimbrone family. He realizes I would never be happy with anyone else. He understands that old attitudes must change in the modem world.'

Ben kissed her again. Francesca's soft lips were wet and delicious like morning dew. Her pointed, exploring tongue was provocative and thrusting. It was Ben's turn to hold back this time.

'Francesca, in a minute you will be telling me off for not controlling my hands in the car.' He reached over and opened the door.

'What are you doing?'

'I'm going into the hotel to book a double room.'

Her eyes widened in shock. 'I cannot go to bed with you before we are betrothed.'

'Oh.' He thought for a moment. 'How do we get betrothed?'

'First you have to ask me to marry you and we have to arrange the date.'

'Darling, will you marry me – tomorrow if there's not enough time left today.'

'We will have to wait for at least a month for Mama to make the arrangements and invite the guests. She would not forgive me if I had a hasty wedding.'

'All right. I suppose I can wait a month.'

'And you must also know the terms of my marriage settlement.'

'What do you mean?'

'I must tell you what I bring to the marriage. With the destruction of the Vitelli, Papa is now quite a wealthy man and he will wish to see that I am well endowed.'

'I already believe that.'

She looked at him suspiciously, aware that she was the subject of a joke. But she continued, 'I also found out yesterday from the lawyers that I have inherited all of Toni's property. So I own, among other things, a flat in the centre of Naples and forty-nine per cent of the shares in a certain wine company in London. I will give those to you as a wedding present.'

That silenced Ben for a moment. 'Well, of course,' he said, 'I only wanted to marry you for your money.'

She poked him in the chest. 'That is why I kept that information to myself until after you had asked me to marry you.'

'Right,' he said. 'Now we've sorted out the unimportant details will you please give me an answer?'

'Can you remind me of the question?'

'Have you forgotten already? Will you come to bed with me?'

Francesca pulled away from him. 'I'll race you there,' she said, swinging the car door open and pushing her skirt down.

Ben leapt out of the other side of the car and the container of shaving soap, which had been lying forgotten on his lap, crashed on to the cobbles and broke in several pieces. It was then that he noticed something strange. The soap had fallen out of the broken dish. He bent down to see what was there. Bedded on its underside he could see another of the Vitelli badges of the Wolf of Hades. Nobody would have guessed that it was there unless they had removed the soap completely from the dish.

Francesca was by his side. 'What is it?' she breathed.

Ben picked out the badge and held it close to his eyes. There were fragments of soap still adhering to the edges and he wiped them away. A slightly rough edge attracted his attention. He looked at it more closely, then pushed at it with his thumb-nail. The badge slid in half and revealed a small chamber in its centre. In it nestled a tiny folded slip of paper.

'I thought it felt less heavy then the other one,' he said.

He removed the piece of paper, unfolded it and smoothed it out on the car's wing. It was covered with fine writing. The language was Italian so he handed it to Francesca.

The girl wrinkled up her nose as she inspected it. 'It is very funny writing and difficult to understand. I think it is a *postilla*. That is the extra part of a *testamento* – you know – where a person leaves his belongings to his relatives.'

'Oh – you mean a will. It's the codicil to a will.'

'That is right. It is something extra when a person is near to death.'

'What does it say?'

'It is very old. The Italian is strange – what you call old-fashioned. But it says something like this:

Be it known that this is the last wish of Alfonso, head of the families of the Vitelli.

I have seen the entrance to Hades. I have come back only to do what must be done. God has shown me that the ways of my younger son Angelo are the right ways. They are the ways of peace. He is to return and is to lead the Vitelli in my place. To this end I give him three parts of all my lands and possessions. The fourth part I give to my elder son Pietro subject to his forswearance of the ways of violence. In future he is to follow the ways of his brother Angelo. If he fails to honour my wishes then I remove his immunity from the Wolf of Hades. He and his kin of the Vitelli will be destroyed and will disappear from the face of the earth. To this pronouncement I give my hand.

She paused and looked up at him.

'Is that all?'

'Then there is his signature and the sign of the witness – a holy father somebody. I can't read his name. And there is the date – the fourth of May, 1866.'

Ben straightened up. 'You know what this means, don't you?'

'The Cimbroni are rightful heirs to the estates of old Alfonso Vitelli?'

'More than that. It explains why the Vitelli wanted to marry you to Dino. It also explains why they kept your father alive. Once you two were married your father's life wouldn't have been worth tuppence – er – two cents.'

Francesca was silent as she absorbed the full meaning of Ben's words. Then she looked up. 'I told you that you were the saviour of the Cimbroni. What else can I do now but marry you?' She poked him in the ribs. 'But don't think that you are *too* important. This little piece of paper changes everything.'

'Well, I don't know if the codicil is legally valid. You'll have to get your lawyers on to that. But obviously Mancino Vitelli knew about it and was worried. Toni must have found it somewhere and threatened Vitelli with it. I guess that's the reason why he was killed. It's uncanny the way the piece of paper foretells the end of the Vitelli. It all ties in with what your grandfather told us. It makes my hair stand on end when I think about it.'

Francesca linked her arm through his. 'None of it is important to me. I will let Papa worry about it when he is better.'

'We'd better give it to him for safe-keeping. He might think it's quite important.' He opened the car door again.

'Hey! What about our double bedroom?'

'I tell you what,' he said, 'why don't we go and tidy up our new flat in the centre of Naples before we go back to see your Papa? That's got a double bed, hasn't it?'

'That will take much too long. We've only got two hours before your plane leaves.'

'Oh, forget that,' said Ben. 'I'll go back to London another day. I think I owe myself a few days' holiday with my betrothed.'